ROMANTIC TIMES PRAISES
NORAH HESS,
NEW YORK TIMES BESTSELLING AUTHOR!

LARK
"As with all Ms. Hess's books, the ending is joyous for everyone. The road to happiness is filled with wonderful characters, surprises, passion, pathos and plot twists and turns as only the inimitable Norah Hess can create."

LACEY
"Emotions leap off the pages and right into the reader's heart. You'll savor every word."

FLINT
"Ms. Hess has once again created a memorable love story with characters who find a place in readers' hearts."

FANCY
"The lively action . . . from the talented Ms. Hess is sure to catch your FANCY."

SNOW FIRE
"Ms. Hess fills . . . each page with excitement and twists. This warm and sultry romance is a perfect dessert for a cold winter day."

JADE
"Ms. Hess continues to write page-turners with wonderful characters described in depth. This is a wonderful romance complete with surprising plot twists . . . plenty of action and sensuality. Another great read from a great writer."

TANNER
"Ms. Hess certainly knows how to write a romance . . . the characters are wonderful and find a way to sneak into your heart."

MOUNTAIN ROSE
"Another delightful, tender and heartwarming read from a special storyteller!"

Other books by Norah Hess:

LARK
LACEY
TENNESSEE MOON
FLINT
SNOW FIRE
RAVEN
SAGE
DEVIL IN SPURS
TANNER
KENTUCKY BRIDE
WILLOW
JADE
BLAZE
KENTUCKY WOMAN
HAWKE'S PRIDE
MOUNTAIN ROSE
FANCY
WINTER LOVE
FOREVER THE FLAME
WILDFIRE
STORM

CALEB'S
Bride

NORAH HESS

LOVE SPELL NEW YORK CITY

Leisure Entertainment Service Co., Inc. (LESCO Distribution Group)

Printed—November 2006

A LESCO Edition
www.leisureent.com
LESCO
65 Richard Road
Ivyland, PA 18974

Published by special arrangement with Dorchester Publishing Co., Inc.

Copyright © 1978 by Elsie Poe Bagnara

Printed in the United States of America.

CHAPTER 1

The rain pelted down for the third day in a row. The drowning earth could no longer absorb the steady downpour and the water gathered in small pools that reflected a gray dismal sky. Then, as though they were lonely, the bodies of water drew together, and mingling and swirling, discovered their united power and rushed forward to find a communal home.

Roxanne Sherwood saw the small stream coming and glanced nervously at her grieving parents, who stood at her side, clinging to one another. She prayed that their tears would hide the onrush making straight for the small open grave.

A raw autumn wind blew across the cemetery. It lashed at black-clad mourners, whipping somber bonnets and beating at bared heads. Roxanne grabbed at her own bonnet and smothered a sneeze.

As if everyone wasn't uneasy enough in the year 1776, British soldiers and mercenaries had brought typhus to the town of Boston. Each new day the horse-drawn hearse, increasingly, made its labored way up the rutted road to the burial ground of the rich. On this wet, blustery day, the weary horses had climbed the long hill for the fourth time.

It was hard to say how many trips were made to the shoddy, unkept graveyard at the bottom of the hill. No one kept track of the poor white or black. They were ignored in death as they had been in life. They were stacked like cords of wood in the carts that otherwise gathered the garbage of the rich. For the poor, living on the outskirts of town, there was no other need for the cart to pass through their winding, haphazard streets. There had never been a scrap of food wasted, a coat or a dress discarded. Only in death could they contribute to the city carts.

And recently, they had contributed dearly. The sodden earth was sprinkled liberally with freshly dug graves; graves that were ugly, jutting mounds, that in some places had given away to the beating rain, leaving nothing more than patches of dark clay. There were no tall stones to grace and mark these graves, nor were there patches of neatly trimmed grass to soften the harsh, rocky earth. There were only tall dead weeds, brown and wet, bending before the wind.

There were, however, occasional wooden homemade markers, carefully carved by loving hands, standing proudly above the weeds and rocks. Some distance away from where Roxanne stood with her parents a tall man dressed in worn buckskins was standing before just such a marker.

A black man, old and grizzled, stood beside him. While the young man stared down at the two open graves, the older man, the pelting rain mixing with his tears, raised his head and said his prayer to the heavens.

"Take them, my Lord, into your lovin' arms," he beseeched. "Give them the joy and comfort that they were denied here on earth. Let their used and wasted bodies once again be strong and straight, and let them dwell in your house, O Lord. Amen."

He closed his tattered Bible and laid a gnarled hand on the other's shoulder. "I'm sorry for your grief, Caleb Coleman." Turning, he made his slow way through the tall hedge, the mud and water sloshing in his broken boots.

Caleb knelt between the two graves, his head bowed in his hands. He hadn't seen his parents for years, and it was only by pure chance that he had crossed the path of a stranger babbling in panic about the typhus in Boston. A childhood memory of a mother tucking him into bed at night, and of a father calling out, "Good night, son," had sent him hurrying the many miles to the place of his birth.

But he arrived too late. They had died that morning, a thin freckle-faced boy told him as he stepped up to the rickety, slanting porch. His heart cold and pounding, he entered the shack and guilt had come rushing over him in waves.

His parents had lived their last years in poverty. Everything in the near-barren room spoke of it. Most of the furniture he remembered as a child was gone. He wondered if it had worn out, or had been bartered for food. Only two straight-backed chairs beside the hearth and the wooden bed holding his parents' bodies stood in the cold, damp room. He knew, without looking, that the kitchen beyond would hold little more.

He had moved slowly to the bed and pulled back the sheet. The fever-wasted bodies he looked down on in no way resembled the parents he remembered: time and hardship had taken their toll, and they were strangers to him. Only the thin golden wedding band on his mother's finger was familiar to him.

The rain quickened, slashing at Caleb Coleman's face. Startled, he jerked, then gave a shuddering sigh. Speaking softly, he murmured, "I wasn't much of a man to you, was I, maw, paw? I always meant to be.

But it seemed like something always came up and I would put off comin' to see you.''

After a few more minutes he rose and took up the shovel leaning against a stunted maple. Slowly and carefully he began to fill the holes. The heavy, wet clay plopped onto the coffins with a dull, hollow sound, making him wince with each thud.

As he shoveled, he tamped the wet earth tightly, making sure it would stay intact. He would not have his parents' coffins exposed to the weather as some of the other poor devils were. He had counted four partially covered graves nearby. The cheap wooden boxes had been hastily lowered into the ground by strangers, then carelessly covered, and now lay under the driving rain as it beat upon them.

The one consolation that softened his grief, somewhat, was that his parents were buried in strong pine boxes, the same kind used by the fancy bastards up on Front Street. He had been charged double the price, he knew, but he would have paid three times that to have his folks buried decently.

But still rankling in his mind was the refusal of three ministers to hold services for his parents in their church. They had looked down their pinched noses at his rough appearance and muttered coldly, ''I am too busy. My time is already taken by members of my congregation.''

Caleb swore bitterly and shoveled faster, muttering, ''Damn such men to hell.''

But in the end he remembered that a better man than they had prayed over his parents, and his mind was eased.

Finally the job was finished and he stood a moment looking down on the mounds. For what earthly reason had they lived, he wondered. They had only him to show for their time of living and, God knew, he wasn't much.

Abruptly he turned on his heel and clapped the dripping coonskin to his head. With his face turned away from the biting rain, he made his way to the stallion tethered by the edge of the road.

Until this day, October 17, 1776, the Sherwood family had escaped the racking grief of seeing a loved one carried to the cemetery. In the past, and more often lately, they had made the long ride, to lend their silent support and sympathy to friends and neighbors. Now typhus had claimed their young son and brother.

Roxanne Sherwood's gaze moved from the flow of water as it gathered momentum to the small pinewood box that hung suspended above the muddy pool the water was making. She shivered and moved closer to her sobbing mother. Poor little Davy . . . to have lived only a scant five years. She swore silently at the British as she recalled the two long weeks of burning fever and raging headaches the little boy had endured.

Gavin and Aline Sherwood were grief-stricken at their loss. Davy had come unexpectedly in their later years and had been cherished as a gift from heaven. After so many unfruitful years following Roxanne's birth, they had almost reconciled themselves to having only one child.

Aline grasped Roxanne's hand now and held it tightly. The typhus must not get her beautiful daughter, too. She had been her constant joy for eighteen years.

Roxanne glanced at her mother and became alarmed at how pale she had grown. She looked too weak to stand, and Roxanne twitched her shoulders impatiently. How long was that old windbag going to keep them in this downpour? In her opinion, the sanctimonious old bastard was only taking advantage of the occasion to preach one of his hell-fire sermons.

When finally some of the mourners—wet and tired . . . and frightened—made motions as if to leave, the long-winded preacher realized his breach of propriety and reluctantly began to close his sermon with a prayer. This, too, would have been a drawn-out affair had not the caretakers, long since grown callous to racking sobs, begun to methodically shovel the muddy clumps of earth onto the little coffin.

Aline gasped her pain and fell against her husband. When the grave was filled and mounded, wet, bedraggled bouquets of flowers were placed upon it. Then friends and relatives gathered around the grieving family to say a last comforting word.

Gavin watched them hurry away and knew that they were anxious to get back to the doubtful safety of their homes. He was surprised that so many had braved the outdoors. All of Boston was afraid these days.

Between them, Gavin and Roxanne helped Aline into the carriage. The driver snapped his whip and they trailed a long line of assorted rigs and carriages down the deeply mudded road. At the foot of the hill the cortege was slowed considerably by a sharp bend in the road, and their driver was forced to halt the team while a lumbering conveyance before them made a careful turn.

Suddenly, Roxanne sat forward and stared. Pulled off to the side of the road, waiting for the procession to pass, was the most magnificent horse she had ever seen. And on his back sat a man who took her breath away.

He would have been handsome had it not been for the absolutely wicked expression on his face. He looked to be about thirty years . . . tall and dark, with black heavy hair hanging to his shoulders. He was well proportioned and showed a careless confidence in his movements as he handled the nervous stallion. He looked like he had just climbed out of bed, his eyes bloodshot and his face haggard. All in all, she thought he was a devilish-looking individual.

He seemed to sense her gaze and glanced curiously her way. His dark eyes riveted on her face and became narrow slits as he studied her. And though in reality they stared at each other only a flash of seconds, it seemed minutes to Roxanne.

She felt herself becoming confused under his penetrating stare and, to hide how he affected her, she tilted her chin proudly and turned a cool look on him. His cold features hardened at her haughtiness and, deliberately and insultingly, he let his gaze travel slowly over her body. Roxanne felt herself blushing, but still could not turn away.

The carriage jerked suddenly and began to move. The stranger lifted a long well-shaped hand to his coonskin and sardonically saluted her. She glowered at him for a moment, then, just as they passed, she looked back and, childlike, stuck out her tongue.

Startled, he gaped at her. Then, laughing uproariously, he stood up in the stirrups and waved good-bye to her. Roxanne smiled and turned back.

"Papa, what kind of clothes was that man wearing . . . the fringes on his trousers and sleeves?"

"They're called buckskins, I believe. Indians and hunters wear them."

"Then that man beside the road is a hunter?"

"I would say so. He has the look."

She wondered idly what a hunter was doing in Boston. Surely he didn't live here. He was too out of

place. Then they were turning into the driveway of
their home and the thought of a fire and dry clothing
erased the hunter from her mind.

A little black boy ran to meet them, an umbrella in
his hand. Aline leaned heavily on her husband's arm
as they climbed the three steps to the large imposing
door.

The servants had hurried ahead of the family and
now fires burned in every fireplace. The rains still fell,
beating against the window and bringing an early
darkness. An old black man moved slowly from room
to room, lighting candles and kerosene lamps. He
prayed silently that their light would help push back
the gloom and sadness that permeated the very walls.

Gavin helped his wife out of her wet, clinging cloak
and led her to the fire. Roxanne watched them huddled
together and knew that they drew comfort from one
another. How else could they stand the thought of the
rain washing away at that lonely little grave.

A young girl, an Irish bond servant, bustled into the
room carrying a tray of food and a pot of coffee.
"Ma'am," she spoke softly, "you and the mister
must eat a bite. You've got to keep your strength up or
you'll get sick, too."

She turned to Roxanne and added, "You, too, miss.
I heard you sneezing up at the cemetery."

Her tone was such that Roxanne didn't argue, but
took up a plate. Aline, however, shook her head
gently. "Not right now, Mara. I couldn't eat a bite."

Gavin would have passed the food by, too, but the
girl looked so disappointed as she left the room he
choked down a few bites of the chicken salad she had
prepared.

The meal was soon finished and Roxanne rang the
small silver bell at her elbow. Mara returned and, see-

ing most of the food still on the tray, shook her head and muttered, "Aye, you'll all get sick," and started toward the door.

Gavin reached out and placed a restraining hand on her arm. "Mara, please bring me paper and ink, and a quill."

Aline gazed a moment into her husband's eyes, then, knowingly, gave a slight nod of her head.

Roxanne missed her parents' silent exchange and asked innocently, "Are you going to write to Uncle Malcolm about Davy?"

Gavin sighed, a deep sound in the quiet room. He looked across the room at his only child and dreaded what he must say. "Yes. I must tell Malcolm about his nephew." Then, clearing his throat, he motioned Roxanne to him. When she stood leaning against his chair, he picked up her hand and stroked it. "Also, Roxanne," he added softly, "to advise him that you will be visiting him until the epidemic is over."

The graceful body went stiff and she jerked her hand away.

Gavin gazed up at her, thinking how very beautiful she was. It was a constant source of amazement to him and Aline that they should have such a daughter. They were a very plain-looking couple, possessing no claim to beauty or to handsome good looks; but with Roxanne it was as though an artist had chosen from their ordinary faces a feature from each and turned it into a work of art.

Aline's drab blonde hair became a glorious gold on the young girl's head, and Gavin's dark-blue eyes became almost purple behind the thick dark lashes that swept her cheeks. The flawless, creamy complexion, however, did come from her mother, as well as the soft, wide mouth.

That wide mouth opened now and objected loudly. "But, papa, Uncle Malcolm lives in the wilderness. A place called Kentucky. I couldn't possibly go there."

Looking at her tear-streaked face, Gavin had a feeling almost of guilt. It must be a dreadful idea for her to accept. He hardened his heart; it had to be. It was much too dangerous for her to remain in Boston.

"I'm well aware of where your uncle lives, Roxanne," he began patiently. "I'm also aware that at this time there is no safer place for you than in the wilds of Kentucky. Not only are there no enemy soldiers there, there is no fever, thank God."

Aline caught her daughter's nervous, twitching fingers and held them still. "It won't be for long, dear, just until the sickness is gone and it's safe again."

She squeezed the fingers gently. "Papa and I couldn't stand to lose you, too."

"But what about you and papa?" Roxanne objected. "What makes it safe for you and unsafe for me? What if you two get sick and I'm not here to tend you?"

"It's not likely that we'll be touched by the fever now, Roxy. Remember, we cared for Davy for two weeks and didn't come down with it. But since you were kept away from him, we have no way of knowing how the fever will affect you."

Roxanne missed the breath of prayer in Aline's last words, hearing only her own words of rejection hanging in the air. But when Aline caressed her silky head and murmured words of endearment to her, she became quiet and nestled closer to the gentle woman, dreading the time when she must leave her.

Mara returned with the writing supplies, and the steady scratching of the quill filled the room. It wasn't a long letter and Gavin was soon sealing it in a black-edged envelope. The waiting maid tossed a shawl around her shoulders and left for the post.

"I asked Malcolm to send your cousin Gideon for you as soon as possible, Roxy," Gavin broke the silence. "In the meantime don't leave the house, and keep away from the servants who go in and out."

Roxanne nodded her head, close to tears again.

The maid was back in a short time, announcing that she had had a bit of luck. "I was just in time to catch the mail carrier on his monthly visit. He said that this will be his last trip; claims it's getting too dangerous with the war and all." She started to leave the room, then stopped to add, "He said he'd get the letter to Mr. Sherwood in three days."

Gavin nodded without comment.

A few minutes later, when the knocker sounded at the front door, Roxanne's spirits lifted as she heard her cousin Mary's cheerful voice. She adored the cousin who was two years her senior. Mary was so sophisticated. She had been married over a year now and was big with child. As she clasped her aunt and uncle in turn, she did so with a genuine feeling of sorrow. "I so wanted to be with you, aunt and uncle. But the doctor and Tom insisted that I shouldn't be out."

"Indeed you shouldn't have, dear," Aline spoke softly to her sister's daughter. "We didn't expect you to be at the cemetery, and you shouldn't be out in such weather now."

"Oh, I'm dressed warmly. And I only had to come a short way. I told Tom I had to see you tonight, no matter what the consequences."

Mary looked at her cousin and moved wordlessly to the young girl and folded her in warm arms. Roxanne dropped her head on the offered shoulder and her tears flowed, uncontrolled.

Patting the shaking form, Mary took a handkerchief from her skirt and wiped at her own tearing eyes. "Don't cry, Roxy. Time will heal our great loss."

When Roxanne made a slight movement of assent with her head, Mary murmured, "Why don't we go up to your room and get you out of these damp clothes. Didn't you know that you were wet?"

Roxanne smiled weakly at her cousin's gentle scolding and followed the slightly plump figure up the winding stairs to her room.

A fire burned cozily in the large, attractive room, which was decidedly a girl's boudoir with its frilly curtains and flower-sprigged wallpaper. Within minutes Mary had helped Roxanne to undress and slip into a soft flannel gown. As she slid between the warm, fluffy blankets, Mary sat on the edge of the bed and sighed.

"You have such a lovely body, Roxanne. I have grown so out of shape poor Tom can hardly get his arms around me anymore."

Roxanne wiped her wet eyes, then giggled. "I'll bet that's not the only thing he can't get around anymore."

Mary slapped at her playfully. "You naughty girl," she giggled back. "But you do speak the truth. Tom used to do an awful lot of complaining about my stomach being in the way."

"What do you mean, used to? Did he give up trying?"

Mary blushed prettily, then leaned over and whispered in her young cousin's ear. Roxanne drew back and stared at her, her eyes round. "You did that to Tom?"

"Yes, I did," the young wife answered defensively. "My stomach has become so big and all. Every night Tom begged me that he hurt so—and I finally gave in and did it. He said that Father John told him that anything done between husband and wife was alright in the eyes of God."

Mary's revelation was totally different from any of her other confided intimacies, and Roxanne was vaguely disturbed. A tingling was stirring in her loins as she pictured her cousin doing this to her husband. Wouldn't her school chums open their eyes at this piece of information!

She smiled to herself, thinking about the naiveness of her young friends. They barely knew where babies came from and had no idea how they got there. She wouldn't have known, either, if Mary hadn't told her. Her cousin had been a wealth of information to her, there was no doubt about that.

But this last information had stunned her. Was that really expected and accepted in marriage? Would she be able to do it, no matter how much she might love her husband?

She felt Mary's questioning look and stammered, "Well, if . . . if Father John said it was alright. Still, I think I'd feel awful sinful doing it."

"Don't be so fast at playing judge, Roxy." Mary was fast to defend herself. "I felt the same way at first. But Tom enjoys it so much, and since I love him utterly, I soon got over it." She paused a moment, then added in a teasing voice, "You'll do it to some man someday, you'll see."

Roxanne blushed red. Unbidden, the tall, rough-looking man of the road slid before her eyes. Quickly she lowered them, afraid of what Mary might read in them.

Mary had noted the confusion that had come over her young cousin and waited patiently. She wondered which one had taken her fancy.

After a while Roxanne looked up and said in a small voice, "I wonder. I doubt if I'll ever have the chance."

Mary arched her eyebrows. Was Roxanne fishing for a compliment? It seemed unlikely. There was no sham or pretense in this young relative. But she asked the obvious question, nevertheless.

"What ever are you talking about, Roxanne Sherwood? You know that there's at least a dozen men in Boston that are crazy about you. You could have your pick tomorrow."

Mary's enthusiasm was too much and Roxanne burst out crying. "Oh, Mary, papa is sending me to Uncle Malcolm until the fever is gone. I have this terrible feeling that I will never see Boston again."

The older woman stared at Roxanne, then, in astonishment, gasped, "What did you say?"

Roxanne stared back, tears tracing a rivulet down her cheeks. "It's true, Mary. I'll be going as soon as my cousin Gideon comes for me."

Mary became all sympathy and gathered the sobbing girl into her arms. Rocking back and forth, she, too, almost cried.

"Oh, you poor little thing. It will be dreadful for you in those hills. Tom was saying just the other day that there's nothing there but crude homesteaders and wild hunters, not to mention the Indians. How will you ever be able to stand it?"

Mary's harshly expressed sentiments echoing through the room only added fuel to spirits already low. Throwing herself back on the bed, Roxanne sobbed loudly. "Oh, Mary, I don't know. But papa insists and there's nothing I can do about it.''

Mary rose from the bed and walked to the window. She pushed aside the curtains and stared down onto the street. The rain still fell, obscuring everything but the soft glow of the street lamp in front of the house. Two British soldiers passed beneath her and she whispered darkly, ''You rotten bastards.''

She turned back and moved to the bed. ''I suppose you're right,'' she said, sitting back down. ''You do have to do as Uncle Gavin says.''

Roxanne sighed, knowing that it was true. ''Please, Mary, let's not talk about it anymore,'' she begged.

''No, dear, we won't. Try to fall asleep now. Things will look better tomorrow.''

Mary remained on the bed, stroking her young cousin's brow until only an occasional sob escaped the sleeping girl.

On the sixth morning after Gavin's letter had been posted, father and daughter had finished breakfast and were taking their coffee in the den. Roxanne stood at the window, slowly sipping the hot liquid.

''It looks like more rain, papa,'' she remarked.

Gavin sighed, thinking of the small grave upon the hill. One of the servants had reported that the grave was still intact . . . but more rain?

The somber silence in the room was broken by voices in the hall. Then a soft knock sounded at the door.

''Come in,'' Gavin invited.

Mara entered the room with a tall gangly youth following behind her. He stopped and stood awkwardly in the doorway, looking uncomfortable and out of place in the richly furnished room. His eyes dropped to his feet, the action showing that he hoped there was no mud on them.

His rough garb and unkempt hair, which hung tangled to his shoulders, spoke of a backwoodsman, and Gavin wondered what the strange young man wanted. But as he continued to stare at the youth, he caught in the dark eyes a glimpse that was vaguely familiar, and for some reason he was pained by the look.

Then Mara was saying in her high thin voice, "This person says that he's your nephew, Mr. Sherwood."

Gavin's eyes went wide and he gasped, "Gideon!" He jumped to his feet and hurried toward the visitor with outstretched hands. "I didn't recognize you, son."

As the warm friendly smile of his uncle greeted him, Gideon swiped the long brown hair from his forehead and smiled back. He grasped the proffered hand and pumped it heartily.

Searching his young relative's face, Gavin knew why he was familiar. Gideon had Davy's eyes and smile. He lay an arm across the muscular shoulders and smiled happily. "It's good to see you, Gideon, after all these years." Leading him toward the fire, he asked, "How was your trip? Did you have any trouble getting into town? Shortly after I sent my letter, the city fathers stopped all people from entering or leaving the town."

"My trip was alright, Uncle Gavin. I left as soon as we got your letter and I made good time. As for gettin' in town, Uncle Malcolm figured that all traffic would be stopped, and he warned me to take only back roads into town and to use the alleys whenever possible."

Gavin smiled. "Trust Malcolm to remember that. As young boys we lived through the typhus once and had the same experience."

Gideon laughed. "Yeah, he don't forget much."

"How is my brother? How has he fared these long years?"

"Right now, he feels saddened about little Davy; otherwise, he's in good health and just like always."

Gavin smiled reminiscently. He knew what the "just like always" meant. His older, widowed brother was still a hell-raiser.

All this time, Roxanne, in the dark recess of the window, had gone unnoticed by Gideon. She took the opportunity to study the cousin she hadn't seen in five years.

Until Gideon was twelve, he had lived down the street from her. They had grown up together, playing and fighting as cousins will. But there had been a deep fondness between them, and Roxanne had been heartbroken when Gideon had been sent to their uncle to make his home. His parents had been killed one winter night when their carriage had slid on an ice-covered road and turned over. His mother and father had been trapped beneath, their necks broken.

The first thing that caught Roxanne's eye was that Gideon's hair hung free instead of being clubbed at the neck like the men in Boston. She recalled that the stranger on the road had worn his hair in the same fashion. Running her eyes over Gideon's body, she saw that he was dressed in much the same way, too, except that Gideon's buckskins were not as fancy as the stranger's. Still, they fit him well and lent a certain grace to his long lanky body.

Then Gavin called her name, cutting short her study. When she walked out of the shadows, Gideon became tongue-tied with shyness. Cousin Roxy has sure growed up, he thought. She'll set them hill men on their ears.

Roxanne's wide welcoming smile put him at ease. After a few words between them, he found that she was the same friendly cousin she had been as a child. In a short time they were bantering back and forth.

The maid answered the summons of the bell. Roxanne smiled at her and asked, "Mara, would you please bring my cousin some breakfast?"

While Gideon put away ham and eggs and hot biscuits and coffee, he tried to answer all the eager questions put to him.

"How are the Indians behaving in Kentucky? Have they gone over to the British yet?"

"Some have . . . mostly renegades. But they don't bother us much. Mostly they steal our animals, and once in a while burn some homesteader's cabin that is stuck away by itself. I think they mainly hunt game for the British soldiers."

Gavin stroked his neat, short beard. It was a habit that warned the family he was worried or uncertain about something. The young couple across the table from him knew what was on his mind. Roxanne hurried to kneel by his side.

"We'll be alright, papa," she urged. "Please don't worry."

Gideon was fast to add his assurance. "Roxy is right, Uncle Gavin. The Indians aren't really on the warpath. We folks in the hills think that they haven't made up their minds yet, and that in the meantime they're only keeping the British pacified."

But Gavin continued to play with his beard, not fully convinced. Finally, he commented, "I hope that you're right, Gideon; but it seems there's danger for you two, any way you turn. The red heathen in the hills, or the typhus here in Boston."

He sighed deeply and stood up. "I'll pray for you children every step of the way."

Moving toward the door, he motioned them to follow him. "Come upstairs and visit your aunt awhile, then tell her good-bye. I want you two on your way as soon as possible."

CHAPTER 2

Two days and one night later, and many miles from Boston, Gideon and Roxanne rode under storm clouds that flew low over the hills. The cool assurance that Gideon previously displayed had almost vanished. He rode with his coonskin hat pushed back off his forehead, anxiously searching the forest.

They came to a wide spot in the trail and Roxanne urged her mare up alongside him. They looked at each other in dismay. "Gideon, we're lost, aren't we?" she asked.

"I allow we are, Roxy," he answered, gazing dubiously back over the way they had come. "I must have taken a wrong branch somewhere along the way."

They reined in the animals and Gideon scanned the sky, his brow puckered in a frown. A puff of wind sent Roxanne's hair blowing across her face and she caught at it impatiently. Tucking it back under her hood, she questioned, "What should we do?"

"We ain't got much time, Roxy. Look how them clouds are followin' us. We've got to find some cover before the rain hits."

There was a pause before he spoke again. Then, "Now we know there's no shelter behind us, but I got a feeling this trail leads to something . . . maybe a cabin."

Roxanne's heart quickened. She certainly hoped so.

Last night they had slept huddled together beneath a great spreading cedar. The large ground-hugging branches had screened them from the biting autumn wind and the bed made by Gideon from soft pine boughs had been comfortable enough. But the mournful yowls of timber wolves calling out their loneliness had petrified her.

Roxanne jerked. The thunder they had been hearing in the distance now sounded almost upon them. Gideon yelled above the rumbling noise, "That thunder means business. We're gonna have one of them heavy fall rains."

A premature darkness was falling and it was hard to keep to the dim trail. Then Gideon reached the top of a hill and shouted above the thunder and wind, "There's a cabin at the foot of this hill." He motioned her on. "The rain's comin . . . hurry up."

They raced in a wild run, striving to keep ahead of the storm cloud that pelted at their backs. Lashing the mare lightly, Roxanne kept up with Gideon's break-neck speed, loving every minute.

Then suddenly, and without warning, they were brought up short by a string of mounted horses stretched across the trail. Roxanne's face grew pale and her eyes went wide in terror. Like shadowy ghosts, a band of Indians had materialized out of the surrounding forest and now blocked their way. Their black eyes inscrutable, and their faces expressionless, they watched the trapped couple's every move.

Roxanne half turned her head and sent a swift glance at Gideon. She saw the tensing of his body and knew that he was equally frightened.

They are going to kill us, raced through her mind. But will they torture us first? nagged her agonized brain. Wild stories of Indian brutality raced through her memory, and she prayed silently, "Please, Lord, send us help."

Behind the string of Indians she glimpsed the faint outline of the cabin she and Gideon had been racing for. A tiny flame of hope flared within her. Maybe there was someone in there who would come to their assistance. But no light shone from the window and no smoke trailed from the chimney. Uttering a small despairing sound, she slumped dejectedly in the saddle.

Then the braves were forming a circle, coming closer and closer toward them. Before she knew what was happening, a red hand that bit into her flesh like steel was laid on her arm and she was being jerked off the horse, thrashing and scratching.

At first they only tried to capture and hold her hands. But their strange grunts and deep guttural words made strange and terrifying sounds and she struggled all the more. Finally, in exasperation, a brave cuffed her lightly on the jaw and she yelled out against the pain as the fight went out of her.

Through the melee of waving arms she saw Gideon pulled from his horse and dragged clear of its trampling feet. The brave holding her gave her a shove and she was clinging to Gideon and experiencing a fear she had never known before. A stupefying tiredness was coming over her, and she thought that she would faint.

Then rough fingers were grasping their wrists and tying them together. Roxanne snapped alert with hope renewed. At least they weren't going to be killed on the spot. Perhaps they would still be able to escape.

The rain caught up with them, coming in a slashing force that soaked their clothes instantly. Without a word being spoken, the braves remounted the ponies and headed into the forest, away from the trail.

With a rope attached to their wrists, and a brave holding it tightly, Roxanne and Gideon stumbled along behind them. The pace was fast and Roxanne's wet skirt clung to her legs, causing her to slip and slide on the pine-strewn trail.

After what seemed an interminable length of time, they finally halted in front of a huge cave. In the semidarkness, it loomed like some monster out of the past. Time and weather had beaten at its entrance, carving an upper covering much like a roof on a porch. Large boulders lay scattered about, tumbled there from years of storms. Large towering pines grew thick, almost hiding the entrance. It was the kind of place that few would ever stumble onto.

A raindove swooped low over their heads, sounding its mournful song. Startled, Roxanne drew close to Gideon and huddled against him. Helpless, with his hands tied, he could only bend his head and lay it on hers. When he would have spoken a comforting word, the brave gave a savage jerk to the rope, bringing them to their knees. Scrambling to their feet, they were dragged headlong into the cave, hastily untied and sent sprawling to the ground.

They sat in almost total darkness, rubbing their raw and bleeding wrists. Gideon could hear his cousin's soft sobbing and drew closer to her. "Oh, Gideon," she whimpered, "what is going to happen to us?"

He pulled her head to his shoulder. "Don't cry, Roxy. I don't think they mean to harm us. I think they're renegades out hunting for the British. They'll most likely turn us over to them."

"But we'll be shot for spies," she wailed, and Gideon cursed his careless tongue. He felt quite sure that if this should happen, the British would shoot him; but he doubted that they would shoot his beautiful cousin. Her golden hair would attract some officer's notice, and certainly her shapely body would hold his interest.

When her hands groped for his, he pressed them and said consolingly, "The British won't shoot you, Roxy."

He sounded so positive that she took hope and moved closer to him, seeking the warmth of his body. Gazing straight ahead, she could see at the edge of the cave's overhang the silhouetted figures of the Indians as they sat close around the flames of a huge fire. She shivered in her wet clothing and wished that she and Gideon had some heat.

Apparently overcome by exhaustion, Gideon now lay rolled into a ball. His even breathing suggested that he slept, and Roxanne wondered how on earth he could sleep at a time like this.

She sighed and settled down beside him, squirming around, trying to make herself more comfortable. The aroma of roasting meat wafted into the cave, reminding her of how hungry she was.

Unbidden came the memory of her last breakfast with ther father. He had looked so sad and careworn. And later, saying good-bye to mama had almost brought the tears to flowing. She had aged so. Her hair had so much white in it now . . . almost overnight, it seemed.

Her eyes teared over. Would she ever see them again?

Suddenly, through her tears, she saw the tall figure of a brave entering the cave and coming toward them. She sat up quickly and poked Gideon sharply in the side. He jerked awake and scrambled to sit beside her, his fingers clutching her arm.

The Indian carried a long, smoking stick and, when

he was a few feet away from them, stopped and tossed it at their feet. While Roxanne gasped in fear, Gideon swooped it up and began to tear at it in quick movements.

For a moment Roxanne stared at her cousin, then slowly realized that he tore at big chunks of meat skewered to the stick. Ignoring burning fingers, she, too, began to tear off the tender morsels, popping them into her mouth.

It wasn't until the last bite was gone and she was licking her fingers that she became aware of the brave's piercing stare. He sat cross-legged in the shadows, his bold gaze roaming over her body. She refused to look fully at him but could not help shooting quick, uneasy glances his way. She shivered, knowing well his look. Since she was fourteen, men had looked at her so.

Once the brave made as if to rise and Roxanne held her breath. Then an older man, seemingly the leader, muttered some word and reluctantly the brave settled back down. But he continued to watch her and she could not relieve herself of the fear that he would not remain there long.

She leaned to Gideon and whispered urgently, "Gideon, do you think that savage means to . . . means to . . . you know what I mean."

Gideon had noticed the Indian's interest in his cousin and had mentally allowed that all men were the same regardless of color. But in this case he wondered if the big attraction wasn't Roxanne's fairness.

Careful not to speak as carelessly as he had before, he answered in an offhand manner. "I think he only wants to look at you, Roxanne. The red man stays pretty much with his own women."

She smiled her relief and squeezed his hand. "Ah,

Gideon, you are such a comfort to me.''

He returned the pressure and prayed silently that his words would prove truthful. Drawing her head onto his shoulder, he murmured, ''Try to catch a little sleep. We probably have a long march ahead of us tomorrow.''

It was some fifteen minutes later that a long shadow fell before them. Roxanne, just drowsing off, sat up startled as the brave settled gracefully beside her. Nervous, she jerked away from him while Gideon jumped to his feet, uncertain what to do.

How could he help her against so many? But the determined look on his face said plainly that he would try.

When the red man lay a hand on Roxanne's shoulder and let it slide down to cup a breast, he feared that the time had come to prove himself. His hill country reasoning asked if he should jump the brave now, or wait and see if the savage meant only to fondle her a bit. And even after Roxanne sent him a quick, pleading look, he still waited. If only she would suffer the caress a moment, it might satisfy the Indian and save their necks.

But when he saw Roxanne's back stiffen and heard her angry order, ''Take your dirty hands off me,'' he sighed heavily. They were in for it now.

The ringing command in Roxanne's voice had, for a moment, startled the brave. He had pulled his hand away as a child would do, caught in a mischievous act. But when she started to rise, the dawning that she was his prisoner returned to him and he yanked her back roughly to his side. And to show that he was her master, this time he slid his hand inside her blouse and began to knead her breast.

Straining away from his probing fingers, she hissed

angrily into his stoic face, "You filthy savage, keep your hands off me."

But her sharp words and struggling body only served to inflame him more, and before she knew it his other hand was clutching the front of her dress. It was then that her anger gave way to a mind-tearing fright. He saw the fear in her eyes and a gloating look of power swept over his face.

He grunted a satisfied "Hah" and slowly and deliberately tore the top part of her blouse to her waist. When her milk-white breasts spilled free, she gave a muted scream and clutched the torn edges together.

But her red tormentor did not want them covered and swept her hands away. In terror, her hands became fists and she pummeled his face. For a stunned moment he allowed this to happen. Then his face grew dark and he grabbed at her waving arms. But she was like a wildcat now, biting and scratching. Furious, the brave gave an irate grunt and lifted a fist to strike her down.

While the clenched fist was still in the air, Gideon made his move. Gathering his long length into a crouch, he let out a bone-chilling screech and sprang on the red muscular back. Each hand grabbed a handful of black coarse hair and jerked backward with all their strength. The brave let out a startled pain-filled roar and strained to pull the clinging body off him.

But no matter how he tried, Gideon stuck there like a burr on a dog. And, to add insult to his predicament, the Indian's companions, noted for their strange sense of humor, were rolling on the ground, laughing uproariously. Their taunts and insults rang in the air, further enraging the brave. He strained his arm almost to the breaking point in reaching for Gideon's swinging hair.

The youth saw the reaching fingers, but too late. The talonlike hands grabbed a fistful of waving hair and Gideon went flying over his head. He hit the stone floor hard and lay still.

Roxanne stared at her unconscious cousin in dismay. Her only source of protection was gone. Her eyes swung back to the figure that once again crouched beside her. Slowly he reached out and his slim fingers began to caress her quivering flesh. Repulsed and horrified, she began to slide away from him, only to come up against the stone wall.

She was caught. Her strength was gone and she was at his mercy.

He grasped her shoulders and pressed her to the ground. She gave a low moan as a sense of hopelessness filled her. This red savage was going to do the things of which cousin Mary spoke.

"Oh, dear Lord, I don't want to learn those things from a savage," she sobbed inwardly. From deep within herself, she tried to find strength and prepared to do battle again.

The Indian had hold of her skirt, trying to yank it past her thrashing legs. Then suddenly, a deep hard voice was hailing the camp. Startled, the brave became rigid, then stood up. Leaning on an elbow, Roxanne stared out into the night. A large horse with a tall man upon its back rode into the firelight. Her eyes went wide as she stared at the rider.

She gasped, "You!" and she knew no more as she slumped onto the ground in a faint of relief.

CHAPTER 3

Caleb Coleman was awake but trying to go back to sleep. He knew he was in no condition to face the day. His eyes burned and his throat felt like he had been swallowing dust.

''Hell, I don't even know where I am,'' he growled out loud.

He became aware of a chill breeze floating through the room and nipping at his body. Blindly reaching for the blanket at his feet, he realized for the first time that he had no clothes on. He leaned on his elbows and cautiously opened his eyes.

At first he could make nothing out through the blurring film that covered them. He rubbed at his lids with a fist, then made a slow survey of the room. It was all too familiar. With a groan, he plopped back down, muttering, ''Hell. Lily trapped me again.''

With one hand holding his head, the other fumbled along the floor, searching for his buckskins. His fingers found them in a wadded heap and hauled them onto the bed. As he went through the pockets, a sharp voice from across the room snapped, ''It's all there.''

He cocked an eye in the direction of the voice and grunted disagreeably, ''That's a miracle.''

A thin body, topped by a head of frizzed mousy brown hair, darted across the room and flung itself onto the bed. Bony arms reached and sought to embrace him. ''Ah, Caleb, don't be mean. You know I wouldn't take your money. Never. I swear."

Roughly, he pushed the woman away and stared up at the thin, ravaged face. "Lily, you'd steal from a dead man," he said bluntly.

"Caleb, that just ain't so." She brought her painted face close to his and added in a coaxing whisper, "Let me please you like I did last night."

His eyes narrowed and he studied the debauched woman, wondering how she could have possibly pleased him. He made a disgusted sound and swung his feet to the floor.

"I'm not that drunk today, Lily."

Lily sat up and screeched out at him, "Damn you, Caleb Coleman, you'll be sorry for this some day. I promise you that."

His buckskins in his hands, he turned slowly and glared down at her. "Are you threatenin' me, Lily?"

Lily didn't pause for breath as she ranted and raved and begged in the interim. But Caleb only grinned and turned a deaf ear to her as he finished dressing.

When she saw that she wasn't going to sway him, Lily became quiet and sat up in the middle of the bed. Silently she watched him lace the long moccasins, then fold them into a wide cuff below his knees. When he stood up and strapped a belt around his waist and adjusted the knife in the pouch attached to it, she spoke quietly.

"Someday you will love a woman, Caleb Coleman." She waited a moment, then added as an afterthought, "And I will ruin it for you."

"That's not likely, Lily." Caleb chuckled and settled the coonskin on his head. Giving her a little wink, he picked up his gear and rifle and slammed the door behind him.

Making his way to the stable behind the one-room

shack, he dodged puddles of water the best way he could. But they were numerous and his buckskins were wet to the knees by the time he reached the stalls.

Overhead, low clouds swept across the sky, promising more rain at any minute. As he entered the barnlike structure, a distant rumble of thunder rolled through the hills. The picture of his parents' graves flashed through Caleb's mind and he thought, God, I hope it don't rain no more.

The stallion stamped his feet and nickered softly when his master entered the dim interior. He was unused to being in such close quarters for such a long time. Caleb stroked the sleek neck and tried to remember what day it was.

The past week was mostly a blur for him. He remembered clearly the two days of hard riding in the rain after his parents' funeral; but once he had gained his own territory and the familiar tavern, events and days became hazy.

He recalled standing at the rough bar, downing one glass of rum after the other, trying to drown his sorrow and guilt. But how he'd ever ended up with Lily, he'd never know.

"The whore must have slipped somethin' in my drink," he muttered to the horse.

He had a deep affection for the stallion and, as he moved the brush gently but firmly over the sturdy gleaming back, he continued to talk to it in low tones. Many times the animal's long swift legs had saved his life. There wasn't an Indian pony in the hills that could catch him.

When the horse had eaten and been saddled, Caleb swung onto its back and rode out into a fast gathering storm. Lifting the reins, he spoke quietly to the mount and it responded in mile-eating strides.

Caleb did not try to hold him back. If his calculations were right, he was already two days late for the rendezvous with the other hill hunters. He hoped that his three partners had waited for him.

Sitting easy in the saddle, he thought with anticipation of the months ahead. The hunt promised to be a good one this year. They were going to hunt in the relatively untouched Ohio Valley. Indians claimed that the streams teemed with beaver and that the forest was still filled with game. He grinned happily. It was even possible they might stay there for a couple of years if the game was really plentiful.

For some time Caleb rode the floor of a valley, crossing swollen creeks and freshly made streams. Then the mighty wilderness loomed in front of him, rising hill on hill. Sodden leaves covering the trail deadened the sound of his passing. His eyes probed the forest around him. In these days of unrest it was best to be prepared. His long rifle was primed and lay handy to his reach.

He was thankful that the settlement didn't have to worry about British soldiers yet. Hopefully they would never have to. Personally, he didn't believe that the redcoats would be foolish enough to venture into the wilds of Kentucky.

But renegade Indians were another matter. These Indians were outcasts, shunned by every respectable tribe in the territory. They managed a living by selling their savagery to the highest bidder of the moment. At this time, England had their doubtful alliance. Several times this past summer he had seen them at a distance, hunting game for the British.

As for the tribal Indians, they still kept pretty much to themselves, moving deeper and deeper into the wilderness as the areas became hunted out. With these

Indians, Caleb was on good terms and had no fear. He had hunted with most of them, had even lived with some of them and slept with their women.

He reached down and patted the stallion's proud arched neck. ''Hell, I have more to worry about from Lily than I do them.'' He chuckled when the horse tossed its head as if in agreement.

He knew that Lily had a vindictive mind and was capable of doing murder if aroused enough. But he grinned inwardly as he thought of her parting threat. Well, she'll never get back at me through a woman. In my thirty years I haven't loved a woman and I'm not likely to at this stage of the game.

Then an earsplitting clap of thunder ended his reverie. Darkness was suddenly descending and a raw wind was blowing in from the north. ''We're in for it, big fella,'' he spoke softly to the nervous animal.

He had no sooner spoken than the rain was on them, coming in a lashing torrent. He hunched deeper into his coat and pulled the collar up around his ears.

Caleb had been riding an hour or longer when he saw the animal's ears suddenly snap ahead. Quickly he leaned forward and was just in time to grab the flaring nostrils and choke off the whinny rising in its throat.

What had the stallion heard or smelled, he wondered. Could it be Indians, or animals? It was hardly likely that any animal would be out in such a downpour.

He rode more cautiously. Then, to the right of him, a horse whinnied. Swiftly reining in beside a huge pine, he took a slow survey of the dim rain-screened forest. Almost immediately his gaze fastened and held on an area of huge boulders and skyscraping pine.

He brushed the rain from his eyes and peered

around the tree. Beneath an outcropping slab of stone, a large fire burned, and the shadowy figures of Indians sat around it.

Moved by curiosity, he dismounted and noiselessly moved forward until he was within a few feet of them. Crouching, he hid, motionless, behind a large rotten log. As he watched, a tall brave stood up and fed more wood to the fire. Caleb grinned broadly. He knew the Indian. A place would be made for him at the fire.

The red man's name was Long Step. It was uncertain whether he was still a member of his father's tribe, or if he had become a renegade and gone over to the British, but for Caleb, it made no difference. He knew that wherever Long Step's sympathies lay at the moment, he would always be a friend to this particular white brother. For more than four years they had hunted together, sharing a mutual campfire.

The other Indians, however, five in all, were strangers to Caleb and he decided to wait a moment before announcing himself.

Then the aroma of roasting meat floated past in the air and his mouth watered. He couldn't remember when he had eaten last. He was in the act of rising and hailing the camp when one of the younger braves stood up and walked away from the fire. He carried a stick with smoking meat in one hand and Caleb, watching curiously, suddenly leaned forward in surprise. The yawning blackness the brave walked into was a cave. He could make it out clearly now as the new wood on the fire flared up.

Slowly he settled back, asking himself, Now what are them red devils up to? He frowned at a sudden thought. Could they have captives in there?

The rain lashed at him, sending rivulets of water

down the gaping neck of his coat. He turned his face to the log, trying to decide what to do. If the Indians did indeed have whites in the cave, would Long Step see fit to release them to his friend?

It would be a touchy situation, Caleb knew, with the decision going either way. Primarily it would depend upon who was in there. If it were some settler or hunter who had, in Long Step's eyes, done him a wrong, only through threat of death then would he release them.

In any case, he decided, before he did anything, he wanted his horse under him and his rifle in his hand. He moved silently in the rain toward the stallion.

Then, with the animal firmly between his legs, and the rifle partially wrapped in an oiled rag, he steered the horse through the maze of boulders, stopping in the shadow of two pines. Through the dripping foliage he peered toward the entrance of the cave. The rain had slowed to a fine drizzle and, along with the light from the fire, he could now see some distance into the cave.

After a moment he grunted, satisfied. His eyes had found the figures of a man and woman crouched against the wall. "I knew them devils had whites in there," he muttered darkly.

His eyes were stopped by the tensely held body of the brave who had carried the food into the cave. His dark eyes never strayed for long from the pair who were hungrily stuffing meat into their mouths.

Knowing that the Indian's interest was in the woman, Caleb strained his eyes and studied her, also. He could not see the faces of the captives, but the ripe curves of the woman's body were clearly revealed by her clinging wet dress. He smiled grimly. He couldn't blame the brave for staring. Any man would stare at such a beautiful and enticing sight.

He swore softly under his breath. "That damned varmint wants to make her his squaw."

He studied the brave a moment longer. He understood the raw hunger on the red face because it echoed his own. To lie between the legs of that curving flesh would be pure heaven. But the Indian could forget about it. Caleb Coleman would see to it that he did.

He eased back in the saddle, his mind racing with ideas of how best to rescue the woman and her companion. The fire was finally allowed to burn low and the braves talked in short, guttural words. Caleb strained to hear what they discussed and was disappointed when they only talked of the day's hunt and where they would hunt again, come daylight.

Then their words were cut off as the woman screamed in terror. Caleb's eyes shot to the shadows and the Indian was gone. He had sneaked unnoticed into the cave and had grabbed the girl.

The firelight showed the woman, tall and slender, with golden hair falling to her waist. The breath gasped through Caleb's lips. "It's her," he whispered, "the girl from the cemetery road."

Before his gaping stare, the brave's hand fastened on the collar of the girl's blouse. With one fast yank, he had ripped the material to her waist. And before Caleb could climb from the stallion things began to happen so fast that he couldn't keep track of them.

The woman's companion, who turned out to be a boy in his teens, had sprung onto the brave's back and clung there like a monkey. The group at the fire was howling their glee and suddenly the young man was sailing through the air. He landed hard and lay still.

Before Caleb could come out of his stupor, the

brave was on the screaming, scratching girl, pinning her to the ground.

The sight of her naked helplessness released him and he was digging his heels into the stallion and halloing the camp. He was conscious of red faces swiveling his way, aware of the astonishment on their faces; but his attention was fastened on the face of the girl.

He saw her eyes go wide and read the silent "You" her lips framed as she fainted.

Long Step unwound his long length in one graceful movement. His dark eyes were unreadable as he looked across the fire at his white brother. Then raising a hand, palm forward, he spoke. "Coleman.. Why do you travel in this rain?"

In a split second Caleb knew how he would free the girl. His voice dangerously quiet, he answered, "I search for my new bride and her brother, Long Step."

Long Step's eyes narrowed, and a low disgruntled murmur traveled around the fire. The leader frowned at them and motioned them to silence. Then turning to Caleb, said stoically, "We no see your woman, Caleb."

Caleb wondered if the brave was being foxy, or if he really did think that another female was his woman. He thought of Lily and hoped that Long Step had not seen him with her. In fact, he hoped that no one had seen him with her. In any event, he would play his friend's game.

Speaking slowly, and willing his words to fall with effect, he said, "I do not speak of the woman at the tavern. I speak of one with hair like gold. I married her this morning and we became separated in the storm." He paused to let his words sink in, then continued. "I have not bedded her yet and I will kill the man who keeps me from her."

Long Step stared at him as though trying to read the truth in his eyes. Then he dropped to the ground and held a whispered conference with the others. Many times the young brave frowned and shook his head vehemently. But each time Long Step seemed to override his objections. Finally, he rose and returned to stand beside Caleb.

"It is possible that we have your bride. There is one here with hair of gold," he began, then was interrupted by the young brave tugging at his leggings. With a look of displeasure on his proud face, the leader bent down and listened to the low spoken words.

When he straightened up, a glimmer of amusement shone in the black eyes. Folding his arms across his bronze chest, he spoke gravely. "If you camp with us and the woman shares your bed willingly, then we will say she is your woman."

Taken off guard by these conditions, Caleb strove to keep the alarm off his face. Not at all sure of the consequences, he still nodded his head. "She will bed with me," he said quietly.

Long Step gazed at him a moment, then made a motion toward the girl.

Caleb swung to the ground. He took his time unsaddling the horse and removing the bedroll. He needed time to think through the action he must take.

Would this city-bred girl go along with what was necessary? A hill-raised girl would recognize the necessity and join in wholeheartedly. She would know of the consequences if she did not. But what of this woman? Would she have any idea of what could lay ahead of her if she repulsed him?

He realized that the Indians were watching him suspiciously and quickened his movements. He pulled the reins over the stallion's head and let them hang. The horse would not stray far. Giving a ragged sigh, he leaned over and picked up the bedroll. Shouldering the rifle, he strode purposefully toward the cave.

The girl lay on her back, an arm flung over her head, nesting in a mass of curls. Her full breasts jutted like ivory mounds in the firelight, and his eyes lingered there. This one had never known a man, he knew instinctively. The eyes and body were still unawakened. How does one go about seducing a virgin in these circumstances? he asked himself.

A hunter with whom he once spent a winter had, one night, out of pure loneliness for his wife, described his wedding night to Caleb. He now recalled the expression in the man's eyes as he told of kissing his young bride, first on the lips, then down the throat, and finally on the breasts. His description of taking a pink nipple into his mouth and sucking it had left a weakness in Caleb's loins. He had never done this to a woman. The personal hygiene of the prostitutes and Indian squaws had never fostered this desire in him. But as he gazed down at the lovely face of the unconscious girl, he knew that he would do things to her he had never dreamed of before.

Then he frowned. He was remembering how the hunter had ended his reminiscing. "You have to get a virgin roused up before you can enter her," he had said. "Still, I hurt her, even though she wanted me and I went slow."

Alarm overshadowed the tenderness in Caleb's eyes. What if I hurt her? What if she cries? For the first time in his life he did not want to hurt a woman.

He sat back on his heels. She was beginning to stir. As he reached to pull her dress together, a soft moan escaped her lips. Then black eyelashes flickered and blue eyes were staring up at him. He smiled at her sympathetically and she whispered in immense relief, "Thank God, a white man."

Caleb dropped his eyes before her look. Would she think so, later? He stood up and began to slowly pace the floor. Once he stopped as though to speak to her and, when she looked at him, his courage vanished and he paced some more.

Then as he passed her for the fourth or fifth time, she whispered, "Is there something wrong? Are you a prisoner, too?"

He shrugged his shoulders helplessly. There was nothing to do but get on with it. He squatted down beside her and she leaned up on an elbow. "I'm not a prisoner," he began, "but in order to free you, I'm going to have to do somethin' that you might not like."

A puzzled frown gathered on her forehead. "I don't understand."

Embarrassment swept over Caleb's rugged features, and he stared at his dangling hands. This was going to be harder than he had thought. When her hand reached out and touched his questioningly, he started and blurted out, "I told them that we were married."

A merry peal of laughter rose from Roxanne's lips. "What a marvelous idea. I think you were very smart to think of that."

He nodded feebly. Just as he thought—she had no idea of what was expected of her. How in the hell was he going to explain it to her?

He reached out and smoothed a strand of hair from her brow. "Are you virgin?" he murmured.

For a moment she stared at him in surprise. Then anger flared in her eyes, and she tilted her head proudly and snapped, "Of course I am." She shot him a fast look. "But I fail to see where it's any business of yours."

A seriousness grew in the depths of his eyes and, before he could speak, the knowledge of his meaning spread over her face.

"No. I won't do it," she gasped.

As her head continued to move in denial, he leaned down and hissed, "Would you rather be an Indian squaw?"

She stared at him, terrified. What he suggested was impossible. She could not let a stranger do that to her. Only a husband had the right. But as his cold eyes bore into hers, she wondered what it would be like to have this rough-looking man make love to her. Stories that cousin Mary had told rushed through her mind, and suddenly the thought of this man doing those things to her caused warmth to spread through her body.

Then a small voice inside her was whispering, You have to do it. Better him than an Indian. Anyhow, you've been eager to know all about it.

The moment was here and, despite her fear, she was weak with the desire that flooded over her. But this man must not know how she felt, she thought, and to hide it from him, she gave a bitter laugh and said, "It seems that I'm to be a squaw any way you look at it."

Caleb gazed at her, uncertain for a moment. Was this her way of saying that she would do it? He rose wordlessly and began to unroll his bedding. When he had finished and stood up, she was standing at his elbow.

"Will you go see if Gideon is alright?" she asked, then paused a moment before adding hesitantly,

"Would you . . . would you also ask him to sleep outside? It would embarrass me to have him see us together."

Her request startled him for a moment. It had never occurred to him that a woman might want privacy at such a time. The other women he had known had never seemed to care. There was a lot he didn't know about ladies.

When he moved to where the young man lay, he found him conscious and staring up at him. Gideon sat up and held out his hand. "I heard you talkin' to Roxy and I understand that it has to be done." He grinned crookedly and added, "Of course, she didn't see it that way, did she?"

Caleb touched the youth's shoulder and grinned back. "She's not hot on it." His face became serious and he whispered, "I'll treat her with respect."

"I'd appreciate it," Gideon answered and left the cave.

But later, when Caleb lay bare beside Roxanne, he doubted if he could keep his word. As he felt the warmth of her nakedness and smelled her perfumed scent, pure lust swept over him. But when he moved a leg against hers and felt her body stiffen, his usual confidence with women deserted him. Like some green schoolboy, he lay quietly beside her, burning inside to take her in his arms.

The fire died down and dark shadows almost concealed them. The Indians still sat by the dying fire waiting for the consummation of the claimed marriage, and he could wait no longer.

With eyes half closed, he turned toward her. Her velvety soft legs came against his and he wondered why he had waited so long. Drawing her to face him, he whispered, "It must be."

She stared into his eyes and her lips trembled as she cowered deeper into the blankets. His hand came up and his fingers gently began to caress her throat. He felt her pulse jumping like a small frightened bird but he was powerless to stop. The smooth flesh slid beneath his hand, urging his fingers downward. Then his long hair was falling on either side of his face as he lowered his head and captured her lips.

At first she lay stiff in his arms. Then the intensity of his kiss was rousing an urgency in her that was equal to his own. Her lips parted eagerly, welcoming his thrusting tongue. When his hand compulsively moved to stroke her breasts, a small breathless moan escaped her lips. A half smile softened his face as he moved his lips down her throat and fastened them on a rigid nipple. Teasing his tongue across it, he thought, the little one may be virgin in her body, but in her mind she is not.

But he, too, was learning new sensations as his hands explored her. He had never before known the intimate curves and valleys of a woman's body, and for the first time realized what he had been missing in the fast coupling of all those other women.

When he could no longer restrain himself, he slowly and gently pushed a knee between her legs, forcing them apart. Then, he hung over her, waiting. Soft arms came up to encircle his neck, and ever so slowly he guided himself into her. Several times he halted when she cried out. But at last he lay against her, their bodies molded perfectly together. Slowly he started a rhythmic movement, watching her face for signs of pain. Her eyes were closed but her lips were slightly parted. He kissed them again. After a moment her legs moved around his waist and she strained to meet him.

He began to move faster and vaguely, in the background, he heard the watching braves give a satisfied grunt as the girl-woman beneath him grasped him convulsively and shuddered helplessly in the grip of passion that tore through her.

CHAPTER 4

Roxanne awakened in the early morning and drowsily wondered why she ached so and yet had a feeling of such well-being. Then gradually she became aware that her head was resting on a hard muscular shoulder, and that the weight of an equally hard leg lay across her own. Then remembrance flooded over her and she blushed as she recalled her abandoned lovemaking.

Slowly, trying not to awaken him, she leaned up and studied Caleb's sleeping face. His features were still harsh, but they seemed somehow softened in sleep. Perhaps the cold eyes, which now lay closed, contributed to that doubtful softness, she thought. His nose is nice, she decided, and the firm lips were beautiful. She remembered those lips moving over her body last night and tingled.

Angrily, she fought the sensation. She had been forced to allow this tall stranger to make love to her, and she was ashamed of herself for enjoying it. He had taken from her what she had saved for a husband. And worse, he was not anything like the kind of man she had always hoped to love. Still, this rough man had tried to be gentle last night, as if gentleness was a new and strange action for him. A smile began on her lips, and she reached out to smooth his tangled hair. But with her hand in mid-air, her conscience nudged her. Your mama would never approve of such a man.

I must get away from him before he wakes up,

the nervous thought shot through her. If he should put
those knowing hands and lips upon her again, she
knew that she would eagerly respond.

His shoulder lay heavy on her hair and it took some
time to slowly ease it away. But at last it was done
and, shivering, she hurried into her clothes. She was
thankful for the light shawl that covered her torn
bodice.

Slipping to the mouth of the cave, she looked out
into a beautiful morning. It seemed almost a miracle
that the deluge of rain had finally stopped.

Her searching gaze found Gideon. He lay rolled in a
blanket, close to the head fire. She did not rouse him.
She was not anxious to face him and maybe see scorn
in his young eyes.

Instead she walked around the sleeping camp and
made her way to a rushing stream some yards away.
Kneeling beside it and scooping water onto her hands,
she splashed it on her face. She gasped at its icy shock
and shook her head vigorously. When she stood up
and began to dry her face on the bottom of her petticoat, Caleb was standing beside her. He was bare to
the waist and his dark skin shone over the rippling
muscles of his arms and shoulders. When he looked at
her possessively out of sleep-filled eyes, she remembered his touch and began to tremble.

To hide the red blush that sprang to her face, she abruptly turned her head away. His lean face hardened as
he studied her. In the light of day she was a haughty
bitch, he thought. Not at all the same warm woman
who had lain in his arms a few hours ago. A glint of
mockery lurked in his eyes. He would break that cool
pride with one stroke of his hand. He circled her waist
with an arm, bringing her tightly against his body.

The hard pressing of his thighs against her caused

Roxanne's heart to surge and a warmth to spread through her. Drawing on every ounce of her willpower, she stubbornly repulsed the signals that urged her to move into his arms and tried to push him away.

The words that he was about to utter faltered on his lips. In anger and pride, he pushed her from him. "It seems my little dove doesn't want to play this mornin'," he sneered.

Steadying herself against a tree where she had lurched, she glared at him, hissing loudly, "I'm not your little dove. I'm not your anything."

Before he could reply, they heard the Indians begin to stir, stretching and yawning loudly. Roxanne glared a moment longer, then took advantage of the interruption to walk away from him. As she hurried past the braves' bold stares, she felt his cold eyes boring into her back.

Throwing herself onto the tumbled blankets, she wondered what would happen next. Now that he had used her, would this unpredictable man go off and leave her with the Indians? Most likely he would after that display of rejection she had thrown at him. "Mama is always saying that my tongue will be my undoing someday," she sighed.

She gazed at the still-sleeping form of her cousin. Although she dreaded it, she wished that he would wake up. The stranger was talking to the Indian, Long Step, and she felt uneasy. They talked in the foreign tongue and she didn't understand one word.

The fear of being left behind grew in her until at last she hurried to Gideon's side. The young man jerked awake. Sitting up and blinking sleepily, he gazed at her owlishly. "What's wrong, Roxy?" he asked.

"I don't know," she whispered back, then nodded toward Caleb and the Indian. "I'm wondering what he's up to. Do you suppose he's going to leave us behind?''

"Naw, Roxy. A white man wouldn't leave his own people at the mercy of redskins.''

"Huh," she snorted, "I wouldn't put anything past that one.''

Gideon hid a smile. He was pretty sure that cousin Roxy wasn't as bitter toward the stranger as she pretended. When she started to rise, he held her back. "They're comin' this way. Wait and hear what they have to say.''

The two men approached the rekindled fire and Long Step raised his hand for silence. In a deep voice, his words carrying, he spoke. "Golden woman belong to Coleman. I watch last night. She welcome him as master. He take her away now.''

Even though a deep relief ran through her that she wasn't being left behind, she felt herself blushing furiously at the Indian's words. She shot a look at Caleb and wanted to beat the knowing twinkle from his eyes. She opened her mouth to refute the brave's words but Gideon lay a silencing hand on her arm. "Do you want to stay with the savage?" he growled under his breath.

The nails of her clenched fists cut into her palms as she bit her tongue to hold back her words. Then silently she consoled herself with ways of erasing the mockery from the eyes that were even now stripping away her clothes.

Caleb led off at a jogging trot, with Roxanne and Gideon bringing up the rear. It had taken quite a while and many strong words from Caleb to regain their mounts. The horses were good sturdy stock and the Indians wanted to keep them. But in the end, Long

Step had decided in his friend's favor, and reluctantly the animals had been handed over.

They traveled for hours through the silent wilderness with no words between them. How much farther did they have to go, Roxanne wondered wearily. The rough, uneven trail was tiring and a throbbing pain nagged at her side. And to make matters worse, she had caught glimpses of a river through the leafless trees and a terrible thirst plagued her. Along with her hunger, she was miserable.

Around noon they came to a hill that was taller than any they had yet climbed. When Caleb reined in and dismounted, motioning them to do the same, she gratefully swung to the ground.

"We'll lead the horses up this one," he informed them. "They're beginning to tire."

Roxanne spoke to Gideon in a tone loud enough for the stranger to hear. "I'm happy to see that at least he has feelings for animals. After all, we mere mortals never get tired."

Looking across his saddle at her, Caleb smiled, an insinuating gleam in his eyes as he said softly, "I'm sorry to hear that you're tired, Roxanne. Perhaps we could take a rest while Gideon minds the animals."

Gideon ducked his head to hide his grin when Roxanne, taken aback by the hunter's words, hurriedly blurted, "I'm not in the least tired."

"Are you sure?" Caleb urged, his voice and eyes sending her messages that confused her all the more.

"Yes, I'm quite sure," she snapped. "Are we going to climb this hill or not?"

Caleb winked at Gideon and led off. Roxanne trudged at his heels, watching his sure feet pick their way over the rocky trail. Her own steps were uncertain and the underbrush picked at her skirt, hampering her every movement. She pulled and tugged and swore under her breath.

Caleb chuckled. "Petticoats have no place on the trail." He turned and grinned at her. "We'll have to fix you up with a pair of buckskins."

"That won't be necessary. We'll be home before long."

He made no answer to her comment, but hidden from her, his face seemed to say, "Don't be too sure."

At last they gained the top of the hill and Roxanne threw herself to the ground. She was exhausted, and the stranger could go off and leave her if he wanted to—she was going to rest. Gideon dropped down beside her.

Caleb, however, walked a few yards away and suddenly lifted his voice in a loud "Hallo." In a short time there came an answering call and, as Roxanne and Gideon watched curiously, three men emerged from the forest.

They were garbed in much the same fashion as Caleb and carried rifles in their hands. "They're long-hunters," Gideon whispered.

The hunters raised their hands in greeting as they slowly approached. They were rough-looking men, and Roxanne regarded them suspiciously as they came to a halt before Caleb. But their whiskered faces spread in friendly smiles and one of them asked with concern, "How did you find your maw and paw, Caleb? Did the fever hit them?"

His voice saddened, Caleb answered, "It got them, Abe. I buried them nine days back."

So that's why he was there, Roxanne thought, as the men spoke in sympathy. "Say now, Caleb, we're sorry to hear that."

They stood a moment in awkward silence. Then, as though Caleb felt her eyes upon him, he looked at Roxanne and said, "Come on, I want you to meet someone."

Roxanne watched them draw near and noted that, although they dressed in the same manner as Caleb, there was a startling difference in their garb. Where Caleb's buckskins were clean, soft, and pliable, fitting his muscular body perfectly, theirs were stiff, wrinkled, and stained, hanging loosely on lank bodies.

"They're a rag-tailed lot," she muttered to Gideon. "Fitting company for him."

When the group was almost upon them, Roxanne lowered her eyes and nervously played with the gravel where she sat. As the four pairs of feet halted near her, Caleb ordered her to stand up and meet his friends.

She glared up at him, ready to lash out with her sharp tongue. But the expression in his eyes warned her to be careful and, with a display of indifference and impatience, she rose and stood beside him.

He lay an arm familiarly across her shoulder. She pulled away only to have him tighten his grip and hold her closer. "Men, I want you to meet my new woman," he purred. "Ain't she somethin'?"

She silently suffered their greedy eyes, like hungry fingers running over her, but inside she could feel the panic and fear building again.

Then, without warning, one of them reached out a grimy hand and laid it on her shawl-covered breast. Startled and sickened, she shrank closer to Caleb even while she wondered if he meant to turn her over to these filthy men he called his friends.

But when she glanced up at him, she saw that his face had grown dark with fury and that his eyes were sparks of ice. Suddenly he put her behind him, then, fast as light, his fist lashed out and the hunter lay sprawled on the ground.

The surprise on the man's face was comical as he leaned on an elbow and complained, ''What in the hell is wrong with you, Caleb? You know we always share our women.''

His voice cold and threatening, Caleb warned, ''I'm not sharing this one and I'll shoot the man that forgets it.''

In shaken relief Roxanne leaned against Gideon. The young cousin put an arm around her, his eyes thoughtful. In the beginning he had liked the strangely cold hunter, had even accepted that what he had done to Roxanne was neccessary. But now it appeared that he meant to keep her, and that put a different face on the picture. He decided that it was time to start laying plans of his own.

Caleb was extending a helping hand to his fallen friend now and they heard him ask, ''No hard feelin's, Jake?''

For a moment Jake stared at him sullenly. Then smiling a toothless grimace, he accepted the out-stretched hand. ''Hell,'' he laughed, ''if she's that special to you, keep her. She's too fancy for my blood, anyhow.''

Caleb chuckled softly. ''She suits me fine.'' Grabbing Roxanne's hand, he urged, ''Come on, let's go get somethin' to eat.''

Roxanne stumbled along behind him, hardly comprehending his words. Her mind was too busy with the ones just spoken between him and the hunter. It was crystal clear that this wild man meant to keep her. Appalled at the thought, her eyes brimmed with tears. Was she never to see her parents again? Would this rough hill man keep her for the rest of her life?

Then they were standing before a dilapidated cabin and Caleb was saying, "Welcome to the Roost."

He swept open the door and pushed her into a room that was rank with the odor of dirty bodies and stale sweat. Roxanne, always fastidious, wrinkled her nose and coughed lightly. Caleb caught her look and, for the first time, realized what a pigsty he lived in. He became embarrassed and swore angrily, under his breath, "Them damned sluts had better clean this place up."

The room was in a dark gloom, with only the feeble light from the fireplace illuminating it. There was a window, Roxanne noticed, but someone had nailed boards across it to keep out the chill of the autumn wind.

Caleb pushed past her and took down a candle from the rough mantel. Squatting beside the fire, he lit it from a flaming splinter. When he placed it on the table, Roxanne gave a start. In the candle's warm glow she saw four women. They were perched like birds on a narrow bench that ran along one wall. Three of them were white, of an undeterminable age, and the fourth was an Indian girl. She looked to be around fifteen and would have been pretty had she not scowled so often.

But Roxanne had never seen the likes of the others. Their bodies were thin and gaunt, almost lost in the short, ragged, and dirty homespun shifts they wore. Lifeless eyes stared out of sunken faces, and she turned to escape their vacant stares.

From the corner of her eye, Roxanne watched the young squaw sidle up to Caleb. With a fawning smile on her face, she laid a timid hand on his arm and murmured, "Welcome home, Caleb. White Star miss you."

Roxanne felt Caleb stiffen and heard his angry

breath suck in. Ignoring the girl's greeting, he loudly ordered food and drink. Then sliding onto a bench that flanked the table, he pulled Roxanne down beside him. While they waited for the meal to be put before them, he placed an arm around Roxanne's shoulder and his fingers stroked her throat and played with the curls at the nape of her neck. The gentle stroking brought a tingling through her body and, in confusion, she looked down at the table.

Then the gnawing hunger that chewed at her was forgotten. It would be impossible for her to eat from this table. Some careless hand had swiped at its surface, but spots of sticky food and grease liberally dotted it. She shuddered, thinking what the plates must be like.

When one of the women, her hands grimy and her nails dirt-encrusted, dropped a chunk of half-cooked meat beside the stack of plates, Roxanne's stomach lurched, sickened.

The woman sliced off a thick slab of meat, placed it in a tin plate, and sat it before her. Roxanne gazed down at the bleeding mass and shook her head vehemently.

Frowning at her repugnance, Jake sneered defensively, "Ain't the food good enough for you, princess? Maybe you'd like roast turkey and trimmin's."

Abe's malicious cackle rose over the rest of the snickering group, and Roxanne caught the mocking gleam in the Indian girl's black eyes.

But surprisingly, Caleb came to her defense. Jabbing at the offending piece of venison, he muttered disgustedly, "This ain't fit to eat."

Gideon, managing to choke down some of the meal, looked at his cousin and knew that she must be hungry. Poor Roxy, how awful this mess must seem to her. Then his eyes brightened. He remembered that in his coat pocket there was a half-eaten slice of cake that Mara had packed for them.

It was mashed and partly crumbled, but as Roxanne drew it from the brown paper wrapping, she knew that it was clean and bit into it eagerly. The familiar taste of Mara's baking brought a lump to her throat, and as she choked, Gideon was fast to hand her a dipper of water.

Everyone noted his deference to her, and an uneasy silence grew in the room. Abe shot a fast look at Caleb, wondering what he wanted with such a pampered doll. Hell, he thought, if a man rode that one more than once a night, he'd break her.

With a scraping of chairs, the meal was finished and the men moved to the fire to smoke a pipe and talk about the upcoming hunt. Roxanne remained at the table unconsciously crumbling a piece of bread while she wondered what the hunter would do next. Did he plan to go on this hunt they discussed? And if so, would he force her to go along with him?

But just as she came to the conclusion that even a wild hunter wouldn't force himself on a woman and make her go with him against her will, a hand was laid upon her shoulder. She stared into hard eyes that silently spoke his intent.

She shook her head mutely and his eyes narrowed as he whispered harshly, "Yes."

He was raising her to her feet when a broad hunting knife came whizzing through the air. Its point struck only inches from Roxanne's hand. Hypnotized, she stared as it twanged crazily before standing still.

A sharp crack of flesh hitting flesh sounded loudly in the room. There followed a screech of pain and White Star lay sprawled on the floor. Caleb stood over her, a mask of fury completely covering his face.

"You red bitch," he panted. "You ever try a trick like that again and it will be your last."

He spun away from her and White Star pulled herself up and sat on a rumpled bed. There was a bitterness around her thin lips and her eyes shot hatred at the girl who was taking her place. A cold chill shot through Roxanne, and she had the sure premonition that she hadn't seen the last of this girl.

Then Caleb's hand was on her elbow, again pulling her to her feet. She yanked her arm away and they stood staring belligerently at each other. With blazing eyes holding cold ones, Roxanne cried out, "I won't! We're not proving anything to a bunch of Indians now."

The room had gone quiet and everyone's eyes were upon them. They waited to see how Caleb would handle his new woman. The men, half jealous of their leader, hoped that the pretty piece would win. And the jaded women prayed that he would smash her beautiful face.

Only Gideon was concerned with the real issue. This time it would be an out-and-out case of rape. He stood awkwardly beside the hearth knowing that he was helpless to aid her. He could only wait around to comfort her later.

Caleb's hands shot out and grasped her wrist. In a voice harsh with his need of her, he muttered, "I want to rest and you're gonna keep me company."

She glared back at him and, in a voice full of contempt she ground out, "You are without decency. I hate and despise you."

She felt his fingers quiver as they tightened around her, and she cringed from the black anger that threatened to strike her. She had gone too far in repulsing him in front of his men. His pride was torn and nothing would save her now.

There followed a tense silence, then wordlessly he was jerking her across the floor. His shoulder struck open a door and she was flung into a room. As she reeled away from him, he slammed the door shut with his heel. She stumbled and barely managed to grab a chair and cling to it. Before she could catch her breath, he was beside her.

His arms went out and slowly he brought her up against him, bending her body to fit his own. "You don't hate me, Roxy," he whispered softly as his lips came down, hungrily searching.

The remembered glow kindled within her and, against her will, her lips stirred and moved against his. She made no protest when his hands removed her shawl, then slowly slid the torn blouse over her shoulders. He swept her into his arms and carried her to a narrow bed in a corner. The afternoon sun struck through a small window directly over the bed and for a moment he feasted his eyes on the beauty of her face and breasts. Slowly, piece by piece, he removed her other clothing, his eyes devouring each disclosed part of her.

He dropped to the floor on his knees and gathered her in his arms and bent his head to take a thrusting breast into his mouth. When he felt the nipple harden and heard her breath quicken, he glanced at her face and saw her eyes heavy with desire. He smiled wickedly and said to himself, Not yet, my little dove. Not until you ask me.

His lips moved over to the other breast and he teased at it with his tongue. Her body was trembling now, but still she hadn't made a sound. He was afraid his ruse would backfire on him for he was on fire himself. He would not be able to hold out against her much longer.

His lips moved hotly down her flat stomach and to the inside of her soft thighs. Instantly her body began to writhe and she fastened her hands in his hair. "Ah, Caleb, Caleb," she almost sobbed.

He brought his head up and looked into her half-closed eyes. "Do you hate me, Roxy?"

"No, my love, no."

"Do you want me to make love to you?"

"Yes, yes."

He stood up and hurriedly stepped out of his clothes. On the bed, he took hold of her legs and, spreading them, hung suspended over her.

"Take it, Roxy," he whispered in a smothered voice. "Show me that you really want me."

Her slim fingers grasped him gently and eagerly guided him into her. He sighed happily and lay still a moment, firmly locked within her. She had given in. She was totally his.

Complete darkness filled the room when at last he relinquished her. Serenely relaxed, Roxanne recalled her cousin's stories and smiled lazily. None of Mary's stories had come near to what she had just experienced. In the privacy of his room, with no prying eyes to watch, Caleb had done such things to her that still she trembled just remembering.

A knock sounded on the door and a nasal voice announced that supper was ready. She felt Caleb rise and fumble in the darkness. The rasp of his flint sounded and a candle sputtered, then flamed. Holding the candle aloft, he let its light play over her body. Shyness flushed her face, but she was too tired to pull the blankets over her nakedness.

He gave her a crooked smile. "I expect you're tired. Can I help you dress?"

She nodded and sat up. He put down the candle and pulled her to her feet. Taking the clothes from the floor, he began to dress her. It was a slow process, brought on by his stopping to kiss some spot of flesh, or taking a rosy nipple between his lips. But at last it was time to put the shawl around her shoulders. Then turning to the table, he picked up a brush. Carefully, he brushed her tangled hair until it lay shining and curling around her face and shoulders. But of the faint smudges under her eyes, brought on by the passion he had aroused in her, he could do nothing about. So kissing each eyelid softly, he led her from the room.

They were met with knowing looks and winks, and Roxanne lowered her eyes against them. Caleb noticed and, strangely, felt anger and irritation with his people. Frowning at them, he snapped, "Tend to your eatin'."

Truly hungry now, Roxanne waited hopefully. Maybe the evening meal would be better. But the same chunk of meat, reheated, was placed on the table.

Caleb stared at it a moment, then rising, stalked to a bag in a corner and dug out half a ham. Slamming it on the table, he unsheathed his knife and sliced off several thick slabs. Stringing them on an iron spit, he roasted them lightly over the hot coals. Then sliding the juicy slices onto a plate, he put them before Roxanne. "Try these," he said, then added, "they're clean at least."

Her eyes thanked him as she dug in, eating heartily. Caleb watched her from lowered lids and, pleased, he smiled.

When the men had once again gathered around the fire to enjoy their pipes, Gideon drew close to his cousin. From the corner of his mouth he whispered, "Roxy, we must get away. I recognize this part of the country and can find my way home. When everyone is asleep, we'll sneak away."

She gave a short nod and Gideon joined the men.

Deep in thought, Roxanne bit nervously on her thumb. A conflict of emotions was running through her mind. Her blood raced at the idea of freedom, and yet her heart was rejecting the thought of leaving the hunter. The past hours had brought such a closeness between them she feared she would be unable to leave him.

Then the reasoning that had been so carefully taught to her returned. This man was not for her, she thought. She could never lead his wild, haphazard kind of life. She glanced around the room, taking in the furniture, the dirt and squalor. Never in a hundred years could she live this way.

But within the hour, she was wavering again. Caleb was sending her glances that made her tremble with anticipation. Then she happened to look up and catch the jealous mockery gleaming in the young squaw's eyes. A feeling of scorn for her weak flesh rushed over Roxanne. In the hunter's eyes, she was no better than the Indian girl. She served the same purpose and was merely replacing the squaw. At some later date, when he grew tired of her, there would be another replacement.

What then? her mind asked. Would she then be turned over to his awful friends? The thought sickened her, and she knew that she must get away from him at all costs.

When the mantel clock struck eight, Caleb rose and stretched. As Roxanne watched nervously, he turned toward her and motioned his head toward the door. She threw a fast look at Gideon and he stared back, his eyes reassuring her.

The bedroom door had barely closed when he swept her into his arms. "Please, no," she murmured beneath his probing lips. "I am so tired."

He drew back and studied her pale, drawn face, and a hint of softness flickered a moment in his eyes. He remembered how he had ridden her delicate body and reminded himself that she was no whore. The little one was probably very tired. Reluctantly he gave in to her wishes.

"We'll get a good night's sleep then. I can wait."

Roxanne lay with her head pillowed on his shoulder, his heartbeat strong and even in her ear. His rhythmic breathing told her that he was asleep . . . had been for some time. Her dress was caught beneath him, and she carefully pulled it free and waited for some signal from Gideon.

Through a wide crack in the wall she gazed at a full moon. That was good. She and Gideon would be able to see where they were going. If we ever get started, she worried. Where was he anyway? Had he fallen asleep?

The stars had grown paler and the first dark gray of dawn had almost arrived before she heard a scratching on the wall outside.

Ever so slowly, and barely breathing, she eased out of bed. Silently she slipped on her shoes and tied the shawl around her shoulders. Ready to leave, she paused and gazed at Caleb's sleeping face in the faint light. Her eyes lingered on his lips and she weakened.

How many times, she wondered, would she regret leaving him. He stirred slightly and murmured her name, and she froze. But he continued to sleep and, step by careful step, she made her way to the door and cautiously opened it.

Loud snores filled the main room and she doubted if they could have heard a thunderstorm. But in her corner, alone, White Star watched with a satisfied grimace as Roxanne opened the door and left.

She stood uncertain on the rotting porch, then Gideon materialized out of the shadows and moved to the steps. Grabbing her hand, together they ran to the cover of the forest. A small glad cry escaped Roxanne. In the light mist her saddled mare stood stamping impatiently among the pines. Gideon's horse, too, stood ready beside the mare.

"Gideon," she whispered, "you are a sly one."

He grinned. "I ain't about to walk."

They led the horses a good distance from the cabin before they mounted and began racing through the forest.

As she rode headlong, branches whipping at her face and body, Roxanne felt relief to have escaped the hunter, but regret as well. Would she ever again, she wondered, experience the shattering pleasure he had given her?

Daylight came and they began to pass through stump-dotted clearings. Gideon looked back at her, his lips spread in a wide grin. "We'll be home soon, Roxy."

CHAPTER 5

The aroma of coffee awakened Caleb. The sun was bright, shining through the window, and he stretched lazily in its warmth. Then he reached a groping hand to the soft body that lay next to him. When his fingers found only rumpled bedclothes, he sat up with a start. His eyes took a swift survey of the room and his lips formed a thin line. "Gone!" he thundered.

His mind clutching at any hope, he mumbled, "Maybe she's eatin' breakfast."

With an impatient grunt he swung his feet to the floor and hurried into his clothes. Then he flung open the door with such force, surprised looks leapt at him. His eyes wild, he shot a look around the room. But only the hunters and their women sat at the breakfast table. The boy was gone, too.

His words rang out, bouncing from the four corners of the room. "You stupid bastards, you let her get away!"

They gawked, only his anger reaching them at first. Then looking to where the boy had slept, they returned his mad stare sheepishly. They could have pointed out that it was he who had let the girl slip out of his bed, but caution warned them that now wasn't the time. Instead, they sat uneasily, their eyes on the floor.

The women slunk into a corner, waiting for the storm that was sure to come. White Star stood to one side, watching Caleb's anger. Her dark eyes penetrated his rage, and she was aware of his pain, which was like a white hot fire eating at him. Jealousy shot through her so strongly that she shook from it. "Someday," she promised herself. "Someday."

But surprisingly, Caleb said no more. His disappointment was so great that words alone could not express what he was feeling. He could only throw them a disgusted look and leave the room. He conveyed his anger, however, by slamming the door so hard that the old cabin shuddered.

Outside, he leaned against its rotting logs, scowling in indecision. Should he go after them? There would be no problem in tracking them. Long Step had taught him the art of tracking and reading signs. A mere boy would give him no trouble at all.

He began to pace the length of the porch with the restlessness of a caged animal. Why had she sneaked off and left him in the middle of the night? He would have sworn on his life that she loved him. Only a woman in love would have responded in the fashion she had. Their lovemaking had been perfect in every way.

Again, anger replaced his hurt. Why should I want to keep a woman that don't want to stay? he demanded silently of himself. Hell, I could get so many women, I could lay with a different one every night of the week.

But a small voice inside whispered, But not like that one.

Tormented and heart-heavy, he struck out at the door, barely missing Abe coming through it. Abe walked a wide circle around him and sat on a bench alongside the wall. Clearing his voice tentatively a couple of times, he began to speak.

"Caleb, I know it's none of my business and you

can stop me if you want to, but it's wrong and dangerous for you to keep that girl here against her will. You
must remember that she's not one of our regular
women. She's a young girl that's been proper raised.
You could get us all in a pack of trouble . . . maybe
even killed." He paused, then added, "You don't
even know who she is."

Caleb had stopped his pacing while Abe talked, and
now he sat down beside him. His friend spoke the
truth, of course. He had known it from the start. But
the girl had got to him, and he had hoped that she
would love him and would want to stay with him.
Damnit, he told himself, how would he get along
without her?

He sighed resignedly and stood up. "Yeah, Abe,
you're right. I'll just trail along behind them and see
that they get home safely. They're likely to run into
trouble again."

"You're thinkin' straight, Caleb," Abe assured
him, slapping him on the back. "See the lady home,
then get back here and take care of White Star. She
was right upset last night."

About to leave, Caleb spun around and snapped
harshly, "Have that red slut gone by the time I get
back here. I don't lay with no killers."

Some minutes later the stallion was saddled and
brought from the shed in the rear. Leading the animal,
Caleb's eyes scanned the ground. At the edge of the
forest he found their tracks; they weren't many hours
old. He swung into the saddle and relaxed in an easy
lope. Looking up at the sky, he made a mental note
that he'd most likely catch up with them around noon.

His fury was completely gone now and he gave
himself over to reliving the past two nights and day.
He had never dreamed that a man could feel the way

he did about that woman. He had come close to telling her that he loved her—and probably had in the heat of his passion. But who knew or remembered what was said then. In their saner moments, however, the cool look of disdain in her eyes every time she looked at him had cut short the words in his throat.

"Is that why I'm so hot for her," he wondered out loud.

But he recalled her soft warm body lying next to his, her faint perfume drifting from the covers, and he knew it was more than that. His feelings for her were deep and strong. For even though he lusted after her almost constantly, he still wanted to take care of her . . . protect her. Right at this moment he worried that Indian enemies might cross her path.

The cold dread of that happening and of what they might do to her made him urge the stallion to a faster pace.

The sun was directly overhead when he caught sight of them. They were halted at a spring and Roxanne knelt before it, cupping water into her mouth. Gideon sat his horse, his eyes wary on the forest. Caleb felt himself suddenly overcome with affection for the boy. "He's lookin' out for her the best he can," he spoke to the horse. "I had no right to be mad at the boy. It's only natural that he'd want to get her away from the likes of me."

He remained hidden in a clump of cedar until Roxanne remounted and they disappeared into the forest. He noted that Gideon seemed to know where he was going so he hung back, well out of sight.

The sun was making its westward swing when Caleb first heard dogs barking in the distance. A homestead is nearby, flashed through his mind.

Before long he came abruptly to a wide clearing. It

led down a sloping hill, fanning out to several acres in a small valley, then halfway up another hill. He smiled grimly, watching the pair tear across a pasture toward a group of buildings.

He dismounted and squatted on his heels behind a clump of red-turning sumac. As he watched, the riders thundered to a stop in front of a large cabin situated at the edge of the cleared land. Gideon swung to the ground and tripped over several welcoming hounds as he turned to help Roxanne dismount.

Laughing together the two walked toward the cabin, and it was then than Caleb saw a tall man with a wide frame standing in the door. When the man moved down the steps and clasped Roxanne in his arms, Caleb's eyes dulled with the jealous ache that shot through him. Then he moved his shoulders in a despairing shrug, he should have known that one like her belonged to some man.

But hold on, he thought, his spirits soaring. That couldn't be her husband. She was still virgin when I bedded her. I'm the man that made her bleed. He laughed bitterly. A hell of a lot of good it done me.

Then the enthusiasm of his first thought was chilled with his second. In all probability she was *going* to marry the man.

When a cold raw wind blew in, his flesh was no colder than the knot in his breast. With a long sigh he rose and turned to the horse. "There's no use hangin' around here," he muttered.

Wearily, he swung into the saddle and turned the stallion into the woods. He rode slowly, his head bent, dreading his return to the cabin now that it was empty of the girl's presence.

The trilling note of a bird brought Caleb's head up sharply. Carefully he studied the trees and leafless underbrush. Long Step had taught him the various birdcalls until even the Indians were sometimes fooled by his imitations. If he wasn't mistaken, that had been no bird that had whistled.

Had he not been so preoccupied with thoughts of Roxanne, he would have known that three braves had trailed him since noon. With faces hard and emaciated, and buckskins dirty and weather-beaten, they wore the well-known look of the renegade.

After he had ridden another five yards or so, a different song sounded to the left of him. His lips firmed: That's two.

When the third note sounded to his right, he began looking for cover. Then a bullet whistled past his head, hitting a boulder in front of him. He whirled in the saddle in time to see a puff of smoke and a horse coming at him on a dead run. A brave, face streaked with vermilion, rode low on its back, a raised tomahawk in his hand.

As the long rifle came swiftly to Caleb's shoulder, from the corner of his eye he saw the flash from a gun barrel in the brush to his right. He squeezed the trigger, the rifle boomed, and the Indian sagged sideways. The Indian hung a moment, then let out a blood-curdling yell before he lay motionless on the ground.

But even before the renegade hit the ground Caleb had wheeled the stallion into the thicker forest, taking a flying leap from its running back. He hunkered down behind a large beech and studied the spot where he had seen the gun's muzzle flash.

It was near dusk now, the darkness coming fast in the thickness of the pine and cedar. From the top of some nearby cedar, he heard the fussy gobble of wild turkeys as the flock roosted for the night. He frowned: How in the hell am I supposed to hear them varmints slippin' around in this racket?

His mouth felt dry and his palms sweaty. He had visions of the two savages squatted somewhere in the brush, or behind some tree, wearing triumphant smiles. "You ain't got me yet," he swore grimly. "And if you do, I won't go alone."

He sat forward. Faintly, there had come the soft thud of unshod hooves clattering away in the semidarkness. Was it one horse or two, he wondered. On the needle-strewn floor of the forest, it was hard to tell.

Taking no chances, he remained immobile for another half hour, straining his ears for a snapping twig or a rustling leaf. Everything was still. The turkeys had settled down and the wilderness was eerily quiet.

The moon rose early, full and bright. Caleb's stomach rumbled. He hadn't eaten all day. And the more his hunger gnawed at him, the more convinced he became that he was a fool to remain hidden any longer. Both them damned Indians are probably miles away by now, he thought. Most likely sittin' by a warm fire, eatin' some homesteader's cow.

His mind made up to leave, he stood up slowly. His eyes took a careful survey of the forest. Nothing stirred. Only an occasional scary hoot of an owl broke the stillness. Flexing stiff and sore muscles, he nodded his head in satisfaction. There were no redskins out there. Hell, what if there are? They won't be able to see me any better than I can see them.

In a half-crouch he darted from his cover, running toward the horse. Too late, midway there, he heard the snapping of a twig and felt the bullet as he ran. His arms flew up, he staggered a moment, then fell face forward. As he fought back the screaming pain of the bullet lodged in his chest, he heard the soft flapping of moccasined feet coming toward him. Then, sensing the Indian squatting beside him, he drew on his last strength and willed his features immobile. Rough hands rolled him over on his back and nimble fingers probed his chest. After a satisfied grunt, the Indian stood up; then his footsteps faded away.

Numbness spread over Caleb, leaving him aware only of the burning hole that ran red with his blood. With shaking fingers he covered the steady trickle, striving to hold it back. I must get the hell out of here, ran through his mind. I gotta get back to my men.

He thought of the full day's ride ahead and groaned. How could he ever do it? He turned his head and, in the full moonlight, saw the stallion just a few yards away. Caleb strained up on an elbow and called softly, "Here, boy. Come give me a hand."

The big horse tossed his head, nervous at the scent of blood. But when Caleb called again, he gave a low nicker and, nimble-footed, made his way to his fallen master.

With one hand grasping the reins and the other still pressing the gaping wound, Caleb painfully pulled himself up. He leaned against the glossy shoulder, shaking the dizziness from his brain. Then catching hold of the saddlehorn, finally dragged himself onto the horse's back.

Only vaguely aware of his actions now, he turned the horse homeward. With each jarring step, he felt the warm blood flow more freely and the forest become a blur before him. Unable to stay erect any longer, he felt himself falling over the mare's neck. A warning voice whispered in his ear, Hang on, just hang on.

When he felt himself going over sideways, he knew that all was lost. Down the trail from behind him came the thundering sound of hoofbeats.

CHAPTER 6

Roxanne walked to a small window and pulled aside the heavy drapes. Outside, the fallen leaves turned slowly in the cool breeze, skipping across the ground and into the spent garden where they were caught and held in a fence row. There would be snow out there before long, she knew.

Would she still be here? she wondered. "God, I hope not," she whispered softly.

She had been here a week, and each day was becoming harder to live through. Her eyes were weary of staring at the endless wilderness that stretched in every direction. The hushed silence sometimes seemed to surround and crush her. She longed for the sound of carriages rattling down a cobbled street and to look out a window and see other houses. When a homesick tear gathered in her eyes, she brushed it away angrily. She should be ashamed of herself. Uncle Malcolm and Gideon were being so nice to her. They were trying to make her visit a pleasant one. She should be glad of the opportunity to get to know her uncle and cousin.

She smiled. Uncle Malcolm was such a rough character on the outside. But he didn't fool her. There was a twinkle now and then in the depths of his eyes that gave away his true nature.

Few people had been allowed to see this softer side of Malcolm Sherwood. It was mostly reserved for his loved ones. He had come up the hard way in the streets of England. At nineteen, he and his two younger brothers, Gavin and Tom, had stowed away in a ship going to America. Several miles out to sea, they had been discovered, but had been allowed to work their passage on the vessel. After a long voyage, they had landed in Boston with little money and only the clothes upon their backs.

But by the end of the day, with a stroke of good luck and much finagling, he and Gavin landed a job with Boston's largest brewery. They found rooms upstairs over a tavern, and young Tom stayed home and kept house for his brothers.

Before the year was out, Malcolm had met the owner's fragile, lovely daughter. They had fallen deeply in love and a year later, after many tears on the girl's part, the father had allowed them to marry.

Through hard work and the determination to show the father that he hadn't been wrong in allowing his daughter to marry him, Malcolm worked himself up to a position high in the brewery. And, always with an eye to Gavin's future, made sure that his brother climbed with him; later, they brought Tom into the business.

After a few years, his father-in-law died, leaving everything to his only child. Through the years, as Malcolm busily and profitably ran the business, a son and daughter were born to them.

Life for him was smooth and beautiful until one winter, when grippe came to the city. In a week's time his beloved wife and two children were gone. His whole world tumbled, and he roamed the streets at night, putting off the hour when he must return to the great, empty house.

Finally, he could no longer stand the loneliness and uselessness of his life. One evening while dining with Gavin and Tom, he spoke of a plan that had been nagging at his mind.

He began by reminding his brothers that he was still a young man. "I am strong and in good health. I have many years ahead of me, and I know that the memory of my Beth will never let me live in peace here in Boston. I've been reading in the paper about a section of land being opened up in Kentucky."

While his brothers watched him curiously, he picked up his glass of wine and sipped at it. Putting it down, he continued, "I'm turning my business over to you two, selling my house, and moving to Kentucky. I'm going to try and start a new life there."

Gavin and Tom had raised loud objections, but Malcolm had brushed these aside and in two weeks had left his old life behind.

He had taken to the wilderness from the start, its roughness being akin to his own nature. In the process of taming his piece of the wilderness, his loss became a dim, pleasant memory. He had in time, even found himself a woman, whom he visited regularly.

Since he was fourteen, women had been a necessary part to his living. Through the years, that drive had not lessened. Even now, pushing sixty, he bedded his woman several times a week.

But again, Malcolm was to know grief. His brother Tom and his wife had been killed in an accident. Their grieving young son was sent to him, looking so like his father that Malcolm had groaned inwardly.

Surprisingly, it was pleasant having a youngster around again. He had not realized how much he missed the carefree sound of young laughter and chat-

ter. In a short time, Gideon was more son than nephew
to him.

Roxanne watched him now, standing tall and force-
ful, showing up the slouched figure of the younger
man with whom he was talking. She had a small
shiver remembering an encounter with that man.

His name was Ez Johnson and he was one of the
four men who worked for her uncle. She imagined that
he was the leader, since it was always he who shouted
orders to the other men and who cuffed around the
women living with them.

Her first encounter with Ez had taken place in the
barn, two days after arrival. She had gone there to tell
Malcolm and Gideon that supper was ready. Her uncle
and cousin were nowhere about, but the barn had been
warm and she had lingered. The pleasant odor of new
hay drifting down had caused her to stop and savor it.
It was a new scent to her and she thought it delightful.
Her eyes roamed over the barn, taking it all in.

To the left of the long main aisle that ran the length
of the building, the horses contentedly munched grain
in a feedbox. Directly across, milk cows and a bull
slowly chewed their cud. A mama cat with two kittens
came and rubbed against her leg. She stooped down
and played with them a moment, remembering her
tabby at home. When she was about to rise, a rustle in
the hayloft caused her to look up. She smiled when
she saw chaff sifting down through the cracks. Gideon
was up to some trick.

Swiftly and silently, she climbed the leaning ladder
and stepped onto the top floor. In the near darkness,
she strained to see her way. Then the setting sun
moved from behind a tall pine and shed its light
through a window in the barn's peak. For a moment

she was blinded by the red glare and squinted against it. Then shielding her eyes with her hand, she saw two figures lying in the hay.

On her back, leather skirt pulled up around her waist, lay the Indian girl, White Star. Kneeling between her bent and spread legs, his hard member in his hands, was Ez Johnson. She had gasped her surprise and, startled, the pair turned to her.

The girl became embarrassed and hurriedly scooted her skirt down to cover her nakedness. But not Ez. Instead, he had grinned wolfishly at her and turned himself so that she could more easily see what he held in his hand. In a suggestive manner he looked down at himself and then up to her. "There's enough here for you too, missy." He leered, making a fist around himself and moving it back and forth.

Enraged, and held motionless like a hypnotized bird, she had stood helpless, glaring at him. Then, to her utter disbelief, Ez with one fast jerk flipped up White Star's skirt and rammed himself into her. As he drove away, his thrusts making the girl cry out, Roxanne was finally released from her trance. She sprang to the ladder and fairly flew down it. His mocking laugh trailed after her, even after she entered the cabin.

Later, she wondered how White Star had found her way to the homestead and why she had coupled with Ez so fast. She would have been surprised to learn that Ez had found the girl in the hay not ten minutes before her own entrance. And that he had said only three words to the girl: "Spread your legs."

She had not mentioned the incident to Malcolm and was now sorry that she hadn't. Every time she ran into the man, his bold eyes stripped the clothes from her body. She was curious to know just how much the young squaw had told him of her and Caleb.

With a long sigh, she turned from the window.

The man on the bed watched her cross the room and his dark eyes narrowed. Couldn't she just once look his way . . . inquire how he felt? The week he had lain here, she had been neither curious nor sympathetic toward him. A slow anger was beginning to build in him. Even a mangy dog would get a pat on the head.

He raised his head a little and looked at her under his lids. If he didn't know her better, he'd swear that he saw a shadow of fear on her proud face . . . or something close to it. He wondered what she had been staring at outside and longed to be able to get up and look. But he was so damned weak. However, each new day found him a little stronger.

He could thank crusty Malcolm Sherwood for that. Malcolm's face had been the first thing Caleb had seen when the fever released him. He had been only vaguely aware of his surroundings the first time he opened his eyes. He knew that he lay in a bed, under a roof. Then a rough voice that matched the face bending over him had stated matter of factly, "Well, stranger, I see you've decided to join the livin'. I didn't think you'd make it there for a while. You must have lost half of your blood before we got back here."

Memory of his fight with the Indians had come flooding back. One of the bastards had shot him. His hand came up to his bare chest and he felt the bandage tied tightly around his ribs.

Giving Malcolm a weak grin, he said, "I'm much obliged to you, mister."

"No need for thanks," Malcolm had grunted, then motioned behind him.

When Roxanne and Gideon came to stand beside

his bed, he could only stare in his surprise. Could Roxanne be thinking of marrying this old man?

He opened his mouth to speak . . . to object, and she put a silencing hand on his shoulder. "Don't talk, stranger," she said coolly. "You must rest and save your strength."

He frowned at her interruption. Why was she pretending that she didn't know him? But of course. She was afraid the old fellow would get jealous.

Well, let him, he thought angrily. It would serve the old goat right—wanting to marry a young girl like her.

Stubbornly, he opened his mouth again, but this time the eyes shot fire as she signaled him to hold his tongue. And while his black eyes glared back defiantly, Malcolm cleared his voice and spoke.

"This is my niece and my nephew, Gideon and Roxanne."

There was a silence as Caleb, stunned, took in his words. For the first time he was ashamed of what he had done to her. Even though she had asked, almost begged, it had been his fault. He had known how to kindle and render her helpless and had done so deliberately. Of course, it had been necessary the first time. But he should have done the decent thing after that and brought her straight home.

But even as these thoughts passed through his mind, he knew that he would do the same thing all over again, given the chance. Now, however, he owed her a debt of gratitude. If she had told her uncle, he'd be a dead man. That rough character would have blown his brains out without thinking twice.

He smiled up at the two young people and joined in the pretense. "I'm happy to meet you both."

Roxanne narrowed her eyes at the sound of amusement in his voice, then turned sharply away.

Malcolm studied her stiff retreating back, asking himself, How has this man upset the lass? He has been nothing but polite. Even from the beginning there had been nothing but hostility from her. Except for one anguished cry when he and Gideon brought the stranger in, she had refused to have anything to do with him.

He turned his attention back to the bed and asked caustically, "What's your handle, stranger?"

Caleb reached a hand to him. "I'm Caleb Coleman, long-hunter."

Shaking his proffered hand, Malcolm said, "We're the Sherwoods and I'm called Malcolm, amongst other things." He paused, then shot another question. "What are you doin' in this neck of the woods?"

Caleb feigned a tired yawn. Sherwood had noticed his niece's behavior and was suspicious. He must channel his thoughts into another vein. "I was out scoutin' for good spots to set my traps, come winter," he lied.

The shrewd eyes studied him a moment, and after a dry grunt, said shortly, "This is my territory around here. You just move on a few more miles."

"I'll do that, Malcolm. I surely will."

"Good."

Malcolm then turned to changing the bandages. He studied the wound closely and nodded his head. "It's comin' along fine. Startin' to close up already. You're lucky you were in good strong health."

When fresh salve and cloths had been laid on the wound, he stood up and said to Gideon, "Give him a shave, son. That'll perk him up."

Gideon had brought the razor and soap, along with hot water, and placed it on a table. Caleb knew that he did it reluctantly, and he felt the boy's dislike keenly as he scraped the whiskers off his face.

I don't blame the lad, he thought. I'd feel the same way if our positions were reversed.

That had been five days ago. Many times since, he had tried to coax Roxanne into conversation. But she answered his questions sharply and to the point, never extending any more information than necessary.

Once he had asked, "What's a dainty lady like you doing in the wilderness? You looked more at home back in Boston."

Her answer, as usual, had been short. "I am here only until the fever is gone from there."

Her answer had cast him in a gloom that lasted the rest of the day. He should have known she wouldn't stay in the wilderness any longer than she had to. It was just as well, he thought. This lonely country would eat at a woman like her until she went mad. This one was made for parties and gay living.

A ragged sigh escaped him. Not that it made any difference to him. Deep down, he had known from the beginning that the girl-woman wasn't for the likes of him. It would be like pairing a highbred mare with a wild, shaggy pony. Even if she should, in time, accept and love this beautiful country, she would never be able to understand him and his woods-queer ways.

But the time spent with her could not be taken away. During nights when he lay with some slut, or sat beside some lonely campfire, he would relive those moments.

Against his will, he admitted that Seth Hale was more her type. According to Malcolm, Hale was a neighbor who had recently taken up homesteading a few miles away. "He's a tenderfoot from Boston," he had added, a hint of derision in his voice.

The city man had fallen for Roxanne and called on her often. He had come courting last night and it had been hell on Caleb, lying helpless in bed, listening to their light chitchat. They talked of plays they had seen and parties they had attended in Boston. They discussed new dances and the present style of clothes. All these things the hunter knew nothing about, and the resentment of Hale within him grew. Besides, there was something suspicious about the fancy homesteader. The man was too elusive about too many questions put to him by Roxanne.

Once she had remarked, "It's strange that we never ran into each other in Boston." And Seth had been so long in answering, Caleb had leaned on an elbow and gazed at him curiously.

Looking uncomfortable and fidgeting in his chair, Seth had finally stammered something to the effect that they most likely moved in different circles, he being so much older than her.

Caleb had settled back down, muttering to himself, If you're that old, why are you smellin' around her now, you bastard?

The first night Hale had left early, with Roxanne walking him to the door. Holding his breath, Caleb had watched to see if he would kiss her. But to his relief, Seth had only taken her hand and held it for a moment. So that's how the gentry do it, he mused. He couldn't visualize himself merely shaking hands with Roxanne. He would have at least had to hold her in his arms and kiss the lush red lips.

Relaxed, he studied the man who gazed down at Roxanne with admiration in his eyes. He was manly-looking enough. He dressed with care, almost as though he still lived in Boston and not the wilds of Kentucky. The man was almost as tall as himself, but fair in coloring, and his hair was a light brown, where his own was Indian-black. His eyes were open and frank, while his were narrow and scowling.

The scrape of the coffeepot on the hearth brought Caleb back to the present. Glancing in that direction, he saw Roxanne pour herself a cup of coffee and carry it to the table. He watched her sip slowly, drawing her lips away from its heat. He lifted himself on one elbow and called across to her, "I could go for a cup of that."

She raised her head a little and looked at him coolly. Then wordlessly, she picked up the cup and walked into her room. The door slammed and he stared at it, his jaw knit in anger.

The blood ringing in his ears, he wanted to get hold of her and slap her beautiful face . . . wipe that contemptuous look out of her eyes. Suddenly, his voice was ringing out furiously. "Bitch! Bitch! Why is it you can only talk to me when I'm between your legs?"

He knew his words were hammer blows to her, but he made no offer to soften them. He must crush her as she had him. His words continued to beat out at her. "Why is it, fancy lady, that when I've got you in bed you can talk to me? Why is it only then you can laugh and moan and whisper wild things in my ears?"

In his fury he had sat up in bed and flung off the covers as though it would give more freedom to his tongue as he shouted his insults at her. But when only silence greeted his outburst, he was suddenly drained. Exhausted, he lay back down.

"By God, if it kills me, I'm gettin' out of this bed tomorrow," he panted. "If I stay here much longer, I won't be responsible for what I do."

The next morning, while one of the women who worked for the Sherwoods made breakfast, Caleb remarked to Malcolm, "I'm gonna get up and eat at the table this morning."

Malcolm didn't answer immediately but studied him a moment. Coleman looked somehow different this morning. His lean, lined face now showed a hardness he hadn't noticed before. Sagely, Malcolm nodded his head. "I expect it's about time. Your wound is about healed . . . ain't apt to break open and bleed."

He helped Caleb to dress, his touch surprisingly as gentle as a woman's. When his moccasins had been laced, Caleb rose slowly to his feet and grew dizzy with weakness. But gradually his head cleared and it felt good to be out of bed. He made his way slowly to the table while Malcolm walked behind him, to lend a helping hand if necessary.

Some minutes later the woman was putting ham and eggs, potatoes, and hot biscuits before him. His old appetite came rushing back and when he had finished eating, he felt close to being his old self again.

He was on his second cup of coffee when Roxanne, followed by Gideon, flounced into the room. The thin gown and robe that she wore so casually hid nothing. The hint of rosy nipples pushing at the flimsy material drew Caleb's eyes like a magnet. Desire, so strong, built in him until his breathing momentarily stopped.

Roxanne was startled to see him at the table, but made no mention of it. And although her greeting to Malcolm was cheery as she sat down across from him, it failed in its attempt to be casual.

"You're late, Roxy," Malcolm growled good-naturedly. "I heard you and Gideon talkin' to all hours last night. You two keep me awake tonight, there's gonna be some head-crackin'."

"Gideon is late, too," Roxanne was fast to point out.

There was an amused light in Malcolm's eyes as he leaned forward and peered at Gideon. "I know that, niece, but oversleepin' is not his excuse. I heard you slippin' out of the cabin at daybreak, Gideon. Must have been somethin' pretty important to get you up so early?"

Gideon squirmed, uncomfortable under the probing eyes that stared at him around the table. When he made no answer to the silent question, Malcolm asked abruptly, "You out lookin' for woodpussy, Gideon?"

Gideon's face became a guilty red, and Malcolm and Caleb laughed loudly. Not understanding the question or the laughter, Roxanne waited for it to subside, then asked, "What is woodpussy, Uncle Malcolm?"

"Woodpussy, Roxanne, means red meat . . . Indian woman."

Caleb shot a surprised look at Malcolm. He spoke mighty strong in front of his niece, he thought. Secretly, he watched her mull over the words, then blush when she got their meaning.

Malcolm finished his coffee and rose from the table. Roxanne smiled up at him and murmured, "I'm sorry I was late, uncle."

She had spoken in a prim little voice, but Caleb noticed that as she glanced at Gideon her eyes were full of mischief. And when Malcolm left the cabin, the two of them covered their mouths, smothering conspiratorial laughter.

Caleb glared at them, jealous of the joke they shared. He, too, had heard them last night: the soft murmur of Roxanne's voice and the deeper hum of Gideon's. They had been playing cards, for he had recognized the sharp flipping sound of the cards as they were shuffled, and the slap of them as they were dealt. Lying in the darkness, he had wanted it to be him in there with her. He wanted to share a time with her, when only each other's company would be enough for them.

Again, it came to him that they had never talked together—had never shared anything except each other's body, the sharing being a flame that was almost unquenchable.

Feeling his gaze upon her, Roxanne glanced coolly at him, her eyebrows slightly raised. Then her eyes flared wickedly and she shrugged one shoulder, allowing her robe to fall open. Deliberately then, her slim fingers went to the thin strap of her gown and slowly slid it down until one firm breast lay bare. She heard the sharp intake of his breath and a mocking gleam shone out of her eyes. Lightly, she trailed a finger over its roundness.

Unconsciously Caleb leaned forward, knowing nothing but the desire to put his hand where hers was. He half rose, then heard Gideon's snicker.

It came to him then that she was allowing Gideon to see her nakedness. Had he seen it before? He had heard of cousins fooling around. Had something been happening every night . . . right under his nose?

In one great lunge he was on his feet, his open hand flashing across her face.

Her head snapped back with its force. Her hand going to her cheek, she stared at him in surprise. He leaned back over the table and jerked her robe together. "Cover your damned self up," he ground out through clenched teeth.

Gideon jumped to his feet and grabbed Caleb's arm. But the angry man turned such a look on him that Gideon quickly pulled his hand away. Spinning around, Caleb made for the door, slamming it shut behind him. Roxanne stared at the shuddering door and wanted to cry. How could she have done such an outrageous thing.

Gideon started for the door, muttering angrily, "Uncle Malcolm is going to hear about this."

But Roxanne's anxious voice called him back. "No, Gideon, let it be. I acted like a damned hussy and I deserved what I got."

She rose to her feet and moved to the water pail. Dipping water into a wash bowl, she wrung out a cloth and held it to her smarting face. She felt the ridges left by his fingers beginning to swell.

"Roxanne," Gideon scolded her. "You know why he done it. He didn't want another man to see your nakedness." He waited a moment, then asked, "Why did you do it?"

"I wanted to punish him for some insults he yelled at me yesterday."

But deep down she knew this wasn't true. She had done it as an open invitation. She had wanted him to sweep her into his arms and carry her into the bedroom. She missed and wanted the feel of his weight pressing down onto her. Every night long hours had passed before she had fallen asleep. Even through the thick walls she was conscious of his presence and longed to go to him.

She sighed and looked helplessly at Gideon. Sympathy showed in his eyes as he said, "Ah, Roxy, you like that rough hunter, don't you?"

"Oh, Gideon, I don't know," she cried, her voice almost a wail. "I hate the kind of man he is, and yet, I'm so drawn to him, I act like an idiot whenever he's around."

"You like him because he's different from the men you have known. When he's gone, you'll forget all about him."

She gave him a small smile. "I hope you're right. Anyhow, there's Seth. Maybe he can help me forget him."

CHAPTER 7

Caleb went no farther than the porch at first. He stood staring blindly across the clearing that served as a yard. He hated himself for what he had done to Roxanne. Her white shocked face kept nagging at his brain. He felt like the lowest kind of an animal.

Slowly he became aware of the sounds drifting from the area of the big pole barn. A great deal of activity went on as horses were let out to pasture and cows were milked. Behind the barn, in a pen, pigs squealed as they fought over the slops in a wooden trough. A few yards distant, a woman scattered corn to a score or more hens and two roosters. They mingled their noise to the rest of the din by squawking and cackling their thanks.

He smiled as long-ago memories of these same sounds came to mind. Clearly he could see his mother milking cows and feeding chickens on just such a morning. He paused to wonder why his parents had given up the little farm to move into the poor section of Boston.

The farm was still there . . . empty and forlorn-looking. It had somehow accused him when he had gone there looking for his mother and father. As a young boy growing up, he had hated the permanence of farm chores and the backbreaking labor. While still in his early teens he had left his parents' home and traveled from Massachusetts to the wilds of Kentucky.

Stopping one night at an outpost, he had become friendly with a youth around his own age. The young man and his father were hunters and traveled with eight others. They had talked long into the night and, when they prepared to move on, his friend invited him to join them. His wild nature had jumped at the chance and hunting had been his whole life ever since.

But now, surprisingly, a nostalgia for those young days tugged at him. He pressed his fingers across his eyes, his mind heavy with remembering. Then, with an abrupt movement, he pulled his hand away and willed his mind to stop its memories. Memories would take you nowhere.

He was relieved to see Malcolm coming from the barn and walked to meet him.

"How are you feelin' by now?" Malcolm greeted him.

"Almost my old self. In fact, I've come to thank you again and to say good-bye."

Malcolm turned searching eyes on him. This was a surprise. He knew that the hunter was crazy wild about his niece and half expected him to hang around all winter. Most likely Roxanne's aloofness has finally frozen him off, he thought drily. It was strange how she treated the man. He'd swear she was attracted to him. He gave an inward chuckle. Missy probably thinks she's too good for him.

He grasped the proffered hand and shook it warmly. "Like I told you before, Coleman, there's no need for thanks. You'd have done the same thing for me." He nodded toward the cabin and added, "Hold a bit, and I'll send you out some grub to eat along the way."

Inside, he caught Roxanne peeking from behind the draped window. He grinned and nodded his head in satisfaction: Just as I figured.

Rummaging in cupboards, he quickly gathered meat and bread and rolled it in an oiled piece of cloth. Then handing it to Roxanne, he ordered, ''Take this out to Coleman. He's got a long ride ahead of him.''

Surprise swept over her face and she asked quickly, ''Where's he going?''

''Said he was goin' home. He's better now and he can't hang around here all winter. The big snows will start soon and he might not be able to get through the gullies and gaps then.''

Malcolm watched her secretly as she fought to hide her disappointment. And when a defiant pride came into her eyes, he grinned proudly and said to himself, A real Sherwood.

He nudged the package at her impatiently. ''Go on, Caleb's waitin'.''

Torn between a longing to see him one last time and a pride that wouldn't let her admit it, she put her hands behind her back and shook her head.

Surprised at her refusal, Malcolm glowered at her. She tried to glare back at him, but when he growled, ''Take it out to him, girl,'' she unconsciously sighed in relief.

I have to mind my uncle, she alibied herself.

Caleb led the saddled stallion from the barn and stopped to adjust the bridle and to tighten the cinch. His thoughts were on Roxanne. For a moment he was tempted to ignore her when he left . . . show her she meant nothing to him. But even as the thought went through his mind, he knew that he would seek her out. He had to look into her face . . . search her eyes. He had to see if there was some sign there that ran in sympathy with his own feelings.

Hell, he muttered inwardly, after that last display of mine, she'll probably spit in my eye.

Behind him, he heard a scuffling of leaves and turned to see her coming toward him. As usual, his face brightened at the sight of her. But when he asked, "Have you come to wish me Godspeed?" his voice held a bantering indolence.

She gave him a stinging glance and retorted, as she thrust the package of food toward him, "I wish I could have done that some time ago."

His hand involuntarily went out to touch her but she quickly stepped back, evading it. The rebuke cut into him and his temper flared. He would have liked to see her face, but she had bent her head and was busily fussing with the fringe on her shawl.

"Look—" he began. But she raised her head so sharply, and the expression in her eyes was so haughty, that the words died in his throat. He wanted to yell once again, Bitch, bitch.

Then suddenly, without intention, he was saying quietly, "I know you pretty well by now, Roxanne. You think that you don't care for me, and most likely you don't. But there's one thing I'm sure of. You lust for me just as strongly as I do for you. Right now you're thinkin' the same thing I am. You're thinkin' that right now you'd like to be layin' underneath me."

She stared into his smoldering eyes and grew weak from the desire that stared out at her. A tingling like fire ran through her, and she wanted to throw herself into his arms. But she caught herself in time and forced her tongue to say coolly, "You are very much mistaken, hunter."

Angry and hurt, Caleb gave the saddle a sharp tug and their eyes met for the last time. He swung into the saddle, lifted his hand in a mocking salute, and rode off.

Malcolm had taken Roxanne's spot behind the

draperies to watch the couple say good-bye. Sure in his mind, he waited patiently for them to declare themselves. When it didn't happen and Caleb rode away, he gave his niece an irritated look and grumbled, "Roxy, you are a nitwit."

About to turn from the window, he caught sight of a rider coming from behind the barn. "Seth Hale," he grunted. "Smellin' around again."

He liked the man well enough, he guessed. Seth was a good neighbor and always willing to help out, but he was a dour person who held himself strictly to propriety. He knew that Roxanne was impressed with his perfect manners, that they reminded her of home, but he doubted that the boring man could hold her interest very long.

She's got too much of me in her. He grinned. Seth's stingy lovemakin' won't be enough for her. Though she don't realize it, she needs a robust man like Coleman.

He glanced after the fast disappearing hunter and noted that he, too, had seen Seth. He gave a low chuckle. That will spoil his ride home.

Roxanne watched the approach of the horse and rider and feigned a welcoming smile. She would allow no one to see how deeply affected she was by Caleb's departure, especially this handsome visitor. Seth would think very poorly of her if he knew she was attracted to such a man.

She studied Seth as he drew nearer. His dress and manner were much the same as those of the men she associated with in Boston. Not at all like wild Caleb Coleman with his Indian buckskins. And Seth's features and countenance were as different from Caleb's as day from night, she noted. Where the hunter's face was cold and harsh, Seth's face was warm and smooth, almost delicately featured. However, the arrogance that shone out of his eyes was a common sameness, shared with Caleb.

She giggled and told herself, It's hard to say which man exaggerates his own importance more.

Speaking curtly to the horse, Seth brought the animal to a rearing halt beside Roxanne. Stepping down in one graceful movement, he bowed slightly to her. His voice gravely polite, he said, "How are you this morning, Miss Sherwood?"

His polite and proper manner was somehow out of place here in the wilderness, Roxanne thought, and her eyes twinkled as she replied, "I'm just fine. How are you?"

He ignored her question and asked instead, "Where is your uncle?"

Malcolm came and stood at her shoulder before she could answer. "Good day, Seth. What brings you over so early in the morning?"

Seth gazed at him a moment, his lips pressed tightly, then turned his gaze on Roxanne. Suddenly the wind was bitter and Roxanne shivered, making her teeth chatter. She had a terrible premonition that Seth was bringing news that would somehow crush her.

When Seth spoke, his voice was gentle. "I was just down to the post and this came in for you by special letter."

Unconsciously Roxanne drew nearer to Malcolm. She sensed his big body go rigid as he accepted the black-edged envelope from Seth.

His movements slow and fumbling, Malcolm mechanically tore it open. His eyes scanned the single sheet, then his nerveless fingers let it fall to the ground.

"Gavin and Aline," he whispered. "They're gone."

Roxanne's heart began to race and panic ran through her. Then she was screaming. "No! No!"

Malcolm pulled her into his strong warm arms and held her tightly. His mouth opened and closed several times before he managed in a harsh, bewildered voice to bring out, "Oh, dear Lord. Why? Why?"

A dull roaring swam through Roxanne's head and everything became a blur. Dimly she heard Malcolm and Seth talking but their words had no substance over the refrain beating in her ears: "They're gone . . . they're gone."

She was conscious of Malcolm's gentle coaxing. "Come inside, honey. It's damp out here and you'll get a chill."

She sensed that he led her into the cabin and sat her in front of the fire. The flames danced and hissed, and an occasional brittle twig snapped, and for a moment she was back home again in Boston. Her eyes smarted from unshed tears and her throat felt paralyzed.

Then silently Malcolm sat down beside her and pulled her onto his lap. She lay her cheek on his rough homespun shirt and a flood of tears washed down her cheeks and her slender body shook.

"Cry it all out, honey," he comforted her, his own weathered face cracking.

CHAPTER 8

It seemed that overnight the weather changed. The temperature had fallen and they awakened to a white and frozen world.

Roxanne, staring out the window, sighed. She felt so restless and fidgety. The passing days had been so uneventful. Maybe somehow the changing weather would have some effect upon their lives, maybe bring some excitement into it.

It had been a month now since Seth had brought them the dreadful news. She had been numb with grief the first week or so and had hardly known what went on around her. Uncle Malcolm and Gideon had been kindness itself, even though they, too, had suffered. Uncle Malcolm's face had aged visibly, and his shock of iron-gray hair now showed more traces of white. His step, which before had been so bouncy, was now more slow and heavy. "We'll all feel better next spring," he had said this morning.

She would not allow herself to think of the future. It was too painful and more than her mind could bear. Uncle Malcolm had squashed all hopes of her going back to Boston soon, if ever.

Last week she finally had the courage to read Cousin Mary's letter. She had skipped the part telling of her parents' deaths, but had read twice the last few sentences, not believing what she read. Mary had written, "The fever is still rampant here and we fear each new day. With death everywhere already, now it appears that fighting may also break out at any time. Our only consolation is that you're safe in your new home. We will miss you terribly and look forward to peacetime when you can visit us."

She had stared unseeing into the fire. To live here the rest of her life. Impossible! her mind cried out.

Then as though he could read her mind, Malcolm had said softly, "God has just about stripped me. I am grateful that he has left me you and Gideon for my old age."

She had made a low objecting sound, and he had leaned forward and asked anxiously, "You do like it here, with me?"

Ashamed of herself, she ran and knelt by his chair. He stopped his rocking and laid a hand on her head. "I'd miss you, girl, if you should leave. I used to get lonesome livin' away up the river here. Gideon, he ain't no company at all—either huntin' or chasin' some girl. I'd forgotten how nice it was to have a woman around the house."

She forced a smile to her face and said, "Thanks for calling me a woman, Uncle Malcolm. I don't think anyone else ever thinks of me as one."

Malcolm's laugh rang out in the cabin. "Come now, Roxy, you know better than that. What do you think Seth and the hunter think you are? A porcelain doll? That Caleb Coleman used to look at you like he'd like to eat you up. Even old Seth gets stirred up once in a while. They know you're a woman, all right."

She had blushed to the roots of her hair when he mentioned Caleb. She was well aware of what Caleb thought about her—one thing only. But Seth? He was a mystery to her. He came calling almost every evening and was always the perfect gentleman. He paid her all kinds of wild compliments, but never offered to do more than to hold her hand. Even when they had the cabin to themselves, he never went further.

Irritated at herself for thinking it, she had tried to visualize the long-hunter merely holding her hand, alone in a room. She suppressed a smile. He would have been all over her the minute the door closed.

Lately, she often found herself impatiently comparing Seth to Caleb, and too often to Seth's discredit. But quickly she would berate herself for wishing that Seth were more like the hunter. She should be thankful that Seth treated her with respect. His intentions were honorable, she knew, and she expected him to ask for her hand any day.

She returned to her chair and teased her uncle gently. "Will you be lonesome if some day I marry and leave you?"

"Not if you don't move too far away," he replied. A twinkle came into his eyes, and he added, "I don't think it's gonna be too long before a certain gentleman comes askin' for your hand."

She had taken her time answering his gibe, letting her fingers trace back and forth on the arm of her chair. Then looking at him seriously, she questioned, "Do you think that Seth's good husband material, Uncle Malcolm?"

Malcolm's face became serious, also. He knew that his answer was important to her. And after giving her question careful thought, he answered gravely, "It all depends on what you're lookin' for in a husband, Roxy. If you mean do I think that Seth will be good to you and provide well for you, then the answer is yes. But if you want excitement in your marriage—good rowdy brawls and wild lovemakin'—then I'd have to say no. Seth just ain't an excitin' man.''

He watched her solemn face for a moment, then teased her. "If you want a marriage that will never be dull, you ought to latch onto the hunter.''

She had jumped to her feet, almost shouting as she cried out, "That crazy wild man? Surely you're joking, Uncle Malcolm. I could never marry anyone like him.''

"Don't speak too fast, Roxy," Malcolm cautioned. "Caleb Coleman, and men like him, are the backbone of this wilderness. We'd be in poor shape without men of his stripe.''

She had jumped to her feet and flounced into her room. Flinging herself onto the bed, she cried herself to sleep.

She turned away from the window now and met her uncle's eyes. He had noticed her unrest and it bothered him. Her independent spirit and youthful vitality were a tonic to him, and when she became quiet and drawn into herself, he knew it right away. He suspected that the wilderness solitude was getting to her. He worried what the long winter months ahead would do to her.

He answered the weak smile she gave him and motioned to her. "Come sit beside me and I'll tell you how I started the homestead.''

Malcolm hadn't finished speaking when the door opened and Gideon came in. He stood on a small rug, stamping the snow from his boots and removing his coat and cap. His cheeks were red from the cold and his eyes shone. He spoke excitedly, "I got a good haul from my traps today. If I do this good all winter, I'll have a good bit of money, come spring.''

"I hope you don't take paper money for your labor," Malcolm warned. "We'll see the end of paper money before this war is over. That's for sure."

Gideon nodded in agreement, then mused thoughtfully, "I wonder how the fightin' is goin'?" There was little news of the war in their isolated part of the world.

"Well, let's not think about it," Malcolm responded. "I was just gonna tell Roxy how I started the homestead."

A smile of anticipation lit Gideon's face. He loved that story. He made himself comfortable at the hearth and Malcolm began.

"First, let me say that it was backbreaking work. When I first come up the river and saw this little valley, there was nothing but great trees stretching as far as the eye could see. Trees that had to be felled and burned before I could build or plant.

"It was early spring, the frost just beginning to go out of the ground. The first thing I did was to build myself some shelter. It was a one-room hut put together with maple saplin' and topped with a sod roof. It was just big enough for my bedroll and gear and an oak stump I used for a seat."

He paused a moment, an amused smile on his weathered face. "Every time it rained, it washed away part of my roof. I wasted a lot of precious time replacing the sod.

"I cooked all my meals outside, and I can tell you that at first they were sorry messes. Then one day an Indian girl came along and showed me how to build a clay oven. After that I ate good. Had hot bread every day."

He paused again and his young kin suspected that he was thinking about the Indian girl. They glanced at each other and winked.

The fire snapped, causing Malcolm to come out of

his reverie. He then continued on with his story.

"Besides the hard work that faced me that first summer, there were also the Indians. They hid behind every tree, it seemed, waiting to steal you blind or take the scalp off your head. But I stuck with it and, when winter set in, I had cleared twenty acres, planted seeds, and reaped a cellar full of food. Just before the first snowfall I finished building this cabin, over the cellar. My fireplace drew good and I was cozy and warm with plenty to eat. In the daylight hours I ran my traps and in the evenin' I . . . "

"You ran your Indian squaw," Gideon interrupted.

Malcolm chuckled. "Where'd you get that idea?" he asked gruffly.

"Oh, I don't know. Kinda guessed at it." Gideon grinned.

Roxanne didn't join in the bantering. Actually, she hadn't fully heard it while she had gazed thoughtfully into the fire. In the warm silence that grew, she turned her head and studied the man who had been strong enough and brave enough to tame the wilderness. He took on a greater importance to her, and she was glad that she came from such stock.

She smiled at him tenderly. "You love this land, don't you, Uncle Malcolm?"

"That I do, Roxy. It's been good to me. It took me when I was so low in spirit I didn't care much what happened, and it made me want to live again."

Vaguely, she heard Gideon, an undertow of excitement in his voice, pursuing the topic of the homestead. He loved the place and the hills, and Roxanne wondered if he always had. Hadn't he maybe, at first, felt the same way as she . . . maybe also shed tears for the life he left behind? If this were true, what had made him finally accept it so completely?

She wondered idly, half hopefully, if this would also happen to her. For some time now, she had found herself enjoying little things. The bluejays and cardinals, for instance, as they fought over bread crumbs she put out for them. And the enjoyment of listening to the woeful yowl of uncle's hound drifting back on the wind as it raced after a coon.

She glanced around the room. She was even beginning to enjoy the running of the cabin. It had been difficult at first. There was so little with which to work. The three-room cabin was a far cry from the many-roomed house in which she had grown up. There were no carpeted floors nor was flowered paper on the walls. The walls were the same inside as they were outside—heavily barked and clay-caulked. The floors were made of wide planks, with colorful Indian rugs scattered about. The furniture was rustic and serviceable, but blending beautifully with the rough interior.

Making a mental inventory of the cabin, she went on. There were no smooth sheets and fluffy blankets—only rough muslin and gay patchwork quilts. The beds consisted of pallets laid on frames and topped with a thick feather mattress. These mattresses were removed in the summer. Gideon had informed her that they were too hot then.

When she had first arrived, total disorder had met her eyes. Soiled clothes were scattered about, as were gear and traps in every corner. The table overflowed with dishes and provisions. She had even found one of Gideon's moccasins under a bag of sugar. Ashes spilled onto the hearth, and she wondered when last the floor had been swept. She smiled grimly, remembering the many days it took to wash the bed linens and rugs. However, in a short time she had, with the help of Lettie, brought order to the cabin. The place was now a charming, clean and inviting home.

In the beginning, though, there had been some trouble with Lettie. It had taken a while to teach the woman to use plenty of hot water and soap on the dishes and to wash the pots last. The first time she saw Lettie place the dishes, unscraped, into the dishpan, she had wondered disgustedly why her uncle and cousin hadn't become sick.

Her biggest problem, however, had been with the menu. No matter what she ordered the woman to prepare for supper, they always sat down to beans and a poorly cooked piece of meat. She was always reminded of that first meal with Caleb, and many of her evenings were ruined when his memory wouldn't leave. Finally, in desperation, she complained to Malcolm.

He had chuckled. "Roxy, you must take it easy on Lettie. She knows nothin' about your ways. She was born to a life that you couldn't even imagine. All their lives, her and them other women over there in the cabin ain't had nothin'. They ain't never known anything but sod shanties and brutal men. Since they were born, meat and beans have been their main diet, and that's all they know how to cook."

He had gazed at Roxanne, a wistfulness in his eyes. "Do you think you could teach her how to cook? I'm just as tired of her grub as you are. Remember, I've been eatin' it longer than you have."

She had nodded. "I'm a fair cook. I'll start with her today."

Surprisingly, Lettie had not only been willing, she was also eager to learn. She had a quick mind that grasped and held every piece of her instructions. The suppers they were called to now were meals to anticipate.

She had suspected from the beginning that Lettie's life wasn't an easy one. The woman always wore one or more bruises on her arms and legs, and it was not unusual for her to have a black eye.

Most mornings the hired woman showed up with dark circles under her eyes, indicating she hadn't slept well. Then one day, the mystery was cleared up. She overheard Malcolm say to Lettie, "You look like you could stand some sleep, Lettie."

Lettie had sighed and answered, "It's that Ez, Mr. Sherwood. He won't let me rest—he's after me all night. If it's not him, it's one of the others. I'll certainly be glad when they leave on the hunt."

"You're lucky you're over here with us, Lettie. Otherwise you might be the one that would have to go on the trail with them."

"Oh, I thank God for that, right enough." She paused a moment. "They voted on takin' poor Bessie. She's beside herself, she dreads it so much. Them varmints will plumb wear her out."

That evening after Lettie had straightened the kitchen area and had reluctantly gone back to the cabin and Ez, Roxanne questioned Malcolm about her and the others.

"Is Lettie married to Ez, Uncle Malcolm?"

Taking a chair opposite her, Malcolm sipped a few times from the coffee cup in his hand. Then, "No, Roxy, she's not. None of them are married over there. They showed up here four years ago and asked for work. The men told me right out that the women were camp followers. Here in the hills you don't ask questions or judge people. They all do their work and that's what I hired them for."

Roxanne was silent for a long time, her mind busy with the awful women in Caleb's cabin. To her surprise, she could not bear the thought of him taking such a creature into his bed. She sighed deeply, trying to picture him in the dismal rundown cabin. How could he share his life with those equally rundown people?

Then, angry at herself for thinking about him at all, she thrust him from her mind. What did she care what he did!

She started, and the three of them looked up in surprise when Lettie announced, "Lunch is ready."

They had idled away the morning.

Until now, the war had been far away and they only thought about it when some traveler brought news of the fighting. But suddenly the post was running low on provisions and they were sharply aware of it.

The British blockade had stopped all boats coming into the states and the cost of supplies was climbing at an alarming rate. The price of gunpowder alone was sky high, going for a dollar a pound.

Malcolm tried not to waste it on small game, and he set traps and snares around the cabin. Rabbits were plentiful, as were the wild turkeys that scratched around in the snow looking for food.

He spoke of his traps now. "Do you want to go with me to run my line, Roxy?"

She nodded eagerly. Anything to break up the monotony of another long day.

Tall oaks stood gaunt and bare, spreading great arms over the snow-swept forest. Roxanne walked behind Malcolm, who was scuffing the snow into white misty clouds. There will be months of this white stuff, she thought, and bitter cold and lonely boredom.

She knew that, now the snow had arrived, few homesteaders would find their way to the Sherwood cabin. From things that Gideon had mentioned, hill people lived a bleak existence. Especially the women. According to him they worked like horses, and the majority had a new baby every spring. She wondered if any of them ever went mad with loneliness.

This loneliness of the hill woman was the main reason she considered Seth Hale as a husband. If by chance she couldn't convince him to leave these hills, he at least knew how a wife should be treated.

Her musing lingered on Seth and, for the first time, she gave serious thought to him. Until now, he had been only a handsome face and a pleasant manner to her. But what kind of man was he really, beneath that calm surface? Did his serene, polite countenance maybe hide something totally different inside? Actually, what was an educated gentleman doing here in the wilderness, homesteading?

Had he come here, as had Uncle Malcolm, to forget some heart-shattering experience. It was highly unlikely, she decided on second thought. His eyes didn't show hurt.

In surprise, she realized that his eyes showed very little. Even desire for her was seldom seen. Only occasionally had she been able to stir him and send a flicker of desire across his face.

Her lips quirked. Last night had been one of those "seldom" occurrences. Gideon and Uncle Malcolm retired soon after his arrival, and she had waited for him to come and sit beside her. But he had made no effort to take advantage of their privacy. He remained in the chair across from her, and she had fumed. What manner of man is he, she had asked herself.

When he prepared to leave at an early hour, she had

made up her mind that she could never spend the rest of her life with such a cold man. But at the door he had surprised her by putting his arms around her and holding her briefly. Her passionate nature responded and she pressed her body into his. His arms tightened and she felt his erection push into her thigh. But just as she was thinking, He's human after all, he released her and quickly left.

She sighed. Seth would never thrill her or set her heart to racing the way the long-hunter did, but he was the kind of man that mama would approve of.

In a matter of two hours, the traps were run. Along with the six rabbits that hung over Malcolm's shoulder, there were also several beavers. Their fur was thick and slick, and he boasted of the price they would bring. When the last trap was reset, he stood up and glanced at Roxanne with a sheepish grin.

"Ruth lives on that next hill. Let's drop in for a cup of coffee."

Struggling up the hill behind him and trying to step in his tracks, Roxanne smiled to herself. She'd bet that he wanted more than a cup of coffee.

She had met Ruth Green shortly after the death of her parents and didn't clearly remember much about her. She knew that Ruth was Uncle Malcolm's woman—had been for many years. He had bought her from a brutal stepfather when she was but fourteen years old. He built her a small cabin a few miles from his own and settled her in. Over the years, he had visited her regularly, instructing her in how best to please a man in bed. After so long a time, it was evident that the teacher was still very adept. For although Ruth was still a young woman, she had never turned to a younger man.

Of course, there is Gideon, Roxanne thought. I don't suppose he counts, though.

It was Malcolm himself who first took her cousin to see Ruth. Gideon had told Roxanne all about it one day.

"I was only thirteen and nervous as hell." He grinned in embarrassment. "Uncle Malcolm marched me into her cabin and in that gruff voice of his, practically shouted, "Ruth, the lad's been playin' with himself. Take him to bed and show him what it's all about.""

Roxanne's eyes twinkled at him. "And did she?"

Gideon rolled his eyes toward the ceiling. "She sure as hell did. I ain't never found her equal since. The things that woman did to me would curl your hair."

She remembered her surprise, and of asking, "Did you go just the one time?"

He had grinned widely and shook his head. "Hell no. I've been goin' regular ever since."

"Does Uncle Malcolm know?"

"Sure he knows. Sometimes we visit Ruth together. He'd rather I go to her than to some slut. You got to be careful you don't pick up some disease from such. Hell, me and him could have them whores of Ez Johnson's anytime we wanted them—that was part of the deal the men offered Uncle Malcolm. But he said he'd break my head if he ever caught me goin' over there."

"Do you think uncle ever goes over?"

"Naw."

Why was it, she wondered, that the natural assumption was a man must always have a woman. Even one as young as thirteen. And why was it, she also wondered, if a woman wanted and needed a man, she was called a whore because of it. She shook her head. It was all so unfair.

Behind her, Gideon studied his cousin, a twinkle in his eyes. "Why don't you have Ruth teach you some of her tricks," he suggested slyly. "The hunter wouldn't have left you if you would have kept him happy in bed."

She sailed across the room and slapped at him. "Damn you, Gideon, what makes you think I want him in my bed?"

He had eluded her striking hand and, still laughing, had continued to tease. "You can't fool me, cousin. I know you care about him."

She had stormed into her room, remaining there until suppertime. But Gideon was right and she hated herself for it.

Roxanne sighed in relief when they arrived at Ruth's cabin.

Ruth must have seen them coming, because as soon as they stepped upon the porch she opened the door, a smile of welcome on her comely face. Malcolm's welcome was boisterous and loud as he swept her into his arms. "Roxy, here, wants a cup of coffee, and you know what I want, woman."

His hand had gone immediately inside Ruth's blouse, and Roxanne could see the kneading of his fingers through the material. She looked away in embarrassment as Ruth laughed and slapped at his hand. "Shame on you, Malcolm. In front of Roxy."

But when Roxanne glanced back, she knew that Ruth's words were only sham. While one arm had gone around Malcolm's neck, her other hand had pressed his head down to her half-exposed breasts.

Then, before her popeyed stare, Malcolm had carried Ruth to the bed and was pushing her skirt up around her waist.

My God, Roxanne thought, hurrying to sit down with her back to them, he's going to make love to her right under my nose.

Amid the noise of the thumping and bumping on the bed, she blushed furiously and would have left the cabin it if wasn't so cold outside.

Then the noise stopped, and gradually so did the heavy breathing. In a short time they were gathered around the table having coffee and cookies. At first Roxanne was too embarrassed to look them in the face. But Ruth and Malcolm acted as though nothing out of the ordinary had happened, and they busily talked about everyday happenings.

She thought, irritated at herself, Why should I be embarrassed? They're the ones that acted like a pair of dogs.

As Ruth poured them a second cup of coffee, she turned to Roxanne and asked, "How are you and Seth gettin' along? Will there be weddin' bells soon?"

Before Roxanne could reply, Malcolm answered for her. "That Seth Hale! I can't understand the man. He's over to the cabin every night and don't do a damn thing but sit there. Any other man, Roxy would have to be beatin' off with a stick."

"Maybe when he starts bundlin' with you, Roxy, he'll break down and become human." Ruth laughed.

"What do you mean, bundle?"

"To bundle means that when it's cold outside, and inside, the courtin' pair gets under the covers to stay warm."

"You mean they sleep together."

"No, not that exactly," Malcolm interrupted.

"They keep their clothes on an' all." He paused to give a short laugh. "Come to think about it, there has been many a lass who lost her underbritches during the course of the night."

Ruth's loud laughter rang out. "That's not all she lost, I'll bet."

Malcolm's deep bass joined her, then he remarked, "I don't think Roxy has to worry about that. Seth's much too proper to ride a filly before the preacher tells him to."

Ruth glanced at him, a knowing smile lifting her lips. "That's what you think," she began, then stopped.

Her companions gazed at her undecided expression. Finally, impatiently, Malcolm growled, "Well, Ruth? Go on."

Ruth hesitated, then laid her hand on Roxanne's arm. "Honey, I don't know if I'm talkin' out of turn, but I think there's something you ought to know. There's a young Indian girl that goes up to Seth's place about every day. I see her cross the river, and Seth always meets her."

Malcolm snorted, "That ain't nothin', Ruth. She probably works for him."

Irritated, Ruth turned to him. "Oh? One day I saw him take her right on the ground." At Malcolm's startled look, she continued, "And I'll tell you somethin' else—that Ez person you have workin' for you, he's smellin' around her, too."

The picture of Ez and the girl in the barn loft flashed through Roxanne's mind. A twinge of anger nudged at her. Seth was giving White Star what she had aroused in him.

But it wasn't until they were on their way home that she realized she wasn't jealous at Ruth's revelation.

CHAPTER 9

Caleb Coleman had ridden his horse hard the day he left the Sherwood place. The sight of smooth, handsome Seth Hale had put a film of rage in his eyes.

"He's what she wants," he had muttered and galloped over the hill toward home.

He was in a hurry, also, to get back to his men, hopefully before they left on the hunt. Thanks to his run-in with the Indians, he was long overdue for the gathering of the hunters. He was sure the main body had already left on the long trek. But there was a chance his own men had waited for him.

It was still a couple of hours to sunset when he clattered to a stop in front of the old, canting cabin. But no noise sounded from within and no smoke came from the chimney. They had left without him.

He led the horse to a shed attached to the rear of the building and grunted with relief when he found that some grain had been left behind. As he tugged at the saddle, his chest began to hurt and he realized that he was weaker than he knew. His legs trembled and his vision blurred.

Inside, he found the cabin much as he had left it. His nose curled in distaste. During the past week he had grown used to brightness and cleanliness, and the dour dank room made his skin crawl. He knelt by the ash-covered hearth and drew his flint and steel from a pocket. After several attempts, the sparks caught a small pile of twigs and burst into flames. He piled on wood until the flames shot up the crumbling chimney. Some of the gloom disappeared and he felt better.

Next, he took up the battered coffeepot and filled it with water from a pail, ground the coffee and threw a handful into the pot. While it brewed on the red coals, he hunted the room for food. When his search turned up nothing, he swore loudly. "Them son-of-a-bitches wouldn't dare go off and leave me without food."

He remembered then the tall sapling outside, where they always hung their meat. Stepping out on the porch, he smiled and nodded his head in satisfaction. Swinging high in the treetop, well out of the reach of marauding animals, swung a chunk of venison. He pulled down the chunk and, with quick strokes of his knife, sliced off two steaks.

Later, eating his lonely meal, he thought of the Sherwoods gathered around their table. He stopped his chewing and remembered how those suppers were. There would be much laughter and a teasing bantering going on between Roxanne and Gideon. Sometimes the good-natured arguing would end on the floor in a tussle. Malcolm would sit and watch them, chuckling softly to himself.

His thoughts swung to Roxanne alone. And as he had promised himself, he sat before his lonely fire and recalled their time together.

Then a log burned through and fell with a crash. Jarred out of his dreams, he gave a long sigh. The room had grown quite dark, and he realized that the sun had set. He rose and lit the stub of a candle and paced the floor restlessly. He'd like to be on his way, but knew it was too dark to find their trail. The moon was only in its quarter and would never penetrate the thick forest. Anyhow, the stallion needed the rest.

He sat before the fire and lit his pipe, then poured another cup of coffee. But he drew comfort from neither and, after awhile, bent over and banked the fire for the night.

He walked into his bedroom and became more depressed. When he stretched out on the lumpy mattress and pulled the damp blankets over him, he thought of the dry warm bed he had lain on last night and gave the pillow a hard whack.

Until now, his way of life had never bothered him. In fact, he had liked the casual existence. Other than a hunt, or a fast tumble with some woman, he had given no thought to tomorrow. It had not bothered him whether his blankets were damp or dry, his food good or bad. But something had happened. He was now looking at his way of life through a different pair of eyes.

He tossed awhile and finally slept.

But his rest had been fitful and he was up with the first gray of dawn. He stirred up the fire and put the remains of the coffee on to heat.

Later, as he munched some parched corn and drank the scalding coffee, he debated his next move. When had his men left? Would he be able to overtake them? The thought of spending the hunt alone did not appeal to him. A man alone in the wilderness could go crazy. The silence that grew in a snow-covered forest could become so intense that it beat at your brain until sometimes you yelled just to hear a voice. And if you weren't careful, you kept on yelling until your voice was raw and only croaks gasped out.

He would have a good chance of overtaking them, he decided. Hampered with the women they would have to make camp every night. But he could keep moving, catching snatches of sleep in the saddle.

When he began to prepare for the trip, he found that he had only his gear to pack. One of the men had gathered his traps and put them on a peg in a corner. He brought out his saddlebag of buffalo hide and laid it on the table. Methodically he began to stow things. Bullets, powder, tobacco, jerked venison and parched corn, and a hatchet were packed neatly. His long sharp hunting knife went into the sheath on his belt.

The eastern sky was turning pink when he closed the door behind him. He stood a moment breathing deeply of the cold fresh air. Then from behind the cabin came the snapping of dry twigs and leaves. He whirled in time to see a young deer flash past him. Its white flag of a tail seemed to wave at him as it bounced off through the forest. He watched its graceful flight and was reminded somehow of Roxanne.

Then in midair the animal gave a jerk and suddenly was lying on the ground, its slim legs thrashing. A loud pop came from the right of Caleb and, as he turned his head, he saw a puff of smoke rising above a clump of brush. As he peered intently at the powdery smoke slowly evaporating in the air, he caught a glimpse of something stirring behind the brush.

When a babble of excited voices burst out, he dropped to the ground and wriggled his way beneath the low-hanging branches of a cedar. The voices came closer and, when he made out the guttural speech of Indians, he froze his position.

Slowly and cautiously he parted the dark-green foliage and looked out. His darting glance found a group of redskins squatting around the fallen deer. Then, his body tensed. A red-clad British officer had come out of the brush and was moving to join them.

What was a redcoat doing in Kentucky? Was he alone, or were there others camped nearby? All these questions swept through his mind as one of the braves knelt and dressed out the deer.

Quickly, he let go of the branches and held his breath. The officer was staring toward the cabin. For a frightening moment he could feel the redcoat's eyes upon him. A disturbing thought went through his mind: I wouldn't stand a prayer's chance against seven of them.

Sweat trickled coldly down his sides as he waited for the impact of bullets. He had never known fear before—had always been contemptuous of death; but now, a fair and beautiful face flashed before his eyes, and he wanted to live.

The drone of the Indians continued, and fifteen minutes dragged by with no one disturbing his hiding place. Caleb carefully parted the screen again and peered out. Two of the braves, the deer slung between them, were halfway to the river. The British officer stood talking to the other four. Caleb gave a shuddering sigh and went weak with relief.

But on the heels of his relief, another thought assailed him, and he frowned. Had he thoroughly killed the fire inside the cabin? Was there, maybe, at this very moment, a spiral of smoke escaping up the chimney? He twisted around, straining to see the cabin and the sky above it. But the tree's heavy branches cut off his view and he could only see a part of the roof.

He turned his attention back to the group and discovered a controversy going on between them. The Englishman kept gesturing toward the cabin while the Indians stubbornly shook their heads and pointed toward the river. Caleb glanced over his shoulder, judging the distance to the shed. There wasn't much shelter between there and his tree. Would he be able to make it to his horse unnoticed?

But while he waited, undecided, the officer threw up his hands in resignation and, before Caleb's surprised stare, he and the Indians turned and walked off toward the river.

Caleb remained under the tree until he heard the sound of oars dipping into the water. He wondered what was their destination and what devilment they were up to.

Their sound faded away and there remained only the drone of the wind, moaning faintly in the trees. What should he do now? Should he keep to his original plans and go after his men, or should be follow the British officer and see where he went.

Duty to the hills and to the hill people dictated what he must do. Caleb crawled into the open and was just in time to see the bark canoe disappear around a bend. The officer was in the bow, shading his eyes from the fully risen sun.

Caleb hurried to the shed and propped open the door. He, too, would be traveling by boat. The stallion would have to forage with the deer.

In a short time he uncovered his canoe, hidden in the tall rushes edging the river, and slid it into the water. He stepped into it and silently paddled to the center of the stream, keeping well away from the shore.

The river was high and fast and he was thankful that he rode with the current. The stream curved and wound so much that it doubled the length of the forest trail, and a man would wear himself out fighting the force of it for any great distance.

The sun moved overhead, beaming down unusually hot for the middle of October. Caleb drew an arm across his face, swiping at the sweat. Off and on at straight stretches he caught sight of the canoe, a small speck moving steadily down the river. How far were the varmints going, he wondered.

It was nearly dusk when he spotted the jutting piece of land where the trading post was located. Then at the same time, he saw the canoe take a sharp turn and move toward the bank. He nodded his head in satisfaction. They were camping for the night. He could now stop at the post and see what rumors he could pick up while having a couple of drinks.

He let his canoe drift silently to the bank. Through the leafless trees, pale lights twinkled in the tavern windows. As he clambered ashore, the moon untangled itself from the treetops, throwing the post into a half light. His eyes took a slow survey of the darkened buildings. No alien movement caught his attention. There were only dead shadows of the buildings and of the tree stumps that dotted the clearing.

A burst of song rang out in the tavern, and he grinned as he hurried to join the revelers.

Caleb hopped upon the porch and lingered to look through a dirty window. Much activity went on inside. The innkeeper rushed back and forth behind the rough bar, filling mugs with ale and short glasses with rum. Sweat poured off his bald head but he was grinning happily. The money in the box behind him was growing. It would be his last big night until the hunters returned in the spring.

Caleb was surprised to see so many hunters. There were a dozen or more gathered in the tavern for that last fling. Most hunters did not drink while on the hunt and very few took along women, and he was not surprised to see them guzzling their drinks and grabbing at every whore who walked by. They had a long winter ahead of them.

In a far corner he saw Lily sitting on the lap of a

burly, bewhiskered hill man. She laughed wildly as the hunter slid a hand beneath her dress and clamped his lips over one bare breast. The stairs leading to the rooms above were heavily trafficked, and he wondered how many trips Lily had already made. When he saw her hand go down the front of the drunk's buckskins, he grinned. She's marked that stupid bastard for her next tumble.

Caleb pushed open the door and a cry of welcome greeted him. Someone from the back of the room called out, "What are you doin' here, Coleman? I thought you left weeks ago. Couldn't you bring yourself to leaving Lily?"

A roar of laughter greeted the man's sally. As though this were her signal, Lily appeared at his elbow, the other hunter forgotten. Her ferret face smiled up at him and she purred, "Well? What about it, did you miss Lily?"

He pulled away from her clinging hand and threw a contemptuous look at her as he growled, "Hell no."

When she would have followed him to the bar, his hand came up and she went reeling backward."

She landed in a hunter's lap. Eager arms came around her waist. For a moment she struggled against them, wanting with all her might to attack the man who had scorned her in front of everyone. But when the man's hand began to paw at her gown, she giggled and pressed into him.

Her fingers fumbled with his fly and she whispered in his ear. On their way upstairs, the hunter called back, "Hey, innkeeper, bring us a bottle of rum."

A pair of hunters moved apart and made room for Caleb at the long wooden counter. It ran over with spilled rum and ale, without a dry spot to lean an elbow on. The proprietor came and stood before him, his wig awry and his eyes a combination of harried hurry and friendly welcome.

"What's your pleasure, Coleman?"

"Give me a glass of that rum . . . heat it a little, will you?"

He drank half of the heady spirits, quickly warmed by a hot poker, then set the glass down. Over the roaring noise in the background, he asked the man to his right, "What do you hear of the war?"

"Last I heard, our army had gone back into the woods. I guess New York and New Jersey are in enemy hands now."

"Hell, if they retreatin', we're gonna have them in Kentucky next," complained the man on Caleb's left.

His partner nodded in agreement. "If it was only the British we had to fight, we could handle them easy. But them damned mercenaries, the Hessians, they're nothin' but paid killers and meaner than hell."

Caleb finished his drink and ordered another. Turning to one of the men, he changed the subject and asked, "Seen any braves huntin' in these parts lately?"

"Naw. Ain't seen any Indians, but I did see a bunch of unshod pony tracks the other day. They must have stole some settler's horse—there was tracks of horseshoes mixed in with 'em."

Caleb hooked his elbows on the counter and looked around. Smoke hung in the low-ceilinged room, striving, it seemed, to blot out the dim lights of the lamps suspended from the rafters. The raucous voices of the men and the high-pitched squealing of the women had reached a fevered high. Many of the hunters had drunk themselves into oblivion and now lay on the floor unnoticed. And of those still on their feet, there wasn't a sober one among them.

Caleb debated the advisability of informing the man at his elbow that the shod horse carried a British officer. But common sense advised against it. The drunken hunters would only lurch out like a herd of stampeding buffalo and scare the scouting party away.

Caleb was satisfied now that the redcoat was spying on the territory's defenses and the people's strength and weakness. It was the officer's job to decide how much danger the hill people held for his soldiers and mercenaries.

It was clear that the men must be caught before he made his report back to his headquarters. And to be sure that it was done, Caleb decided, he'd best go after the man alone.

He downed his drink and slipped unnoticed out the door. As he stood accustoming his eyes to the darkness, he tensed. In the corner of his eye he had seen a slim form glide from the corner of the building and melt into the shadows of the trees. He caught a glimpse of two swinging braids and swore softly under his breath.

What in the hell is that red bitch hangin' around here for? he growled inwardly.

He intended to follow her and force the reason from her. But then he decided that she was most likely only spying on him because of jealousy. I'll attend to her later, he thought, and stepped off the porch.

He made his way cautiously to the river and stepped into the canoe. This time he kept close to land, hugging the river bank. The moon was directly overhead now and he would be a sitting duck in the middle of the stream.

His paddle hardly made a ripple as he slowly dipped it in and out. Sometimes he let the canoe drift while he listened intently to the night noises. It was during one of these pauses that he heard the definite sound of a loud yawn.

He swung ashore and held his breath as the canoe lightly scraped the gravelly bottom. An owl hooted from a nearby tree and, farther down the river, its mate answered. There was no other sound.

Crouching to the ground, Caleb made his way through the underbrush that edged the bank. Then excitement filled him and his heart pounded in deep hard beats. Just a few yards in front of him, a small fire burned. Lying close to the fire, and in a circle, lay six blanket-covered bodies. One lone brave paced back and forth, standing guard.

The Indian, his eyes glazed from the want of sleep, turned and walked in Caleb's direction. He smothered his surprise—the sentry was a young man who used to run with Long Step. He wondered when the brave had gone over to the British.

When the sentry turned to retrace his steps, Caleb wriggled forward, coming to rest behind a large boulder only feet away from the sleeping men. His eyes slid over the bodies and stopped when they came to rest on the red coat covering the officer. He rose to one knee, his hand going instinctively to the knife in his belt. His arm drew back and at that moment, high on a hill, a wildcat let loose a scream that fairly curdled his blood. The sleeping men sat up as though propelled by springs and, stupefied, stared at him.

Taking advantage of their surprise, Caleb came erect, the knife nestling in the palm of his hand. Then, as though the blade had life of its own, it was hurtling through the air and plunging into the Englishman's chest. A dark stain spread around it, looking black against the red of the coat.

The officer's mouth formed a silent objection, then

his eyes went wide and he slumped forward. In a wild scramble, the braves tumbled out of blankets, their astounded eyes on Caleb and the long rifle he pointed steadily at them.

Long Step's friend was the first to speak. "We bring you no trouble, Coleman."

"Then why are you scouting for the British?"

Sensing that they wouldn't be shot on the spot, the other braves regained their tongues and the air was full of their denials.

"The English pay much money for scouting. But we red men don't care about war between palefaces and we lead him in circles . . . show him nothing."

After pondering the Indian's answer, Caleb decided that in all likelihood they spoke the truth. The Indian man had a devious mind. They were a tricky people and it would tickle their sense of humor to take the officer's money and give him nothing in return.

He lowered the rifle, and their relief made hissing sounds as it rushed through their teeth. Caleb walked over to the fallen man and, with a foot, rolled him onto his back. He was still young, his face unlined. For a sad moment he thought of the parents across the ocean and of the pain they would suffer when their son did not return to them.

Then abruptly he turned and ordered sharply, "Bury him."

In a matter of minutes a shallow grave was scooped out of the damp gravelly soil and the young officer rolled into it. Hurriedly it was filled, then leaves and twigs scattered about. All evidence of a grave was erased.

Leaning against a tree, Caleb watched the braves draw sticks for the man's gear in a nearby pile. He made no move to stop them. Taking a part of the slain man's property would make it unnecessary for him to caution them to silence.

The Englishman's saddlebag gave up few treasures, so the dividing was quickly done. Soon, the mists from the river had swallowed the red men from view.

Caleb listened to the dip of the paddles a moment, then struck off through the woods. At last he could get on with the business of finding his friends. He hoped that his canoe would be safe until his return in the spring. Time was too precious now to take the slow way by water.

Everything was quiet at the post as he skirted it. Even the tavern was still and in darkness. He smiled, thinking of the aching heads tomorrow.

It was near daylight when the dim outline of his cabin came into view. He debated sleeping for a few hours before going on. But no, he decided, he might sleep too long and his friends would only be farther away.

Luckily, the stallion had remained in the warmth of the shed. As he threw the blanket over the strong back, he talked to it as though it were human. Slipping the bit into its mouth, he led the animal outside. Swinging into the saddle, he gently nudged a shiny flank and they took off in the direction of the Ohio Valley.

The sun was high when he stopped on a hill and looked down on the Sherwood homestead. He saw figures moving about, but none were female. "Miss High and Mighty is most likely still in bed," he muttered and urged the horse on.

By noon he struck a wide-beaten path and grinned broadly. His friends traveled this route. Standing out plainly on the trail was the print of a cracked shoe. Abe's gelding wore such a shoe.

Caleb rode steadily, not stopping to eat. When hunger gripped him, he munched some of the parched corn he had put in a pocket.

It was around dusk when he discovered that bare hoofprints of Indian ponies were covering the shod tracks of his friends' horses. There were many, perhaps a dozen or more. He hauled the stallion to a walk and carefully surveyed the forest. Them bastards are up to no good, he thought darkly.

Keeping his eyes glued to the trail, Caleb gave a sharp grunt when the pony tracks veered off the trail and disappeared into the deeper part of the forest. Involuntarily, he shivered. There was a threat of death around him, and he felt his scalp tingle.

Without conscious thought he leapt from the saddle and dropped behind a tree, crouching motionless. He waited, listening, but nothing stirred. Still, he had that sure feeling that he was being watched.

Then, in the duskiness of the woods, he heard soft scudding noises and, without more warning, lithe bodies were swarming over him. With one great yell and his knife flashing, he was rolling on the ground with them. He thrust out at the nearest flesh.

From the tangled mass, Caleb drew himself to one knee. Then there was the sound buckskin makes when cut and a pain in his thigh so excruciating that he feared he'd lose consciousness. He grew limp and melted to the ground. Through bleary eyes he watched moccasined feet gather around him. Forcing himself not to give in to the screaming agony, he stared up at the surly visages that were black with smoldering hate.

He saw the savage thrust of the foot coming toward his chin and was helpless to move. As he passed out,

questions rang in his mind. Was this ambush acciden-
tal, or had the renegades been warned he was riding
this way?

The picture of White Star, slipping through the
forest, flashed before him.

CHAPTER 10

Roxanne's long legs stretched out, keeping pace with the pair of horses that plodded in front of her. The sturdily built team pulled a sledge filled with a cord of wood.

She had been helping her uncle with this chore for close to a week now. Four days ago he had announced at the breakfast table, "We gotta get a lot of wood in, Roxy. There's a smell of snow in the air and, when it comes, it's gonna be a whopper. We won't be able to get to the woods then."

Actually, she had been helping Malcolm with all the chores for three weeks. Gideon had accidentally stepped into one of his own traps. His ankle was so badly bruised and swollen that he could neither pull on a boot nor walk. The work hands were all gone on the winter hunt, and there was no one but herself to help.

Of course, there was Lettie . . . and the other two who had been left behind. But those unfortunate women were so run-down and puny in their strength that Malcolm didn't have the heart to ask them to do strenuous work.

But Roxanne was strong and healthy. She could toss the chunks of wood as easily as Malcolm could. Besides, he liked her company. He liked the ring of her laughter, which was spontaneous and infectious. She made him feel young again, and his step was much livelier when she was around.

But today he was alone, hunting. This morning he had decided that he'd best not put off any longer hunting some deer or buffalo. There was no way of knowing how long the next snow might keep them in. One year he had been snowbound for a month and his meat supply had barely lasted.

"Anyway," he had said, grinning at his niece and nephew, "I ain't seen Ruth for a while. I'd better drop in and see how her wood is holding out. And drop her off some fresh meat."

Roxanne and Gideon had passed amused glances, and Gideon had called after him, "I sure wish you could take Ruth something for me."

Malcolm had chuckled and retorted, "You're gonna have to wait your turn, boy," and slammed the door.

Today was the first time that Malcolm had allowed Roxanne to handle the team alone. She was enjoying her first responsibility and called out many unnecessary orders to the docile plow horses.

It had been tiring work, loading a cord of wood onto the flat sledge, then strapping it to hold fast. But Malcolm had taught her well, and she had accomplished the task without too much trouble. She had received only two pinched fingers and ten cold toes.

Dressed in a pair of Gideon's buckskins, she was warm and comfortable. She enjoyed the feeling of complete movement they afforded, and it was a relief not to fight petticoats in the chill wind that had sprung up earlier. A long rifle rode importantly on her shoulder, and she felt a smug pride in the fact that she knew how to use it.

Both Malcolm and Gideon had been her teachers. Malcolm had cautioned her, "Pay attention to what I tell you now. There ain't no powder to be wasted."

So, she had listened carefully and watched closely as he poured bullets and measured powder. For over a month she had walked around with a sore shoulder. But gradually she got the hang of it, remembering to hold the stock firmly against her shoulder when she fired. She did not become as good a shot as her male relatives, but Malcolm allowed that she would be able to hit an Indian or a redcoat if she had to.

The icy, rutted tracks now changed course and led down to the river. The path here was smooth and level, and she could take her attention off the horses. She smiled. Several yards ahead, three deer were gathered at the river's edge, breaking the silence as they rapped sharply at the frozen water with dainty hooves. But the outer limit, a three-foot width all along the river, was frozen solid. After awhile, they turned from it and began to nuzzle in the soft snow.

For a moment Roxanne debated trying her luck at bringing one down, then shook her head. She would never be able to make herself pull the trigger on the beautiful animals. Anyhow, Uncle Malcolm would be bringing home more than enough.

In the distance, coming from the direction of Seth's place, she heard faintly the shrill barking of dogs. She wondered idly if he were going out on a hunt. And, as she so often did, she let her mind linger on him, wondering what kind of husband he would make. He was always kind and considerate, but there still remained the standoffish quality that uncle had described.

Then, too, there were times when he was almost gay—giving her compliments and chatting about Boston. But if she should put too many questions to him about his past, he became evasive and his smile forced. She found this especially true when she spoke of the war or complained about the king's actions toward the colonists. A defensive, uneasy expression would cross his face, and she would wonder why he acted as though her words were a personal insult to him. She tried to stifle these thoughts, telling herself that he felt guilty because he wasn't fighting for this new country.

But he shouldn't feel that way, she mused. There are many who aren't fighting, including Caleb Coleman and his hunter friends.

At any rate, she hoped and believed that after marriage all this would change. That he would grow used to her ways and perhaps mellow a bit.

He had proposed a week ago today. Before giving her answer, however, she had not been able to resist teasing him.

"Are you quite sure it's me that you want to marry, Seth?"

He had been holding her hand, and at her words, brought it to his lips. "Quite sure, Roxanne. I was sure from the first time I saw you."

"You're absolutely sure that you don't favor someone else?" she prodded.

She felt a slight tensing of his hand as he cautiously answered, "What makes you say that?"

She peeked at him from under lowered lashes. "Aren't you awfully fond of a certain Indian girl?"

Her question had brought a sullen flush to his cheekbones, and he had flung her hand from him. "Surely, you joke," he replied coolly.

Doubts had come to her then. He didn't seem the kind of man who would be attracted to an Indian squaw. Ruth must have been mistaken. In all probability she had seen Ez Johnson with White Star.

She put a hand on Seth's arm and said softly, "I ẅ only teasing. I will be honored to be your wife."

He had drawn her into his arms and kissed her. It seemed for a moment that his hands would move to caress her. But then, he was gently pushing her away and saying good night. And although, only last night, Uncle Malcolm had invited him to stay and bundle her, he had made some excuse about having to get back home.

She suspected that Uncle Malcolm was a little disappointed in her choice of a husband. And Gideon—he left no doubt in her mind that he didn't like her choice. He had said quite plainly, "He's not the man for you, Roxy. He's gonna be mighty stingy with himself. He ain't gonna be at all like the hunter."

A flutter had moved through her breast, but she had firmly pushed it back. She was determined to forget the wild hunter, and she snapped angrily, "I certainly hope that he's not."

Gideon had given a small snort and retorted, "Sure you do, Roxy."

Roxanne tensed. A whippoorwill had swooped through the forest, its cry trilling behind it. Two months ago she would have hated its mournful sound and would have most likely started to cry. But now she liked hearing it. As far as that went, there were many new things she was beginning to see in a new light.

She could not pinpoint how it had all come about, but suspected that many small things had snowballed into the awakening of the good and simple things going on around her. She had found herself worrying, along with Uncle Malcolm and Gideon, that a sickened horse might die and had even fretted that an overload of snow on the cabin's roof might break the beams. She had climbed the slippery roof one day with Gideon and helped to break loose the snow and ice. And after the first snowfall, she had thought nothing of helping her cousin shovel the snow against the cabin, to keep out the whipping winds.

And more surprising, she found herself enjoying the evenings spent before the fire. While Malcolm spun tales of Indians and wolves, she and Gideon listened wide-eyed as they cracked nuts or roasted chestnuts. Sometimes they played cards, and many times they merely sat in quiet talk.

They had had few visitors the last several weeks; but when an occasional neighbor and his family did struggle through the snow for a visit, she derived much pleasure from their company. She now knew enough about pioneer life to converse easily with the women.

At first the women were self-consciously aware of their drab garb and weather-roughened skin and hands, and had been ill at ease before her pampered beauty and bright clothes. But as she had continued to chat in her open, friendly way, it was not long before their own tongues became as glib as her own. She knew that Malcolm was proud of her ability to mix with his friends, and she was glad.

Suddenly the wind picked up and blew sharply across her face. Strands of hair whipped loose from her scarf, stinging her cheeks and eyes. She noticed then that the forest was growing dark and threatening. Scanning the sky, her heart quickened as she studied the low, murky clouds. A blizzard was brewing and she had at least another mile to go.

Near panic made her voice harsh as she cracked the whip over the horses' backs, urging them on.

She had not gone far when the first icy pellets hit

her face. Within ten minutes, it was snowing in earnest, a white sheet in front of her. The surrounding trees became a blur and the trail was fast becoming obscure.

"What if I become lost in this white hell?" she groaned aloud. Only last week Uncle Malcolm had spoken of hunters and settlers getting turned around in a snowstorm and becoming hopelessly lost in the wilderness. Many had frozen to death.

Then a tiny well of hope bubbled inside her. He had also said, "The old-timers know how to bury themselves in the snow and wait out a storm."

Maybe she could do the same thing. But I'll keep going as long as I can see the trail, she thought. I can't be too far away from home.

She struggled on, half closing her eyes to protect them from the driving snow. She became weary and her boots felt like lead. Finally she stopped the team; she had to rest and catch her breath. Leaning against the stacked wood, she strained her eyes to locate some familiar object. But vision was blocked at times after only a few rods and she gave up the effort.

She sighed and came away from the wood. "I've got to go on," she whispered and called loudly to the restless horses. She raised her arm to crack the whip and a long drawn-out howl of a wolf rent the air. As one, the horses reared up, their front legs pawing the air. Before she knew what was happening, they were lunging through the forest, the sledge bouncing crazily.

Stunned, she stood looking after them, desolation descending over her. Then she was struggling along, shouting for them to stop. But the wind carried her voice back into her face and the panic-held animals raced on.

The snow came to her knees in many places, and several times she fell. Then she became aware that somewhere along the way she had dropped the long rifle. The image of a gray, shaggy wolf made her push on.

She was able to keep the bouncing sledge in sight and when it became lodged between two trees, she gave a glad cry. But when she staggered up to it and saw how tightly it was stuck, she gave a despairing moan.

"Now what?" she wailed aloud. "I'll never be able to get it loose."

Then she smacked herself in the forehead. She was hit with an idea so simple that she cursed herself for not having thought of it before. She would merely un-hitch the horses and ride one home. Uncle Malcolm had said that a horse could always find its way home.

Speaking in soothing tones, she drew near the straining, terror-stricken team. But just as she reached to take up the reins, the animals gave a great lunge, snapped the singletree and, before her unbelieving eyes, disappeared into the forest.

The deathly yowling of the storm pressed around her, and she stood with sagging shoulders while hope-less tears ran down her cheeks. Then, impatiently, she dashed away the salty rivulet that threatened to freeze on her face and straightened her back. She must move on. She must keep her blood circulating or she would freeze to death in her tracks.

But which way should she go, her mind asked. Gid-eon had mentioned, once, something about the moss always growing on the north side of a tree trunk. But all the trees around here were cedar, and the branches were too snow-laden to see through to the bole. Any-how, she didn't know in which direction the cabin lay.

Giving a ragged sigh, she moved out in the direction she felt was right. Faintly, behind her, the cry of a wolf drifted on the air. She tried to walk faster, terrified that it followed her.

Her feet became leaden and she was stumbling, sometimes falling, and always struggling. Then her heart gave a leap. She had spied footprints ahead. She would follow them; they had to lead to shelter. But after a few feet, she wilted and hopeless tears again brimmed in her eyes. The tracks were her own. She had been walking in a circle. She was totally lost.

She sat down on a tree stump, her head in her hands. There was nothing left but to bury herself in the snow. "But how does one go about it?" she whimpered. "Do I literally dig a hole, or do I burrow into a snowbank?"

Her hair was frozen across her face and she gazed through it, seeking a bank of snow. But the forest floor was one big sheet of white without a bump to mar its surface. She sighed and struggled up. She was so tired . . . almost at the end of her endurance. Maybe she would lie down and rest a moment. She lifted her eyes and stared blindly into the forest, searching for a tree she might crawl under. She took a few faltering steps into the whiteness and suddenly a large shape loomed in front of her. Startled, she stopped and peered at it. Then, gasping a sound of relief, she managed to walk the last couple of yards to a rough, run-down cabin. Flinging open the door, she sprawled on the earthen floor.

For long moments she lay there, her breath coming in gasps. Outside, the wind built to a howling pitch, making the old building shudder and the fireplace ashes to blow onto the crumbling hearth. Slowly she raised on an elbow and, for the first time, saw the weak, fluttering flames in the fireplace. Uneasiness ran through her. She was not alone. Human hands had built that fire. Suddenly she felt their presence.

A stealthy sound coming from behind Roxanne caused her to jump to her feet and peer around. When a shadowed form appeared by the door, she let out a small cry. Her first impulse of movement was checked as the faint light from the fire shifted across the face of the figure and she recognized White Star.

The girl's soft moccasined feet had made no sound as she moved to the door and now closed it. "Thank God," Roxanne cried out. "I was afraid that there were Indians in here."

She immediately realized her blunder and, stammering, sought to rectify it. "I . . . I mean that . . . that there was a man in here."

A slow cunning smile crept into White Star's eyes. Her lips curled slightly and she grunted, "I know what you mean, Miss Sherwood."

"Oh, you remember me then . . . know who I am?"

The girl's eyes flickered, then she looked away. Roxanne wondered if she was remembering the day in the barn with Ez, or the night that Caleb had slapped her because of a white girl.

When White Star answered, her words indicated that she remembered both times. Hot jealousy stared out of the young squaw's eyes as she muttered, "Yes, I know who you are. I also know the two men who are in love with you."

"Two men?"

"Yes. Two."

"But there is only . . . " The rest of the sentence died in Roxanne's throat. A rough hand had come from behind and grasped her shoulder. In the darkness she had been blinded to all but the plainly seen figure of the girl. She had not seen the man in the shadows.

White Star stooped to the pile of wood at her feet and threw a large chunk of pine on the fire. It caught quickly and light brightened the room. Turning, Roxanne stared into the wolfish face of Ez Johnson.

"You!" she gasped.

"That's right, missy. Good ol' Ez."

"But I . . . but I thought you were on the hunt."

His jeering laughter was loud in the cabin. "I am, missy. I'm always on the hunt. Huntin' for tender pieces like you. I knew that if I waited long enough, you'd come to me."

Overcome with cold terror, she stared helplessly. His lips spread in a leering grin, and there was no mistaking his intent as his eyes ran over the tight-fitting buckskins.

He licked his thin lips and Roxanne threw a pleading look over her shoulder to White Star. "Please help me," she begged.

But the hatred that stared back at her said plainly that there would be no help coming from that quarter. A mocking, derisive laugh burst from Ez's throat. He knew also that the girl would never help her.

Taking advantage of his momentarily loosened grip, Roxanne yanked herself away from him and darted behind a table. Her eyes full of contempt, she hissed at him, "I'd die before I let you touch me."

His retort was a string of vile words as he lunged across the table, grabbing at her. She twisted away from his reaching hands, only to come up against White Star. The squaw was strong and held her firmly. Then Ez's hands were upon her, furiously ripping at her clothes.

She struggled and strained away from him and, in

impatience, Ez's foot came out and tripped her. As she hit the floor, he was on top of her and they were rolling in the dirt. Fury replaced her terror and she was like a wildcat, biting and scratching as he strove to hold her down. She opened her mouth wide and screamed piercingly.

Ez swore his annoyance and cuffed her hard across the face. And while her head swam dizzily, he tore off her coat and blouse and yanked off the buckskins. She lay bare and exhausted before him.

With his hands he pinned her shoulders to the ground and roughly pushed a knee between her legs. She shuddered at what was happening to her and, with her last strength, struck out at him, screaming at the top of her voice.

The last ringing sound of Roxanne's cry still lingered when the cabin door banged open. A magnificent brave, tall and broad-shouldered, stood in the opening. White Star's eyes grew wide as she went limp against the table.

"Long Step," she whispered.

In one fast swing the Indian's eyes scanned the room. His eyes fell on the couple on the floor and, fast as a striking snake, his hand went to the sheath at his waist. Held helplessly by Johnson's body, Roxanne watched in fascination as a short, broad knife came over Ez's shoulder and plunged into his chest. She gasped as dark-red blood spurted out and sprayed her breasts. Ez reared slightly, rolled his eyes, and with a deep sigh fell forward, onto her.

For one wild moment, Roxanne knew that she would faint. Then Long Step was flinging the body off her and helping her to stand. He grabbed up the blanket that Ez and White Star had lain on and draped it tightly around her nakedness. Then swinging around to the Indian girl, he gripped her arm in a viselike hold and shot words at her in his native tongue.

A dreaded fear in her black eyes, White Star whimpered and cringed away from him. Shielding her face with an arm, she whined, "I did not touch her, Long Step."

Her eyes blazing at the Indian girl's lie, Roxanne took a step toward them and cried out, "You lie! You caught and held me for Ez."

Caught in her lie, the girl darted furious sidelong glances at the white woman she hated so intensely. With a burst of strength she wrenched her arm free and sprang out of Long Step's reach.

"What white woman doing out alone, anyhow?" she muttered darkly.

Long Step advanced on her, his hand raised threateningly. She gave a frightened cry and darted past him, racing for the door. As it slammed after her, Roxanne reached out a hand and stopped the brave. "Let her go, Long Step. She's not to blame."

For a moment the red man studied the white woman. The honesty of her words shone out of her eyes. The paleface did realize that White Star could not help herself.

He nodded his head solemnly. "White man has touched the girl and spoiled her life. Her dignity is gone for all time."

His manner was calm now, almost gentle as he led Roxanne to a bench beside the fireplace. Squatting down, he piled wood onto the fire until the flames danced high. Then laying a hand on her shoulder, said gravely, "There is enough wood and you are safe here. You stay. I go get your man."

Her hand came up to cover his. In a voice that was shaky, she said, "Long Step, I can never repay you for what you did for me tonight."

The tall brave grunted, "No need to pay," and without further words, bent and slung Ez's body over his shoulder and strode out of the cabin.

CHAPTER 11

Through the opening of the lodge, Caleb watched the squaws as they bustled around the campfire, cooking a mountain of food. Thirty braves and numerous squaws and children would eat it.

He was a prisoner in a renegade camp—had been for two months now. He sighed and looked up at the towering snowcapped pines surrounding the camp. They had carried no snow the first time he opened his eyes and seen them.

During the first four days of his captivity he had experienced intense pain. He had rolled and tossed in a high fever and had had no idea where he was. Gentle hands had tended him, bathing his thigh and changing the dressing. In his delirium he had thought that it was White Star who handled him so carefully. He recalled swearing at her, "Get away from me, you red bitch. You did this to me."

But when he finally came back into the conscious world, an Indian girl, whom he did not know, squatted beside him, changing the dressing. His thigh was swollen twice its normal size, and an ugly red surrounded the knife wound. It was burning hot to his touch, and he had muttered, "If gangrene sets in, I'm done for."

The girl stayed with him through the day and night, tirelessly bathing the wound with a solution made from the bark of some tree. Toward morning the swelling began to go down and the leg was cool to the touch. Then the fever had left him completely, but his body was gripped in a chill that shook him uncontrollably. The girl had stood up and quickly stepped out of her doeskin shift and, to his amazement, picked up the covers and slipped in beside him.

Taking him into her arms, she whispered, "Little Doe will keep you warm."

Caleb smiled now. She had continued to do so ever since.

His eyes picked her out of the group of squaws. Her slim body moved gracefully as she went about her allotted chores. He felt a stirring in his loins. Little Doe was delightful in bed. He had experienced his second virgin, and in the long cold nights he had coached her carefully in the ways that he enjoyed.

He remembered that other virgin he had enjoyed so much, almost to the destruction of his very being, and his body was stilled. What was she doing now . . . this very minute? Was she helping Lettie to make their meal? His eyes grew stony. Maybe she was married by now and was preparing Seth's dinner.

He groaned inwardly, remembering her golden hair spread out and her slender arms reaching for him. He couldn't bear the thought of her doing that to Seth and, determinedly, he pushed her from his mind.

His mind continued to dwell on Seth, however. He'd swear that he had seen the man in camp at least twice. Each time Seth and the renegade chief had been engrossed in serious conversation in the shadows of the campfire. And he had definitely seen White Star . . . several times. His suspicions were stronger that it was she who had attended him those first few days.

But he still didn't trust White Star and believed that

she was behind his capture. As he had asked himself a dozen times, he asked again, But why? What did she have to gain by it—to obtain revenge? Also, what did the renegades want of him? Of what use could he be to them?

He had gone over it all many times, but still could not figure it out. He was treated well, even to having the chief's youngest daughter for his squaw. He grinned. The sly old wolf probably had her there to keep an eye on him. However, he had discovered, while still convalescing, that his lodge was guarded at night. The Indian wasn't leaving it entirely up to Little Doe.

But other than the guarding at night, as long as he didn't leave the confines of the camp he was allowed complete freedom. Once, when he had wandered into the forest, a half-dozen braves had come breathing down his neck.

He stretched out on the fur pallet and reached for his pipe. There had to be some way of escaping. He had to get back to the settlement and learn what was going on.

A wind whipped up, scattering the snow from the pines. His stomach rumbled and he was impatient to eat.

When the old squaw motioned to her husband that the meal was ready, Caleb hurried outside. The chief, looking very dignified in his ragged blanket, strode from his lodge. When he had been served, the braves gathered around the blackened pot that swung over the fire. When all were served and sitting around the fire, Caleb approached for his share of the stew. He was a prisoner and must be treated as such.

Little Doe brought him his bowl, generously filled

with the tenderest pieces of the meat. He smiled his thanks and she squatted beside him, waiting for any request he might make.

The stew was tasty, but he couldn't get used to eating with his fingers. And the slurping and chomping that went on around him fairly turned his stomach.

Since the Indian man makes no conversation while eating his food, the meal was soon finished. With satisfied grunts, the red men filled their pipes and leaned back, relaxing. At a nod from the chief, the women and children divided what was left in the pot and hunkered down to eat outside the circle of warmth.

Through the curling smoke of his own pipe, Caleb studied the Indian chief. He was a strange man, not easy to know. The old brave did not act like an enemy, nor did he act in a friendly way. But the cold eyes that looked out of the stoical face warned that he would not hesitate to kill if he felt it necessary.

Everyone turned at the sound of racing feet on the snowpacked trail. A young brave, a runner, emerged from the forest, his long easy lope eating up the distance. He dropped beside the chief and spoke softly in a rapid voice. The chief listened intently. The runner finished and the chief turned to Caleb and ordered curtly, "Coleman, go to your lodge."

Caleb gave an indifferent shrug of his shoulders and, with Little Doe at his heels, made his way back to the lodge. Inside, he threw himself on the pallet and stared intently at the excited, jabbering braves.

Although he pretended indifference, he was anything but. There was something in the wind. Something big was about to happen and somehow he must learn what.

The braves remained around the fire for the rest of

the day. Sometimes they talked quietly, then again loudly as they argued some point. Caleb strained his ears to hear them, but the lodge was too far away for him to make out their guttural speech.

Then great dark clouds suddenly gathered in the sky, bringing an early darkness. And when the wind built to an angry gale, the snow came. It arrived with such force that the meeting was hastily broken up, and the Indians rushed to their separate quarters. Caleb noted, however, that the leaders went with the chief to his lodge. A grim look came over his face. They would finish plotting their devilment there, he knew.

The lodge stood about ten yards from Caleb's, situated in a grove of pines. If he could only make his way to the shelter of the trees, he could come up behind the lodge and hear clearly what they talked about. He gave his shoulders an angry jerk. How in the hell was he supposed to do that with Little Doe watching his every move?

Black of night came and the wind still howled, stronger than before. The outside world was a white sheet, making the shoddy village appear ghostly. Then, as Caleb stared through the snowy blanket, he tensed. A white man had just materialized out of the misty forest and slipped into the lodge.

Caleb's heart raced and the blood pounded in his ears. He must learn who that man is. How? He stood up and paced the floor. How was he to get away from the young squaw? His eyes fell on her, sitting before the fire, sewing a shirt for him.

He smiled. There was a way. A way so simple that if he had thought of it before he could have been away from here weeks ago.

He stretched out on the furs and motioned the girl to him. She came eagerly and curled up beside him.

With practiced fingers he began to stroke her body. When he sensed that she was weak with passion, he leaned on an elbow, hovering over her. She gave him a tender smile and closed her eyes for his kiss. He gazed at her a moment and then his clenched fist rose and swiftly clipped her on the chin. A fleeting remorse flashed across his face. He felt her go limp and took his arms from around her. "I'm sorry, Little Doe," he whispered.

Impatient now, he started to rise. Then he stiffened and sank to his knees. Someone was outside the lodge. Was he being guarded after all? He had noticed the absence of the sentry and had supposed that because of the weather they had not thought it necessary to watch him.

Then, over the noise of the wailing wind, came a tearing sound directly behind him. He twisted around and, amazed, watched a long shining blade slice through one of the pelts covering the lodge. As he stared wide-eyed, the blade disappeared and long brown fingers took its place. Slowly the sides were pulled apart and Caleb smothered an exclamation. The face of Long Step appeared in the opening.

The red man looked warningly at his white friend, cautioning him with his eyes to keep silent. His eyes fell on the unconscious girl and, after giving a satisfied grunt, motioned Caleb to join him.

Caleb stepped over the girl and slid through the opening. Long Step touched his arm and nodded his head in the direction of the forest. Caleb shook his head and whispered, "Somethin' is goin' on at the lodge. A white man just went in there and I want to see who it is."

Long Step grabbed his arm and hissed in his ear,

"You can find out about that later. Your woman needs you now."

Caleb peered at him in the darkness. "Woman? What do you mean, my woman?"

"The golden one. Your wife."

Roxy needed him? That was hard to believe. He was the last man in the world she would need . . . or want. He looked sharply at the brave. "Why does she need me?"

Giving his arm a tug, Long Step urged, "Come with me. I'll tell you on the way."

As they made their way through the storm, Long Step recounted what had happened in the cabin.

Rage was surging through Caleb in waves before the brave had finished his story. That someone like Ez Johnson should put his grimy hands on Roxanne's beautiful body was almost too much to bear. For a split second he was furious with Long Step for killing the man and depriving him of the pleasure.

It was after midnight when they saw a dim light winking through the snow. Caleb sighed. He was dog-tired and his leg throbbed. He glanced at Long Step and marveled at his endurance. The man must be exhausted.

Then the cabin was before them and Caleb rapped sharply on the sagging door and waited until a well-remembered voice asked cautiously, "Who's there?"

"Me and Long Step. Who were you expectin'?" he retorted.

He heard her exclaimed surprise, and his spirits dropped. He was right. It had been Seth she was expecting.

A rusty bolt scratched and the door swung open. Caleb stared at her, unable to get his fill. She still wore the blanket wrapped around her, and much of her long smooth legs showed below it. Her golden hair fell in tumbled curls around her shoulders, and the firelight striking it made it seem alive.

He swallowed the lump in his throat and brushed past her. "Who were you expectin' to show up with Long Step?" he threw over his shoulder. "Ain't I still your man?"

He hasn't changed, she thought, irritated. Just as hateful and arrogant as always.

She wanted to hurt him suddenly. To wipe the cool assurance off his face. In a voice coldly impersonal, she retorted, "You aren't *my* man. You never were."

He lowered his eyes to hide the hurt that leapt into them. After a moment of struggle, he was able to remark insolently, "Oh? You mean that Seth, 'the gentleman,' has taken my place?"

She swung around to face him, her eyes stabbing into his. "If you insist on putting it that way, the answer is yes. We're to be married in the spring."

There followed a tense silence. Caleb's rugged countenance stiffened. Her words had cut him to a degree he hadn't thought possible. But after fighting silently with himself, he managed to ask in a calm voice, "Is that so? Did you tell him that I've been there first?"

His insulting words slapped against her face, then with her fists clenched she was shouting at him, "I hate you, Caleb Coleman. I hate you so, it hurts."

Caleb seemed unperturbed at her outburst. He had heard those words from her before. He started slowly toward her, a feline grin on his lips. The gleam in his eyes said plainly that she had pushed him too far. She clutched the blanket tightly and began backing away.

Unwittingly, her backward steps were in line with

the sagging bed. Caleb continued to grin as he stalked her. In a low caressing murmur, he spoke. "Roxy, darlin', you know that's just not true."

The backs of her knees came against the bed and she cried out in a small voice, "Oh, no."

In the ensuing battle of trying to fend him off and still hold onto her concealing blanket, Roxanne lost. With one great sweep, Caleb ripped it out of her hands. She grew weak again from the hunger that leapt to his eyes as they took possession of her nakedness. Finally, she pressed her head into the dirty straw-filled pillow and closed her eyes against his need.

. She trembled as his hands smoothed the hair from her forehead and then moved down her throat. His fingers lingered a moment on her fast-beating pulse, then moved to cup a breast, gently kneading and stroking. She felt his hair brush her face and his lips claim hers. The pressure was gentle at first, then all restraint left him. His kiss became hard and demanding, forcing her lips apart.

She wanted to cry out, Get away from me—I don't want you! But the words would not come and all she could murmur was, "Oh, Caleb, Caleb." At this moment, all that mattered was being in his arms.

She relaxed and responded wantonly, eagerly accepting his exploring tongue. Reluctantly, she let him rise and hurry out of his buckskins. When he hung suspended over her, her hand came up and gentle fingers stroked him, then guided him into her. His hands clasped her buttocks and brought them up until he fit snugly between her legs. Holding her firmly, he began a slow movement, in and out, causing her to moan her pleasure with each downward thrust.

Then his driving body was becoming urgent and

his movement faster. He dropped her back onto the bed, and her legs came up to clasp around his waist. Their heavy breathing mingled and rushed through the room. Then with one great thrust their bodies stiffened together, jerked spasmodically, and became still.

His passion spent, Caleb rolled off her and leaned on an elbow. He looked into her eyes, still soft from the ecstasy he had aroused, then drew her hand to his throat, pressing his chin against it in a caressing movement.

For the merest fraction of a moment, she smiled tenderly at him. Then a small voice within her whispered, You have let him use you again. How could you forget the honorable man who has offered you marriage.

Her face went cold and she abruptly pulled away. In a voice thinly veiled in sarcasm, she asked, "I suppose you'll tell Seth about this."

When he made no response, she turned her head and looked at him. There was an expression on his face that held her eyes. For the first time his guard was down and she could see beyond his arrogance. His dark eyes, filled with dull pain, looked almost pleadingly at her.

But then, almost immediately, he reverted to his old self. His laugh was a wild cold sound, and, when he said calmly, "You'll never marry Seth Hale," she almost believed him.

She gave a short "Huh" and rose from the bed, wrapping the blanket around her body. She moved to the fireplace and picked up her buckskins. They were dry now but hopelessly torn. What was she to wear home? She felt Caleb's eyes upon her and tossed the clothing to the floor. Let him worry about it.

Long Step lay curled in a ball before the fire, his

breathing even, in a deep sleep. Roxanne piled more wood on the fire. The brave had been her good friend tonight, and the least she could do was keep him warm.

The night wore on and the storm continued. Caleb made many trips to the shed outside, bringing in armloads of wood. Long Step had awakened, refreshed and relaxed. He now sat before the fire, mending the torn seams of Roxanne's buckskins. As he jabbed the bone needle, threaded with thin rawhide, into the soft buckskin, he muttered, "Squaw's work."

If it were squaw's work, Roxanne wondered why the brave carried such items as needle and thread in the small pouch at his waist. She deduced that the red man most likely didn't have a squaw of his own, and thought it a pity.

There was little said between the Indian and Caleb, and Roxanne spoke not at all, except to thank Long Step when he handed her the finished garment.

Although Caleb did not speak to Roxanne, he watched her every movement, the same pained look on his face. Once he looked at her as if determined to speak, to explain his feelings. But her face was so cool and remote-looking that his courage seemed to vanish.

Toward dawn Roxanne, dressed now, went to the window and gazed out. The howling wind was beginning to die away. She gave a relieved sigh as she listened to it moan through the dips in the hills.

She discovered that the wind was taking the snowstorm with it, and she opened the door to look out. The night was still black, without a glimmer of a star; but over in the east a pinkish glow was beginning to fan out in the sky. She closed the door and announced, "The snow is stopping and dawn is coming."

In the first light, they closed the door behind them for the last time. Caleb walked in front of Roxanne, with Long Step bringing up the rear. Struggling along behind Caleb, Roxanne fell into a dismal depression. Against her will, she longed for Caleb to speak to her, to say anything—even if it were something hateful. Once they reached her uncle's place, she might never see him again. And if she did, she would be a married woman, most likely.

But Caleb kept his silence, and she stumbled along, an occasional tear blinding her and making her miss his tracks she was trying to walk in.

Suddenly, Long Step gave a warning grunt and Caleb stopped so short that Roxanne bumped into him. The two men, their heads alert, listened intently. Roxanne strained her ears—for what, she did not know.

Without warning, the air was full of bloodcurdling yells. Rifle shots whined through the silence, ricocheting off trees and rocks. The next thing Roxanne knew, Caleb had yanked her down behind a huge boulder. Her head hit a rock with a thud and she lay stunned and helpless. As though in a dream, faintly and far away, she heard Reverend James singing a gospel song.

Poor old man, she giggled to herself, he doesn't hear well.

Then the song stopped and there was no sound but the crunching of snow as a group of Indians milled around several yards ahead of them. Vaguely, she knew that Caleb was crouching beside her, his long rifle at his shoulder. A slight stirring behind her said that Long Step also had a rifle trained on the renegade braves.

She jumped involuntarily when two rifles boomed in her ears. Loud yells filled the air, then moccasined feet pounded off into the forest.

Caleb peered from behind their shelter. Two bodies lay sprawled in the snow. He grinned his satisfaction. Then, hastily pouring powder and bullet, he and Long Step waited for the next charge.

They had little chance of outfighting them, he knew, and his hand went to the knife at his waist. Should he plunge it into Roxanne's heart now? She was barely conscious and would have no idea what he intended when he took her into his arms.

A cold tremor went through him at the thought. Would he be able to do it—to still her life for all time? But the knowledge of what the red men would do to her chilled his blood even more, and slowly he began to withdraw the knife. Long Step saw what he intended to do and nodded his head solemnly.

Then he stopped with the knife half-unsheathed. The preacher's song had started up again and was coming closer. He let the knife slide back in place. An idea had come to him. Two ideas, in fact. And one was so strong it left him weak.

He touched the Indian's shoulder. "I'm gonna try to get to that crazy old preacher," he whispered. "Keep me covered."

With the help of his elbows, Caleb inched along on his stomach, from boulder to boulder. Sometimes the snow almost covered him, in drifts as high as three feet. Finally, he caught sight of old James struggling slowly in snow to his knees.

When the man of cloth drew opposite him, Caleb called his name as loudly as he dared. Thankfully, the preacher either heard or sensed his presence for he made his way to Caleb and squatted down beside him. They conversed for a few minutes, then James nodded his head and followed Caleb back to the shelter.

Roxanne swam between semiawareness and a somnolence. Crazy and weird thoughts flashed in and out of her mind, causing her to smile, then frown, and sometimes to cry out. She was a child again, happy as she sat on her father's lap. Then she stood at her brother's small grave and tears ran down her cheeks. And finally, she dreamed that she and Seth were being married and that rifles were popping and acrid smoke was burning her eyes and throat. Seth gripped her elbow, urging her to say, "I do." She giggled and kept repeating, "I do, I do."

Then there was a lull in the racket and Caleb was shaking her awake. "Roxy! Roxy, can you hear me? Can you understand me?"

She shook her head a couple of times and found that her mind was more clear. The short nap had helped. She looked at Caleb and nodded her head.

He leaned her back against a boulder and spoke quietly. "I want you to go with the preacher, Roxy. Me and Long Step will keep the varmints busy while you and James slip away."

She peered at him a moment, her eyes anxiously searching his face. "What about you?" she asked. "Isn't it dangerous for you to stay here? Why don't we all slip away?"

Her questions were childishly innocent, and he suppressed a smile. He'd give anything he owned if he could slip away with her. But it would be an impossible feat. She and the preacher would never be able to outrun the red devils.

He patted her arm. "I'll be alright. Me and Long

Step want to stay and see how many of them bastards we can pick off.''

It seemed for a second that she would argue some more. Then she sighed and nodded her head. ''You be careful. You hear me?''

The preacher touched her shoulder and motioned her to follow him. Caleb watched them start off and grew weak in relief and bitter regret. He was seeing that golden head for the last time. A deep sigh caught in his throat. At least he had known her, if only for a short while, he thought, as he turned back to Long Step.

As fast as they could fire and reload, Caleb and the brave started a barrage of shots in the general direction of the Indians. They might not find many targets but they would at least keep the enemy behind cover.

On stomach and elbows, Roxanne and the old man crawled from behind the sheltering boulder. Slowly inching their way, they moved from snowbank to boulder and to snowbank again.

Once Roxanne looked back over her shoulder and saw several bodies sprawled in the snow. Caleb and Long Step were making a good accounting of themselves.

It seemed to Roxanne that they had been crawling for hours. Her knees and elbows were rubbed raw and her head was aching with a relentless throb. When she felt that she could go no farther, the preacher rose to a knee and cautiously looked around.

''I think we're safe now,'' he whispered and helped her to her feet.

The area was familiar and her heart sang. Home was just a short distance away.

CHAPTER 12

Gideon became bored with just sitting and rocking. He was an outdoor person, and he hated being cooped inside. Time dragged at him, making him restless.

And not having had a woman for such a long time added to his unrest. Even now, there was a bulge in his buckskins that throbbed and nagged at him. His glance fell on Lettie and he slowly rubbed himself. The woman had certainly changed since the men had gone off on the hunt. She had gained weight and it showed to advantage in the new curves of her body. Her face had filled out and she looked ten years younger.

"Hell," he thought, "I'll bet she's not a great deal older than me."

He took to studying her closely every time she made a trip to the fire. Beside her other improvements, he noted that she was also clean and neat. At lunch today, when she leaned forward to set a bowl of soup before him, her hair had smelled fresh . . . like Roxy's soap.

He watched her now as she came and knelt by the hearth and fed wood to the fire. Her dress stretched tightly against her hips and buttocks and, as he watched those curves move as she adjusted the logs, he felt his hardness leap under his hand. Again it bore in on him how long it had been since he had lain with a woman.

He stretched his good foot forward and gently

nudged her. She looked up, her eyes questioning. He gave her a crooked grin. "I was wonderin', Lettie, if you miss Ez. He's been gone a long time . . . a long time for a woman to be without a man."

Lettie smiled inwardly. She had wondered how long it would take young Sherwood to proposition her. For over a week now she had secretly watched his discomfort and had deliberately put herself before him as much as possible. She gazed at him a moment, then smiled.

"Are you suggestin' that you take his place?"

Gideon let his gaze go boldly to the deep cleavage that showed at the top of her half-buttoned blouse. "Yeah," he drawled. "I was thinkin' along them terms."

"What would your uncle say to your beddin' me? I don't think he'd like it."

He grinned up at her. "Who's gonna tell him? I won't."

Lettie grinned back. "It's for damned sure I won't. He'd send me packin' so fast, my head would reel."

Gideon spread his legs apart, slowly unlaced his fly, and pulled it open. Startled, Lettie stared at the hard pulsating muscle. He was unusually large for a lad his age. In fact, he was larger than Ez or the other three hunters. Actually, she couldn't remember ever seeing any man that was as large as him.

Lettie looked uncertain for a moment. She was taking a chance with her job. Malcolm Sherwood would run her off the place if he caught her messing with his nephew. Then she shrugged her shoulders: What the hell. It's what I've been wanting.

She stood up and stepped out of her dress. She wore nothing beneath it and Gideon gasped as she moved forward and knelt between his legs.

She cupped a breast in each hand and leaned forward to envelop his hardness between them. For a minute or so, she rolled them up and down his hard length. Gideon moaned and leaned back in the chair. This thing with the breasts was something new to him, and now Lettie was sucking him, deeper and deeper, and he felt as though he was going crazy. His hips began to rise and fall in rhythm with her movements, and his breathing was ragged.

Lettie stood up quickly and bolted the door. When she turned back, Gideon had moved to the bed and lay naked, waiting for her. He was young and hungry and the sun was well into the west before he was sated.

Dressed once more, Gideon made his way to the window and looked out. "Good Lord," he exclaimed, as he tried to peer through the white sheet that slanted against the glass panes. Lettie was tugging at the door and having a hard time opening it.

He had heard the wind rise when he and Lettie were on the bed, but had heeded it only vaguely. He looked at the clock now and frowned. Four already. Roxy should have been home hours ago.

Lettie staggered back into the room, her arms full of wood. "It's murder out there," she gasped.

"Yeah. I'm worried about Roxy, Lettie. Do you think anything has happened to her?"

Lettie deposited the wood on the hearth and dusted off her hands. "I been thinkin' about her, too, but let's not get too hasty. If she knows to let the horses have their own way, they'll bring her home."

Hope flared for Gideon. Then he sighed heavily. Uncle Malcolm had told her that one time, but she might not remember it. He had only mentioned it in passing and it might not have registered with her.

He limped back to his chair beside the fire and

cursed the ankle that kept him from searching for his cousin.

Lettie came and stood beside him. "Mr. High and Snooty will be here before long," she encouraged. "And if Roxy's not here by then, he'll go look for her."

"That's true," he agreed and felt better. His thoughts turned to Malcolm and he wondered if he was alright. But he dismissed the thought that anything could go wrong with his uncle. He's all cozied with Ruth right now, ridin' hell out of her.

Night came early and Gideon waited for Seth's step upon the porch. But hour after hour dragged by and Seth didn't come.

"Damned city man won't come out in the storm," he fumed to Lettie.

Lettie made a light supper but neither ate much. The wind howling around the cabin and moaning down the chimney oppressed them and made the food stick in their throats.

The night wore on, and Gideon hobbled back and forth between window and hearth. Once he struck out at the wall. Why in the hell did he even look out the window? It was total black out there.

Lettie fed the fire and kept the coffeepot going. Twice when she had gone for wood, she heard the distant howling of wolves and shivered. Poor tenderfoot girl, out there alone with them. I won't tell Gideon that I heard them, she thought.

But Gideon had heard them and was almost frantic with the additional worry. As if the blizzard isn't enough, he almost sobbed, them hounds of hell have to be out there roamin' around.

The clock slowly ticked away the time and, when it struck four, the storm had begun to abate. By the time the sky turned gray it had stopped altogether. Gideon stood staring out the window, wondering if it were too late for Roxanne. Was she lying out there, frozen and still?

She wouldn't know to keep movin' . . . keep the blood circulatin', he muttered to himself.

He gave a sudden start, then groaned deeply and bowed his head on the windowsill. Lettie heard him and hurried to his side. She peered through the window, then clutched his arm. Standing in front of the barn, their heads drooping wearily, was the team of horses. But there was no sledge, or Roxanne.

"I must do somethin'," Gideon cried out, his eyes wild.

Not fully aware of his actions, and against Lettie's protestations, he shrugged into his coat and moved onto the porch. His gaze found an extra foot of snow on the ground and drifts that were double that. How could he ever go for help?

His shoulders slumped dejectedly and he turned to reenter the cabin, but stopped short. A series of shots came ringing from over the distant hill. The cold air carried sounds so far that it was difficult to judge their distance, but hope sprang within him. There were hunters out there, and maybe they could hear him. Cupping his hands to his mouth, he called as loudly as he could.

When Lettie, standing at his shoulder, heard his "Help, help!" she opened her mouth and joined him as two more shots rang out.

While the rifles continued to pop, they yelled themselves hoarse. Then Lettie touched Gideon's arm gently. "It's no use, Gideon. The wind is blowin' our words right back in our mouths. I doubt if our voices reached three yards."

Defeat came into Gideon's eyes and he nodded dumbly.

But their cries had carried plainly to Malcolm coming in from the other direction. He tried to hurry, his mind racing with all the horrible things that could be happening at the cabin. But the snow, well past his knees, slowed him. As he struggled, he envisioned the cabin in flames, Roxanne captured by Indians, or maybe Gideon scalped by the red varmints.

Finally, the homestead came in view. His eyes fell on Gideon and Lettie. It was Roxanne, then. His heart pounding, he called out to the pair, "What's wrong? Where is Roxy?"

His face blanched as both, talking at once, informed him that Roxanne had been gone since yesterday morning. After a moment, he lay a comforting hand on Gideon's shoulder and turned to Lettie. "Wrap me up some meat and bread, Lettie, and I'll go lookin' for her."

They followed him into the cabin, and Lettie bustled about while he eased himself into a chair. He was exhausted. He stared into the fire, cursing himself for spending the night with Ruth. "I could have made it home and none of this would have happened."

Lettie handed him the package of food and a cup of coffee. Nodding his thanks, he drank the coffee in one long swallow and left the cabin.

He would go first in the direction of the shots, he decided. He was curious about them. They had been going on too long to be coming from hunters. There was a battle being waged somewhere over the hill.

He was halfway up the hill when he saw the pair descending. He recognized Roxanne's blonde head and, with a yell that echoed the forest, broke into a stumbling run. He clasped her in his arms and, his eyes blinded in tears, reached a grateful hand to Reverend James.

Roxanne's tears mingled with his and her crying mounted until he became worried about it. "Roxy, girl, what happened? Could it be that bad?"

"Oh, Uncle Malcolm, it was awful. I got lost in the storm, then the horses ran away. Finally I found this old cabin and Ez Johnson was there and he tried to . . . tried to . . ."

Malcolm's body went rigid and his eyes took on a terrible look. "Roxy, did he . . . did he?"

He could not bring out the rest of the words, but Roxanne understood the unfinished question and was shaking her head. "No, Uncle Malcolm, he didn't. Long Step came along and killed him with his knife."

Malcolm drew a long breath and held her closer. Smoothing back her hair, he murmured soothing words to her, trying to calm her.

Preacher James touched his arm and spoke anxiously. "Malcolm, a bunch of redskins have Long Step and the hunter penned in among them boulders on the other side of the ridge. They could sure use the help of your rifle."

Concern came over Malcolm's face and he quickly put Roxanne away from him. "Buck up, girl," he said sternly. "Stop your cryin' now and get along to the cabin."

He turned to the preacher. "Go with her, James. Lettie will give you something to eat and a change of dry clothes."

Without further words, the burly hill man was plowing through the snow, taking the hill in long strides.

Caleb watched the pair wriggle out of sight and his chest rose in relief. Let them red hellions come now.

They'd have one hell of a fight on their hands. He wasn't going down easy. Not now, by God!

"Make your shots count, friend," he breathed to Long Step.

As though they were beginning to tire of the game, and intended to bring it to an end, the Indians drew together, surrounding the chief. The two watching men knew that it would be but a matter of minutes before they came charging at them.

Beside Caleb, Long Step dug in his elbows and brought the rifle to his shoulder. "Give 'em hell, Long Step," Caleb murmured.

They hadn't long to wait before the circle was broken. The braves swung onto the backs of shaggy ponies and formed a line, facing them. Swiftly, Caleb counted fourteen and frowned. He hadn't known that many were left. Two against fourteen didn't have a chance in hell.

They waited, not speaking nor stirring. They knew that the Indians might hold this position for several minutes. It was their way, to stretch out time and play on their adversaries' nerves. Then, when they felt that their enemies' resistance was nearly gone, they would charge.

But Caleb was an old hand at fighting them and their ruse would not work. As for Long Step, Caleb didn't believe that the man had a nerve in his body.

Nevertheless, when the air was suddenly split with a chorus of high chilling yells and the ponies came charging, both men's bodies snapped alert. But it was only a reflex, and each man picked his target and pulled the trigger.

Their rifles boomed in unison and two more ponies were riderless. The remaining Indians slackened their pace long enough to view their fallen brothers, and Caleb and Long Step worked furiously to reload their weapons.

As they worked with sure, practiced fingers, a short squat brave suddenly threw up his arms and tumbled to the ground. Almost simultaneously, directly behind them, came the sharp report of a rifle.

The unexpected shot brought the Indians to a standstill, and silently they stared at a spot several yards behind the trapped men. While they gaped and began to jabber excitedly, Caleb and Long Step had reloaded and brought down two more Indians. The odds were getting better and Caleb's hopes were building.

The chief gave a hoarse command and the braves wheeled their mounts and raced off through the forest, bent low over the ponies' necks. At the edge of the forest, the chief turned and shook his fist, and Caleb was not surprised to recognize the seamed face of the old renegade who had kept him prisoner for two months. He nudged Long Step. "That old chief really wants me, for some reason."

When the riders were out of sight, Caleb turned around and his lips spread in a wide grin. Malcolm stood beside a huge beechwood, white gunsmoke swirling around him.

"I got that bastard," he shouted his satisfaction.

"You sure as hell did," Caleb shouted back. "Me and Long Step was about done for." He stood up and went to meet Roxanne's uncle. "How did you know we was here? Did Roxanne get home alright?"

"Yeah. I met her and the preacher about half a mile from the cabin. She was worn out and almost scared to death. The preacher said that you was trapped up here and I hurried on as fast as I could."

They met and Malcolm held out his hand to the Indian. "I owe you one, Long Step," he said gravely.

They shook hands, then the three squatted down. Caleb laid a hand on Malcolm's shoulder. "You saved our bacon, Malcolm. This makes two I owe you."

Malcolm gave a curious laugh. "Don't fret about it, Caleb. I'm savin' up to ask you for a big favor someday."

"Just ask, Malcolm. Anytime, anything."

Long Step grunted in agreement, and Malcolm smiled his thanks.

Caleb's face slipped back into its cold mold as he said to Malcolm, "How much do you know about Seth Hale?"

Malcolm pushed back his coonskin and scratched his sweated front hair. "I don't know a great deal about him," he began slowly. "He showed up here about six months ago and bought out a homesteader that couldn't make it.

"He's a cool one . . . real closemouthed. Never lets anyone get close to him. Why do you ask?"

Caleb didn't answer until he had primed the rifle and closed the breech. Then laying it aside, he said, "I strongly suspect that he's mixed up with the British. Maybe not directly. He might only be supplyin' them with food through the Indians. I'm almost certain he's involved with the renegades."

Malcolm looked surprised. Then slowly his face showed acceptance of Caleb's words. That could explain many things. Times that Seth disappeared from his place for weeks at a time without explanation. Not that it was any business of his where the man went, but neighbors usually informed each other when they were going to be gone for any length of time. They would want an eye kept on the place.

He looked at Caleb and said quietly, "I wouldn't be at all surprised. He never wants to talk about the war."

Caleb found a seat on a boulder. The other two followed him, and Malcolm brought his pipe from a pocket. He filled it, snapped his flint and, after a couple of puffs, handed it to Caleb.

"What are you gonna do about it, Caleb?"

His eyes gazing thoughtfully through the tobacco smoke, Caleb answered slowly. "I'm not sure yet. For starters, I'm gonna move into the old cabin that Roxanne stumbled onto. I can keep my eye on him from there."

"I meant to ask you somethin', Caleb," Malcolm began. "How come you didn't go on the hunt?"

Caleb gave a short laugh. "Been a prisoner in a renegade camp the past two months. Them Indians that we was fightin', they're from that camp."

Malcolm started to say something, but stopped. Long Step had the pipe now and after a puff or so passed it back to him.

Malcolm dragged on it a moment, holding the warm bowl in his hand, then cleared his voice and said, "There's somethin' I think you ought to know, Caleb. Seth asked Roxanne to marry him and she said yes."

Caleb's eyes went hard and a muscle in his cheek twitched. Long Step glanced at him. "Huh," he grunted.

Malcolm averted his eyes and drew on the pipe in quick, short puffs. A silence followed, then Caleb stood up and adjusted his collar around his ears. "He'll never see the day," he said tersely and, shouldering the rifle, walked off in the direction of the old cabin.

CHAPTER 13

Caleb did not go directly to the old cabin as Malcolm had thought. Rather, he had passed it and continued to the cabin that he shared with his friends.

He hoped that his stallion had returned. Besides, he had left some old traps. They were rusty and some of them broken. Still, he felt that he could oil and mend them enough to use. He must make a pretense of trapping if he were to fool Seth Hale into thinking that he was only a trapper with no other interests. The man was shrewd, and he must be very careful if he was to catch him at anything.

A little past noon, he arrived at the cabin. Almost immediately he saw the horse. With broken reins dragging in the snow, the animal cropped at the dried windswept grass growing alongside the cabin. Caleb smiled in relief. He hadn't really expected to find him here. An Indian would kill for a piece of horseflesh like that.

He called out a greeting as he moved toward the stallion and wondered what had become of the saddle. Most likely scraped off against some tree, he thought.

The horse whinnied a welcome and trotted to meet him. Caleb put an around its neck, "Hi, old man," he murmured. "You've had a tight two months of it, haven't you?"

He stood back and ran a critical eye over the animal. The once-sleek coat was now thick and shaggy, and the mane and tail were full of burrs. Where once had been a firm belly, only sunken spots and bony ribs showed through the rough hide. "Don't worry, old fellow, I'll get you fat in no time," he promised.

It took him but minutes to gather up the discarded traps. He looked at them dubiously. It'll take a lot of bear grease and wire to get these things working properly, he thought inwardly.

Slinging them over his shoulder, he swung onto the stallion's bare back. He had not gone far when he reined in and sat listening intently. Had he heard the slithering sound of a moccasined foot? Peering closely through the trees, his eyes fastened on the long ears of a rabbit protruding from behind some brush.

He brought the rifle up to his shoulder. The unsuspecting rabbit gave one hop, spun in mid-air and lay still. He had his supper.

It was growing quite cold and the sun was about to set when the old cabin loomed in front of him. He gave it a careful survey as he approached. He didn't want to run into any of Ez's friends. But it spoke of emptiness and he relaxed and studied the building.

It was long and low, consisting of a single room. One lone window looked out to the east, as though the owner had planned on the sun awakening him in the morning. Inside, he knew there was a dirt floor with a crumbling chimney in a corner. The yard was filled with rubbish, making small uneven mounds under the camouflage of snow. Tall brown weeds, edging the path to the door, bent before the wind.

His new home for the rest of the winter. A weariness settled over him and his shoulders drooped. "What a way to live," he muttered.

He neck-reined the horse to the rough shed in the back. Dismounting, he led it into the dim interior and rummaged for something to feed the animal. Finally, from the floor and from the small loft, he gathered enough hay to at least put a small dent in the stallion's hunger. Tomorrow he would visit Malcolm and pick up some supplies for himself and for the horse.

Inside, he soon had a fire blazing, casting a rosy glow on the dirty windowpanes. He stood up and studied the rickety bed in the corner. He shrugged. It would beat sleeping on the floor, he guessed. Stripping the bedclothes from it, he spread them over a chair to warm and to drive out the dampness.

Stepping outside, he cleaned and dressed the rabbit. Inside once more, his clothes steamed while he squatted before the fire roasting the rabbit to a golden brown.

When he had eaten every piece and thrown the bones into the fire, he leaned back and wished strongly for a cup of coffee.

But he had the comfort of his pipe, he thought, as he carefully filled it and lit up from the fireplace. And sitting in a homemade rocker, his stockinged feet almost in the ashes, he puffed slowly and let his mind dwell on Seth Hale. If the man was conspiring with the enemy, he was playing for high stakes and would be a slippery customer to pin anything on. If this was true, what had they promised him, Caleb wondered.

Damn the leeches that would prey on this wonderful country in its time of trouble, he thought bitterly.

The colonies were in upheaval at this time. They had few real leaders, very little money, and no clear idea of how to handle the British. What they didn't need at this time was a countryman plotting with the enemy. It was imperative that Seth be stopped—if he were up to no good. Caleb had no desire to see the hills overrun with redcoats.

He leaned forward and knocked the dottle from his pipe. From this moment on, he would make it his business to know exactly what Mr. Hale was up to.

Roxanne's shivering had gradually ceased, and she now lay comparatively quiet. She was slowly accepting the fact that the past twenty-four hours had been real and not a nightmare. That such things took place in the hills—and that one must always be on guard against nature and man!

The latch lifted and she leaned on an elbow to gaze at her uncle standing in the door. He smiled and crossed the room to sit on the edge of her bed. "How are you feelin', honey?"

She smiled wanly. "Pretty nearly my old self, Uncle Malcolm. My nerves are still a bit shaky, though."

"I'm not surprised. That was a hard thing for a city girl to go through. Lucky thing that Indian came along."

"I know it. I never thought I'd be glad to see that Indian . . ." She had started to say, "again," and caught herself just in time. She and Gideon still hadn't told Malcolm about their experience with the Indians, and of the time spent with Caleb.

There was a pause, during which Malcolm stared nervously at his feet. Then he turned toward her again, and at her questioning gaze, said, "It was good that Coleman came along, too. Long Step couldn't have held all of them off."

With averted eyes, Roxanne played with the edge of the blanket. Finally she muttered, "I suppose so."

Aggravated at her attitude, Malcolm shot her an impatient glance. What ailed the girl, anyway?

"There ain't no supposin' about it," he growled. "Long Step might have saved you from Ez, but Caleb saved you from the Indians."

He paused, waiting for her response. When none came, he brought up a new subject concerning Caleb. "I sure am glad that Caleb is settlin' down so close to us. Makes me feel a sight safer."

His words startled her. "What do you mean, close to us? Isn't he going back to the hunt?"

"Naw. He figures he'd never find his partners. He's gonna finish up the winter, trappin' around."

Roxanne's answer was a loud "Huh."

But Malcolm caught the excited gleam in her eyes. The stubborn little mule is glad, he thought to himself as he left the room. He closed the door, smiling.

Roxanne pulled herself up until her back rested against the headboard. Caleb was only a hill away. She felt herself grow warm as she remembered the night last spent in his arms. Would Seth ever be able to send her to such heights?

Somehow, she doubted it. So far he had shown no great passion toward her. She had a feeling that the act between them would be very punctilious. She feared that missing would be the wild abandon that she and Caleb shared.

Her face blazed red as she remembered the things that Caleb had done to and for her. And even as she squirmed, she wished that his strong lean body was lying next to hers at this very minute.

A knock sounded on her door and she jumped guiltily. Did her thoughts show on her face? She waited, composing her features, then called out, "Come in."

Gideon swung open the door and smiled at her.

"Do you feel like comin' to the table, or do you want Lettie to bring you in a tray?"

"I'll come out. It's getting lonesome in here." She threw a robe around her shoulders and followed Gideon's hobbling progress to the table.

At first Roxanne wondered at Lettie's radiant face as she moved about, bringing food from the fire and placing it on the table. But as she mused, she remembered that Ez had been her man. His death had released her from a brutal life.

When Lettie set a bowl of soup in front of her, she caught and squeezed the woman's hand. "Lettie, I'm so glad that you are free of Ez and will never have to go back to that cabin if you don't want to."

Lettie smiled at her, then looked at Malcolm. "That's up to Mr. Sherwood to say, Roxanne."

Feeling three pairs of eyes anxiously upon him, Malcolm put down his fork and scratched his head thoughtfully.

Roxanne noticed an eager gleam in Gideon's eyes as he watched their uncle and smiled inwardly. As Caleb would say, "Gideon and Lettie had been mixin' it up."

"Well, Lettie," Malcolm began doubtfully, "I wouldn't mind you stayin' here, but I don't know where you would sleep."

"Look, Mr. Sherwood." Lettie leaned over the edge of the table at his elbow. "I can make me a pallet on the floor. I'll even sleep on the bare floor . . . anything—just so I don't have to go back there." She paused, blinking her eyes rapidly to hold back the tears that threatened to choke her.

"Mr. Malcolm," she began again, "just because Ez is gone, don't mean them other varmints will leave me alone. They'll just pick up where Ez left off."

She straightened up slowly and her voice was a whisper as she added, "I'd rather kill myself than go back there."

In discomfort, Malcolm looked away from the misery in her eyes. It wasn't right that a human being should have to look that way.

He cleared his throat loudly and said gruffly, "There's no need for you to sleep on the floor, Lettie. We'll set up up a cot in here."

Three sighs of relief mingled together. A single tear ran down Lettie's cheek, and she started to reach a hand to Malcolm's shoulder. Midway, she stopped. Her thanks would only embarrass the crusty hill man. But as she picked up the empty soup bowls, her eyes slewed to Gideon and they exchanged knowing looks. Roxanne caught the glances and looked quickly to see if Malcolm had noticed. But he was busy cutting into his deer steak.

That evening, after Lettie had made up her narrow bed, Roxanne and Gideon drew her into a card game and she became part of the family.

The next morning Roxanne awakened with the pale winter sun in her eyes and the aroma of coffee in her nostrils. She leaned on an elbow and listened to the morning sounds. From the barn came a variety of noises: the lowing of cows, the neighing of horses, and the fussy clucking of chickens.

I should be up and helping Uncle Malcolm, she thought vaguely. But the bed was warm and the room cold, and she snuggled deeper into the blankets.

In the main room she heard the low murmur of Lettie's and Gideon's voices intermingling with soft laughter. Her lips quirked—she could imagine what they talked about. Gideon had only one thing on his mind.

Their chatter stopped and Roxanne sat up in bed when a knock sounded on the door. "Why is Seth calling so early?" she muttered, almost complaining, as she slipped on her robe. She fumbled for slippers, then gave the belt around her waist a tight twist and walked toward the door.

As she entered the other room, she stopped short. The early visitor was not Seth. Caleb, with the freshness of outdoors about him, stood wiping his feet on a small rug placed by the door for that purpose.

As usual, whenever she saw him, Roxanne's heart began to race and a trembling took hold of her. Quickly, she stuck her hands behind her. Not for anything would she let him see how he affected her.

Caleb's eyes flickered briefly over her, holding a moment on the thin-clad breasts. Then politely, "Good morning, Miss Sherwood."

His cool formality surprised and somehow offended her. She ignored his greeting and asked sharply, "What are you doing here?"

He took his time answering, first letting his gaze roam pointedly over her body. As her face grew red in confusion, he drawled, "Don't get yourself in an uproar, miss. I didn't come to see you."

He turned to Gideon and asked shortly, "Is your uncle around?"

Gideon's answer wasn't friendly as he answered, "You'll find him in the barn."

Caleb said thanks, but his eyes were on Lettie. With a crooked, teasing grin on his lips, he coaxed, "Come with me, Lettie. There's a lot of nice soft hay over there."

Lettie grinned back at him, but shook her head. Inside, Roxanne fumed. She knew that Lettie would have gone with him in a minute had she been alone.

Caleb leaned toward Lettie and murmured lowly, but loud enough for Roxanne to hear, "You don't know what you're missin'."

Roxanne gasped when he looked over at her, as if to confirm his words. But before she could fling a biting retort at him, he had opened the door and quietly closed it behind him.

Outside, Caleb gave a pleased laugh when a heavy object from within slammed against the door. "The little wildcat don't like to be ignored," he said softly to the door.

In the barn, he found Malcolm finishing the last cow. "Hey, Coleman," the older man greeted him, setting down a pail of milk. "What brings you out so early?"

"Hunger," Caleb laughed. "There ain't a damned thing in that shack to eat. Not even any hay for the horse."

"Well, I can remedy the horse's hunger, but I'm kinda low on provisions myself. In fact, I was plannin' on goin' to the tradin' post today."

"Good. I'll go with you. In the meantime, if you'll loan me some hay and a bite to eat, I'll appreciate it."

After Caleb forked down some hay for the stallion, they walked toward the house. "What happened to your saddle?" Malcolm asked.

"Got lost while the Indians had me. Do you think you could loan me one for a while?"

"Sure. Got a couple extra ones in the barn."

They entered the cabin and Malcolm handed the milk to Lettie. "Before you strain this, Lettie, would you mind fixin' Caleb some breakfast?"

A sulky Roxanne lounging at the table jumped up and went to sit before the fire. When Malcolm announced that he was going to the post with Caleb, she retorted snappishly, "I wouldn't go nowhere with that no-account."

Malcolm hid his grin, thinking, Caleb has sure ruffled her feathers this morning.

But Caleb let his smile show as he remarked casually, "I don't recall asking you to come with me."

And as he turned to tease Lettie, Roxanne abruptly rose from her chair and hurried to her room, slamming the door behind her. Malcolm and Caleb looked at one another and winked.

Later, as they rode toward the post, Malcolm questioned, "What did you say to Roxy this mornin' that riled her so?"

Caleb gave a dry chuckle. "I think that's it. I didn't say much of anything to her."

Malcolm chuckled, too. "That would do it. Her face looked like a rainstorm, didn't it?"

Caleb made no response, but his heart was singing. He had gotten through to her, even if only in anger.

They arrived at the post and tied their mounts to a hitching rack. There were several other horses fastened there, their tails turned to the wind, and Caleb remarked, "Seems to be a lot of people out of provisions today."

"Naw, it ain't that," Malcolm drawled. "Today is Saturday. The men will be in the tavern swilling ale."

Caleb grinned. "You want to stop in for a couple?"

Malcolm grinned back. "Don't mind if I do."

As Malcolm had predicted, the rough plank bar in the dimly lit room was crowded with men. The earthen floor, heavily covered with sawdust, reeked from spilled rum and ale.

Malcolm took a great breath. "By God, Coleman, I like that stink."

As they stood accustoming their eyes to the darkness, the hill men called out friendly greetings and made room for them at the bar. Ale was placed in front of them and Malcolm tipped his tankard eagerly.

As Caleb raised his own to his lips, his glance fell on a man at the end of the bar and his body grew tense. Malcolm sensed his tightened frame and followed the direction of his gaze.

Seth picked up his mug of rum and moved up beside Malcolm, giving Caleb a cool nod. "I'm meeting my sister Nell here today," he opened the conversation. "She's coming from Boston and will be making her home with me."

Malcolm hid his surprise and remarked, "That's nice." But inside, he was saying, Roxy won't like this. She won't want no female under her feet.

He took a swig of ale, then asked, "Did your sister mention how things were going in Boston? Did she say if the British are still there?"

After a pause, Seth answered shortly, "General Howe is still occupying the city."

Caleb asked, "He's been there close to a year now, hasn't he?"

When Seth was again slow to answer, Malcolm interposed. "It ain't gonna do him any good. Since last April, General Washington has kept a tight land blockade around Boston. He'll have Howe out of there before long."

As Malcolm spoke, he watched Seth from the corner of his eye. The man's face became flushed and anger sparked the narrowed eyes. Malcolm poked Caleb with his elbow, and Caleb nodded and chuckled silently.

He debated annoying Hale with some more war talk, in the hope that the man's anger might let something slip. But he realized that Seth might catch onto what he was doing and would be warned.

Instead, he ordered another round of drinks. Just as these were put before them, from outside came the drumming sound of galloping hooves.

Seth hurried to the door and looked out. "She's here," he exclaimed and stepped outside.

Malcolm picked up his mug and smiled slyly at Caleb. "Let's go take a look at the filly."

They moved with the other men to stand on the narrow porch that flanked the building. Seth was helping his sister to dismount. When she stood on the ground, a low murmur went through the men. She was strikingly attractive, with dark skin and black hair. Her riding habit revealed a body that was softly curved and inviting.

As Caleb studied her, he made a mental note that her breasts were larger than Roxanne's. "Let's go meet her," he murmured to Malcolm.

Seth introduced Malcolm to her warmly. "Nell, I want you to meet my fiancee's uncle. He's also my closest neighbor."

He ignored Caleb, even to the point of turning his back on him. But Nell's sparkling brown eyes were looking at Caleb questioningly.

Malcolm placed a hand on Caleb's arm and said, "Miss Hale, I want you to meet a friend of mine. Caleb Coleman, long-hunter."

Nell gazed at Caleb and her eyes kindled. She slid them down the length of his body, stopping for a fleeting moment at a spot below his belt buckle. She blushed and looked away from the bulge that was building there. When she brought her eyes back to his face, a knowing look shone in them.

Later, when she and Seth rode away from the post, Malcolm jabbed Caleb in the ribs and remarked,

"You can get between them legs any time you have a mind to."

Caleb laughed, realizing he had been breathing heavily. "Yeah, and none too soon."

Malcolm laughed loudly and whacked him on the back.

They finished their drinks and stepped into the adjoining room of the store. They quickly made their purchases of flour, coffee, sugar, and salt. Caleb had to buy extras, such as bacon, beans, baking powder, and a couple of pots and a skillet.

The storekeeper, a Scotsman, totted up the bill and, rummaging a moment beneath the counter, came up with a couple of cloth bags and tossed the items inside. He looked askance at the paper money the two men handed him, but after a hesitation, reluctantly took it.

"Don't know if this is any good or not," he grumbled, stowing it in a box that was half full.

Malcolm and Caleb were halfway home when through the trees to the left they spotted the red flash of Nell Hale's roan. Caleb reined in and motioned for Malcolm to do the same.

Two sets of tracks led off the broken trail, leading to a dense thicket where Nell sat her horse. She patted the nervous animal's neck as she peered anxiously straight ahead.

Malcolm whispered, "Where do you suppose Seth is?"

"I don't know, but I mean to find out. Let's swing around the lady and see if we run into him."

They urged their mounts into the smooth expanse of snow, swinging well away from the woman, then moving in a half circle when they were out of her sight. After ten minutes of plowing through drifts that sometimes reached the animals' chests, they cut Seth's trail. Silently they veered and followed the fresh track.

Malcolm was first to spot Seth. He signaled to Caleb and they moved to the shelter of some tall sumacs. Together they dismounted and, from the secrecy of the bushes, watched him. It was obvious that he waited for someone. And though he was several yards away, they could tell he was uneasy as he paced back and forth.

Then both men caught their breaths and held still. Into the slight clearing rode Caleb's old enemy, accompanied by three braves. From the manner in which Seth and the chief greeted one another, there was no doubt that they knew each other well.

The chief slid to the ground while the braves remained mounted, their black eyes searching the forest. Caleb and Malcolm froze into position, praying that the density of the bushes would hide them.

As Seth and the Indian hunkered down and talked in low tones, Caleb strained his ears, knowing that it was a wasted effort. He swore impatiently under his breath. Something very important to the hills was being discussed by those two, and he was on fire to know what it was. He fought back the urge to confront Seth and to demand point-blank what he was up to.

Some minutes later, Seth handed the chief a packet. Caleb peered intently, trying to see what it contained. But the Indian didn't open it; rather, he quickly stored it in a pouch at his waist. But Caleb felt that only money could be in the long, narrow package. It was too small to hold anything else of value.

The two men conversed for a few more minutes, then stood and shook hands in the white man's fashion. It wasn't until after they had remounted, and Seth was turning his horse to retrace his steps, that Caleb and Malcolm realized he would see their tracks. Caleb gave a disgusted grunt. What in the hell had they been thinking of? Only a real green-horn would have forgotten that the man would return to his waiting sister.

What to do now? raced through Caleb's mind. With Seth alerted that someone was on to him, he would be so careful in the future that it would be impossible to catch him in his mischief.

Malcolm touched his arm in sympathy, and Caleb's mind was made up. He would shoot the bastard. He could at least stop his future work with the Indians. As he lifted the long rifle and cocked it, he thought, Maybe Malcolm can get the old chief.

As if Malcolm read his mind, he nodded his shaggy head and brought his own rifle to his shoulder. They waited. Another few yards and Seth would see their tracks. Simultaneously they took aim on the men and their fingers tightened on the triggers. Then suddenly the chief was calling some word to Seth.

Seth reined in and, after a slight hesitation, called back, "How far is it?"

The wind was at the watching men's backs and they couldn't hear the Indian's answer. But to their relief, Seth turned his horse again and followed the Indians.

"Whew, that was close," Malcolm said.

Caleb drew an arm across his sweating face. "Yeah. I thought for a minute there we'd have to kill them."

The horses stirred, anxious to get back to warm quarters. Caleb glanced at the darkening sky. He wanted to follow Seth and the Indians, to see if they met anyone else.

He turned to Malcolm. "I'm gonna follow them. See if they meet up with some redcoats. Would you drop off my supplie. at the shack?"

"Sure thing, Caleb, but oughten' I go with you? You might run into more than you can handle."

"I don't mean to fight them, Malcolm. I just want to trail them and find out what they're up to."

Malcolm nodded and swung into the saddle. As Caleb handed him the bag of provisions, he said gruffly, "Take care of yourself, Coleman. I gotta feelin' I'm gonna need you real bad one of these days."

Caleb looked into the weatherbeaten face. A deep respect and fondness for this rough hill man had grown in him, and he said gravely, "I'll be there if you need me."

He gave the stallion a whack on the rump and it moved off.

Caleb had gone only about a mile when he came to a small clearing in a stand of walnut trees. He halted the horse and studied the trampled snow covering a small area. Almost immediately, he spied the shod horse prints leading off alone, going in the opposite direction.

He pushed back his coonskin and surveyed the forest narrowly. Why did Seth turn back? he questioned silently. For what reason did he follow them in the first place?

He debated a moment who to follow. He wasn't long concluding that in all likelihood Seth had returned to his sister. Following him would be a wasted effort. As for the Indians, there was no telling what they might lead him to. He pulled down his cap and lifted the reins.

He smelled the Indians' campfire just as dusk was coming on. The stallion became nervous and his ears pricked up and his nostrils flared. He smells Indians, Caleb thought and leaned forward to pat the quivering neck.

Riding around a small hill, he reined in sharply. They were camped by a spring that ran from under the hill. Huge boulders and thick-spreading cedars hemmed in the spot like a large room.

The fire leapt high, silhouetting the figures around it. Caleb slumped in the saddle, fighting his disappointment. They were alone. Silently, he rode the horse at a walk around the hill. He would keep watch on them, anyhow. They might still rendezvous with the British.

He stepped down from the horse, unsaddled him, and tied him to a tree. He debated building a small fire, but decided against it. It's a cold camp for me, he thought. There may be more of the varmints skulking around out there.

Picking two boulders away from the wind, Caleb hunched down between them. The faint aroma of roasting meat made his stomach rumble; saliva gathered in his mouth.

CHAPTER 14

When Malcolm returned home, he made no other mention of Seth than to say he had met his sister, Nell. He looked at Roxanne's scowling face and remarked, "Looks like you'll have company when you move in with Seth."

Roxanne asked suspiciously, "What do you mean?"

"Well, Miss Hale hasn't come for just a visit. Seth told me and Caleb that she's gonna be makin' her home with him."

From the corner of his eye, he watched his niece's back stiffen and her chin take on a stubborn tilt. She didn't like the idea, and Malcolm was glad. Anything that put a stumbling block in the path of that marriage was alright with him.

And to make a bad matter worse he, with twinkling eyes, remarked, "I don't think you have to concern yourself with that too much, though. She and Caleb sure took a shine to each other. I wouldn't be at all surprised if them two don't get together."

Gideon tried to hide his laugh, but it turned into a large snort, followed by a strangling noise. Roxanne jumped to her feet and swatted him sharply on the head as she flounced to her room. The door slammed behind her, making the cabin shake.

Hot tears scalded her eyes as she threw herself across the bed. "Damn him, damn him," she whispered furiously and pounded the pillow with her fist.

This morning she had longed with all her being that he ignore her sharp tongue and, instead, carry her off to the bedroom. There was a time when he would have done just that. What had happened? What had changed him? Had he grown tired of her, tired of her inexperience? Would he seek love with Seth's sister?

She gulped. "If she's anything like her brother, Mr. Caleb Coleman will be in for a surprise."

Her mind dwelled on Nell Hale. What was she like? Would she be cool and polite, like her brother, or would she be warm and friendly? Uncle Malcolm had mentioned that she looked to be in her late twenties and was very attractive.

She sighed and rolled over on her back. Miss Hale was also most likely well schooled in the art of pleasing a man.

Before she realized it, her tears were no longer from anger but stemmed from a deep sense of loss. She loved Caleb Coleman completely, and he didn't care in the least.

When Malcolm knocked on the door later and announced that supper was ready, she called back that she wasn't hungry. Not for the world would she have them see her tear-swollen eyes!

After crying herself out, Roxanne fell into an exhausted sleep. It was dark of night when she awakened to the squeak from her door. She leaned on an elbow and counted the striking of the clock. Eleven. The soft slithering sound of stockinged feet whispered across the floor. She peered through the gloom and, through the shaft of moonlight slanting through the window, saw Lettie and Gideon pass into his connecting room.

She grinned. Impishly, she debated calling out Gideon's name and demanding to know what he was doing up at this hour. She stiffled a giggle, picturing the look on his face as he tried to explain Lettie's presence to their uncle.

Instead, she slipped off the bed and made her cautious way to the door. Fixing her eye to a large knothole, she had a clear view of the couple before the fire. She grinned again. They had wasted no time in disrobing.

Now I'll see if the young rooster is the great lover he claims, she thought.

Gideon stood up from laying some wood on the fire and Lettie came to him immediately, winding her arms around his neck. Roxanne was surprised at how shapely the woman had become. Meat covered her bones, giving her curves she had never had before. Her breasts were large and firm, and Gideon now began to fondle one, while his mouth came down on the other. When he slid a nipple into his mouth and began to tease it with his tongue, Lettie made little noises in her throat and writhed against him. Her arms came from around his neck and her hands disappeared between their bodies. Gideon moved away from her enough so that she could fondle and stroke him.

Fascinated, Roxanne watched him grow large and throbbing in Lettie's hands. Then breathing heavily, Gideon raised his head and placed his hands on her shoulder. And before Roxanne's wide-eyed stare, urged Lettie to her knees in front of him.

"Don't tease," he mumbled and forced her mouth open. He grasped her chin and plunged himself between her parted lips. Lettie closed her lips over him and grasped his buttocks.

Roxanne barely breathed as she watched the hired woman's mouth slide smoothly up and down. This is what Cousin Mary had told her about. This is what she had done for her husband.

In a short time Gideon was jerking in spasms while his hands held Lettie's head firmly. Then he was still, and Lettie rose to her feet. Taking his hand, together they moved to the bed. Lying down and facing each other, Lettie began to stroke him until he was hard again. Unceremoniously, he climbed between her waiting legs and rammed himself into her.

Roxanne held her breath, afraid that Malcolm would hear the thumping and bumping as Gideon slammed against the eager body.

She remained at the knothole, waiting to see if Gideon returned any of Lettie's acts. And though she once again pleasured him with her lips, Gideon never went below her breasts.

Suddenly, Roxanne was aware of the cold. There had been no fire lit in her room and it was icy. She fumbled in a drawer for a gown and hurriedly put it on. She had barely climbed into bed and pulled the covers over her when the latch to Gideon's room lifted and Lettie scurried across the floor.

When she heard Lettie's cot squeak in the main room, Roxanne slid out of bed and strode purposely into Gideon's room. There was something that she had to learn about.

Gideon was just dozing off, an exhausted, contented look on his boyish face. When Roxanne sat on the edge of the bed, his eyes flew open and he raised himself on an elbow. "Roxanne!" he exclaimed in a whisper. "What's wrong?" Then his eyes narrowed suspiciously. "What do you mean by waking a person at this hour?"

"There's nothing wrong," she whispered back,

"and I didn't wake you. I know that Lettie just left you."

When he began protesting that she had been dreaming, Roxanne lay a finger across his lips. "Hush up, Gideon. I've been watching you."

Sitting up quickly, he almost shouted, "What?" At Roxanne's alarmed face, he lowered his voice and continued angrily, "You've got a hell of a nerve doing that."

"Oh, tish," she hissed. "Don't get so riled up. I only wanted to learn something."

When Gideon saw that she wasn't going to tease, he puffed himself up importantly and smiled smugly. "Well? Did you learn anything?"

"Not really. Cousin Mary had already told me about . . . about what Lettie did to you."

Gideon interrupted her in a teasing tone. "And Caleb showed you the rest."

She blushed and slapped at him. Gideon dodged away, laughing softly. "What else did you want to know?" he asked, more seriously.

She dropped her eyes and toyed with the edge of the blanket. When she began to speak, her voice was hesitant. "I'm curious . . . I'm curious why you didn't do to Lettie . . . what she did to you."

Gideon gave a disgusted snort and threw himself back onto the bed. "Hell, Roxy, a man don't do that to a whore. He only does that to somebody he likes . . . maybe loves."

Her face took on such a bewildered look that he smiled humorlessly. "You don't know much, do you, Roxy?"

She looked away and answered, "I guess not."

Gideon sat up. "I think it's time I educated you,"

he began. But his next words were cut off sharply by the sonorous voice of Malcolm booming through the walls.

"What in the hell is goin' on in there? You two stop your jabberin' and get to sleep."

Their eyes crinkled at one another, and Roxanne clapped a hand across her mouth to smother her giggles. She stood up and whispered, "Good night," and moved to the door. But before she closed it, she paused and called softly across the room, "Are you sure about that, Gideon?"

For a moment Gideon's face was puzzled. Then he gave her a sleepy grin and whispered loudly, "Dead sure, Roxy. Good night."

Roxanne snuggled deep into the feather bed and a gradual warmth spread over her. As she drifted off to sleep, she hugged a special knowledge to her breast. Caleb must feel something for her. For he had done to her what Gideon wouldn't do to Lettie. Her last waking thought was, Could she bring herself to do what Lettie had done? She sensed that Caleb had wanted her to.

The next morning, after sleeping late and having a leisurely breakfast, Roxanne found the time moving slowly. After several trips to the window and staring out on the white world, she plopped herself into a rocker and stared moodily into the fire. She was so bored, so restless. For over a month now, not one homesteader had broken trail to visit them.

"The distance is too great in the wintertime," Malcolm had explained.

She drummed nervous fingers on the arm of the chair. She had to get out of the cabin for a while, if only for a walk. But where could she walk? Down to

the barn? Out to the spring? There were no other broken trails . . . excepting, of course, the one leading to
that miserable Caleb Coleman's place . . . and to
Seth's cabin.

Her face lit up. Of course! She would go visit Seth.
As she dressed, she admitted reluctantly that the
thought had been in her mind all along. She was curious about Nell Hale. She wanted to see for herself
what kind of woman she was, and just how attractive.

When she came out of the bedroom with her coat on
and a scarf tied around her head, Gideon looked at her
questioningly.

"I'm going to visit Seth," she remarked. "I want
to look over his place and see how I can fix it up, once
I've moved in," she continued, her eyes daring him to
say anything.

And for a moment she thought he would forgo his
teasing, for his face held an excited expectancy as he
shot a fast glance at Lettie. But then his eyes took on
the old sly twinkle. "You gonna look Caleb's new
heartthrob over, too?"

She glared at him a moment, then swishing to the
door, called back sarcastically, "You'd better drop
the latch behind me. You can never tell when Uncle
Malcolm may come busting in."

But Gideon wouldn't be riled. Her gave her a lazy
grin. "Thanks for the reminder, cousin. Lettie will
take care of it."

The mare made good time on the snowpacked trail
and within a half hour Roxanne was knocking on
Seth's door. The dark-haired woman who answered
her rap was still in gown and robe. Her hair tumbled
around her shoulders in loose curls, and her face was
soft with sleep. Roxanne looked at her and hated her

immediately. She could see where this curvaceous, attractive woman would attract Caleb . . . or any other man.

The woman's eyes smiled at her and a slim hand came out in friendly greeting. "You have to be Roxanne," she said in her throaty voice. "Come on in, out of the cold."

And although she felt anything but doing so, Roxanne tried to respond in like manner. Forcing a smile to her lips, she said, "And you are Nell, of course."

They stood a moment, looking at each other, knowing that they would never be close. Two beautiful women seldom were.

"Seth has told me so much about you, Roxanne," Nell said, reaching to help remove her coat. "I am so pleased that at last he's marrying and settling down."

Roxanne smiled her thanks and walked to the inviting fire. It wasn't until she started to sit down that a movement caught her eye in the dark shadow of the chimney. A young Indian girl squatted there. She peered closer and recognized White Star. Giving a startled exclamation, she stepped back.

In the act of hanging up Roxanne's wrap, Nell turned and asked anxiously, "What is wrong, Roxanne?" Then seeing the young squaw, also standing now and looking ill at ease, she continued, "Did White Star startle you?"

"Yes, she did," Roxanne retorted sharply, holding her hands together to stop their trembling. "I'm surprised to see that one in this house."

Nell hurried to her side and, placing an arm around her waist, said gently, "Didn't you know, dear, that the girl cleans house for Seth?"

"No, I wasn't aware of it. And I wonder if Seth is

aware that this girl tried to do me harm a short while ago?''

Nell's eyes grew wide and she looked at the darkly sullen face of White Star, who stared down at the floor. ''Is this true, White Star?'' she demanded.

''I no touch her,'' was the guttural reply. ''It was Ez Johnson who hurt her.''

''You lie!'' Roxanne cried out angrily and took a step toward her. ''You caught and held me for him. Only Long Step's appearance saved me.''

While Roxanne talked, Miss Hale had moved to the door and now stood holding it open. ''I think you'd better go, White Star,'' she ordered. ''And I'm sure my brother won't want you back here.''

The girl hesitated a moment, then slouched to the door, her black eyes shooting hatred at Roxanne. She passed outside and moved off through the forest.

Nell closed the door and shivered. ''I didn't realize what kind of people lived in these hills,'' she said lowly, as though to herself.

She took a seat next to Roxanne and patted the younger girl's knee. ''I'm sure Seth knew nothing about this. It must have been a terrible experience.''

''I wouldn't care to go through it again,'' Roxanne answered.

They talked of other things then, discussing new styles in clothes and laughing at how out of place they would be in the hills. But when Roxanne brought up parties she had attended and the plays she had seen in Boston, Nell grew noticeably ill at ease.

Finally, she remarked sharply, almost rudely. ''I'm sure we traveled in different circles, dear, there being so much difference in our ages. Shall we talk of something else?''

Her words caused Roxanne's happy chatter to die

away, and she stared down at her clasped hands, feeling like a young schoolgirl.

A silence grew between them. Then both started talking at once. They laughed lightly, and Nell said, "You go first."

"I was only going to ask if typhus is strong in Boston."

"No, thank God, it isn't. It has finally run its course. The city is almost back to normal, considering that British soldiers throng the streets night and day."

It wasn't until they sat at the table, having tea and cookies, that Caleb's name was brought up. When Nell said, "I met the most handsome man at the post the day I arrived," Roxanne almost choked on the gingersnap she had just bitten into.

She gave a small cough, then said weakly, "You did?"

"Yes," Nell answered, her voice hushed and eager. "He looked all man, with the very devil looking out of his eyes. Seth says that he's a long-hunter and pretty wild. His name is Caleb Coleman. Do you know him?"

"Yes, I know him," Roxanne answered shortly.

Nell noticed the strange quietness that came over her, but didn't let on as she continued to talk about Caleb. "I believe that he lives quite close, and from the look he gave me, I expect him to come calling soon."

Roxanne gave her a sidelong look and thought to herself, Is that why you're still in your gown? But she fought back her anger and managed to say quietly, "I'm sure he will. There aren't many like you, here in the hills."

Nell smiled at her compliment. "Thank you, dear. I'm certainly glad that Seth has *you* all tied up. I have a feeling that you're just the type that long-hunter would be attracted to.''

Roxanne felt herself blush and become rattled. She muttered something to the effect that she doubted it.

They gazed at each other a moment, while the clock ticked loudly and the fire snapped. Then Roxanne turned her head away and exclaimed, ''It's getting late and I must get home. Darkness comes fast in the hills.''

''The time has gone so quickly,'' Nell complained, rising with her. ''I hope you will come again soon. I know that Seth will be sorry that he missed you.''

Roxanne brought out the mare from under the sheltering pine where she had tied it. Swinging into the saddle she looked toward the cabin to wave, but the door was already closed. She shrugged her shoulders and nudged the horse onto the trail.

It wasn't until she had gone some distance that she realized she hadn't invited Nell Hale to visit her. Even though she didn't like the woman, that was a terrible breach of etiquette. She reined in the mare and sat nibbling on her thumb as she debated whether or not to return and issue the invitation.

She decided that she had better. Mama would be ashamed of her if she knew her daughter had been so rude.

She was turning the mare around when, from a rise several yards ahead, a flash of brown caught her eyes as it disappeared behind a boulder. She leaned forward and peered intently. But nothing moved in the rock's vicinity, and she made a mocking sound at herself. I am getting fanciful, she thought.

Lifting the reins, she moved on; but several yards beyond the boulder she plainly saw White Star striding along with the free grace of an animal. ''Well, I'll be damned," she muttered, "she's going back to Seth's place."

Roxanne spoke quietly to the mare and turned it off the trail and into the concealing forest. Keeping well behind the girl, she followed to the edge of the clearing. There Roxanne reined in and watched.

White Star's steps didn't slacken or falter as she stepped upon the porch and knocked. For the first time it occurred to Roxanne that maybe the girl meant harm to Nell Hale. She was jabbing her heel into the mare's flank when the cabin door opened. Nell, a smile of welcome on her face, stood there. Her lips moved and she pulled White Star into the room.

Roxanne sat staring at the closed door, her mouth wide open. What was going on there? The words of Uncle Malcolm's Ruth shot through her mind. Was there something going on between Seth and White Star, after all? It was all too plain that Nell's display of outrage had been only for her benefit.

She turned the mare around and headed for home. I'll certainly have this out with Seth, she thought angrily, urging the mare to a pace that was dangerous on the slippery snowpacked trail.

CHAPTER 15

The night was cold and Caleb slept little, merely dozing off and on. It was a relief when the Indians rolled out of their blankets before dawn.

He waited until they were out of sight before standing up and stretching sore muscles. The stallion was browsing on tufts of tall dead grass and seemed content. His own empty stomach growled and he was tempted to try the grass himself.

He checked his rifle, then climbed into the saddle. The Indians' trail ran south until it came to a long, tall hill, then turned abruptly west, in a straight line. After an hour or so, their trail came out of the forest and into a small valley that was full of ravines and boulders. In the distance, in thin spirals, smoke reached into the cold air.

The main Indian camp was near. Caleb stepped out of the saddle and tied the horse to a low bush. When the last Indian disappeared into a ravine, he ran, bent over, to crouch behind a boulder.

He waited until he heard the returning warriors being greeted by the children, then moved swiftly to a drifted snowbank and peered over. At the bottom of the ravine was the sprawling camp. He recognized many of the squaws and old men, and his eyes searched for Little Doe. She was not in the group, and he hoped that she wasn't out in the woods somewhere and would stumble onto him.

The braves tied their shaggy ponies to some bushes nearby, then gathered in a close circle around the fire. The older braves, who had been left behind to guard the women, now joined them. The chief began to talk, his voice excited and his hands making many motions. Caleb strained to hear his words but could not make them out.

Dropping on all fours, he crawled for several yards, well out of sight of the campfire, and slid down into the ravine. Then in a half-crouch he slipped cautiously through the scattered boulders and brush until he came up behind the chief's lodge. But he had no sooner positioned himself behind a thick stunted cedar when an old squaw announced that it was time to eat.

Flattening himself to the ground, Caleb swore helplessly as he watched the circle break and the braves hurry to a hot meal.

He admitted reluctantly that he would learn nothing here. His best bet was to keep an eye on Seth. Sooner or later the man would give himself away.

He squirmed his way back to the stallion and mounted. Turning the horse homeward, he made his plans as he rode along. He would begin by visiting sister Nell—tonight, he decided with a grin.

When he finally reached the old rundown cabin, it was at the end of a long tiring day. In a hurry to get home, he had made the mistake of breaking new trail instead of keeping to the one made by the Indians. Many times he was forced to dismount and lead the animal through snowdrifts that sometimes reached to its broad chest. In the end, his straight course had taken him longer, and his leg muscles, seldom used, screamed in agony.

As he rode around to the back of the cabin, he followed the tracks of a team of horses and the running imprint of sledge runners. The marks stopped at the shed door and he leaned over to pat the weary horse's neck. "I see that Malcolm has brought you some hay, old fellow."

Dismounting stiffly and leading the animal inside, the hay's fragrant scent reached him from the small loft. He unsaddled his mount and pulled down its supper. Then fastening a blanket over the wide back, he made his way to the cabin.

Inside, the cabin was cold and dismal. Leaning the rifle in a corner, he hunkered down by the hearth and built a fire. He was weak from hunger and, as he filled the blackened coffeepot with water and coffee grounds, his fingers trembled. Placing the pot on the flames, he turned to making his supper. He smiled in appreciation when he found that Malcolm had stored all his provisions in the proper places. It would be no hard chore for squirrels and other small animals to invade the rotting cabin and make off with his food.

When he had salt pork sizzling in the frying pan and corn pone baking in an iron kettle, he removed his hat and coat. As he hung them on the head of the bed, his eyes fell on the pillow that still held the imprint of Roxanne's head. He had intentionally left the pillow indented, but now he leaned over and fluffed out her mark. He must keep the thought of her away. He was going to concentrate on Nell Hale now.

There's a high-steppin' filly, he said inwardly. I won't have any trouble gettin' her into bed.

He finished his meal, eating directly from the pans, and poured his third cup of coffee. Leaning back in the chair, he loosened his belt and sighed. He had eaten too much and too fast.

The small stub of candle was flickering, ready to go out. He rose and searched the shelves for another. He located a dozen, lying next to the sugar canister. By this time the candle had gone out and he lit the new one at the fire and stuck it into the holder.

Then, as he haphazardly washed the frying pan and kettle, he debated whether to visit the Hale place tonight. He was bone-tired and might fall asleep on the attractive Nell.

But by the time he had carried in several loads of wood and stacked them neatly beside the hearth, his supper had digested and he felt better.

He washed up at the wobbly dry sink and scraped the three days' growth of whiskers off his face. Changing into a clean shirt and giving his dark hair a swipe or two, he was ready to go courting.

He hated disturbing the stallion after such a strenuous day; but once saddled and on their way, he discovered that the animal, too, was rested. It tossed its head impatiently and pulled against the reins, eager to go faster.

When Caleb arrived at the Hale clearing, he reined in and made a slow survey of the place. The sky was clear, and the pale cold moon bathed the area in a soft light.

Nothing stirred around the cabin, and the only sound was a long-drawn howl of a wolf as it roamed the hills. A feeble light glowed from the cabin window and he saw Nell pass before it. He gave his wicked grin and gave the horse a jab with his heel.

Riding the stallion behind the building, he dismounted. Attached to the cabin was an open-end leanto, and he led the horse beneath its shelter. Smoothing his clothes, he moved to the front and knocked on the door.

Nell peeked out the window at him; he touched his coonskin in a light salute. She swung open the door, a welcoming smile spread across her lips.

"Well, now," he murmured, his eyes lazily traveling the length of her body.

She still wore the gown and robe, and standing in front of the firelight her curvy shape stood out clearly. Her eyes twinkled and her lips quirked at the corners as she stepped aside and invited, "Come in out of the cold, Mr. Long-Hunter."

As he handed her his cap and coat, his eyes took a quick turn of the room. She was alone. "Where is Seth?" he asked, taking a seat beside the fire.

Nell gave a short laugh. "He's gone courting."

Caleb's face darkened as he tried to hide the stiffening of his back from Nell. He wouldn't get very far with her if she saw how her words had cut him.

But by the time she had hung up his coat and poured him a mug of cider, he had controlled his features and was able to speak in his normal voice.

"I hear tell he's gonna marry that hellcat. When's it supposed to happen?"

Nell gave him a sidelong glance. Had she detected anger, and maybe disappointment, in the hunter's voice? But looking at him closely, she found his face smooth and his eyes fastened on her breasts. She gave a slight shrug of her shoulders. She must have imagined it.

Pulling a chair close to his, she sat down and answered, "In the spring sometime, I think. I believe that Seth said March or April."

Caleb noted the thinly veiled antagonism in her voice and hid his smile. Miss Nell Hale was jealous of the beautiful Roxy.

He stretched his legs to the fire. "He's gonna have his work cut out with that one," he drawled. "She's got a temper like a catamount."

A flicker of jealousy ran through Nell and she glanced at him suspiciously. How did he know so much about Roxanne Sherwood? "Do you know my brother's fiancee that well?" she asked coolly.

Caleb felt the telltale red wash over his face and he swore inwardly. This woman was as slick as her brother and he'd have to watch every word with her. He picked up her hand as his smooth tongue began its work to erase her suspicions.

"I don't know her too well," he began. "I've only seen her a few times; but during those times, I've seen her hop all over her uncle and cousin. Course, they tease her a lot."

He glanced at Nell and noted that she still looked ruffled. He leaned toward her until their shoulders touched. "Me and her didn't take to each other a'tall. I can't abide a sharp-tongued woman," he added.

He hid his grin as her face took on a smile and she leaned into him. "You mean to say that a big handsome man like you couldn't get that little girl to eat out of your hand?" she murmured.

Caleb ignored her comment, for as her words purred out she had arched her shoulder, causing her robe to fall open. One large breast stood free of the low-cut gown, and his eyes were riveted to it. She rose and slid onto his lap. Wrapping her arms around his neck, she brought her lips down to his. Her tongue grabbed his thrusting one and began to suck urgently as she rubbed herself against his growing hardness.

Caleb's breathing became short and heavy, and he began to knead the exposed breast, tweaking gently at the nipple. She moaned softly and reached down to unfasten his buckskins.

His eyes flared and he grinned wolfishly. Hell, she's nothing but a fancy whore, he thought. He gazed down at Nell questioningly. He noted that she avoided his eyes and realized that now perhaps she regretted her wantonness. To calm her fears, he pulled her closer. He must continue to play the game if he was to learn anything.

He drew her head onto his shoulder and whispered, "You're wonderful. I've been lookin' for someone like you for a long time."

Her attitude changed immediately and she began to stroke him again. She was kissing and nuzzling him now, when from outside came the sound of a horse's hooves.

"My brother," Nell snapped angrily. She rose hurriedly to her feet, quickly closing her robe and tying it.

For the first time, Caleb liked Seth Hale. The man had saved him from the most embarrassing moment of his life. He pretended to be angry at the interruption and swore strongly as he pushed himself back into his pants.

But Nell's anger, however, was real. Her eyes were heavy with her need, and when Seth stepped upon the porch, Caleb whispered, "Honey, we'll make up for it tomorrow night."

This pacified her a bit and she squeezed his hand. When Seth entered the room, they were sitting calmly before the fire. The two men nodded briefly at one another and Nell looked at them curiously, wondering at the coolness between them.

After passing a few remarks, touching on the weather and the supply shortage at the post, Caleb allowed that it was time to get home.

Nell walked him to the door; but under her brother's disapproving stare, she merely shook hands and invited Caleb back again.

CHAPTER 16

Roxanne returned from her visit in a foul mood. Before Gideon's and Lettie's amazed stares, she threw off her coat and swept to the fireplace to slide the coffeepot onto the red coals. Still without a word, she rose to her feet and marched to her room, slamming the door loudly.

Gideon looked at Lettie and raised his eyebrows. "What's got into her?"

Lettie shrugged. "Maybe she had a spat with Seth."

"Naw, I don't think so. Seth never riles her that much, one way or the other. I wonder if she ran into Caleb. Now, he strikes fire from her."

Before they could say more, Roxanne was back in the room, pulling the coffeepot toward her. "Do either of you want a cup?" she half growled, taking the pot to the table.

Still staring at her, Lettie and Gideon shook their heads silently, and she poured one cup.

Taking a deep swallow, she swore in anger and pain as the liquid burned her lips and throat. Gideon snickered and Lettie shook her head at him. Roxanne glared at her cousin but said nothing.

She remained in her pout until Malcolm came stamping in from running the traps, his booming voice calling out a cheery greeting. He shrugged out of his coat and tossed his coonskin on Lettie's bed.

Then standing with his back to the fire and rubbing his rump in its warmth, he grinned at Roxanne. "Saw Seth out by the spring before. He sends his regards and will be over tonight to visit you."

Roxanne's reply was a grunt. "Hah."

Malcolm's eyes took on a teasing gleam. "Run into Caleb just now. He was comin' from the Hale place. Yep, made his first visit to Miss Hale." He paused a moment, then added, "Looked all tuckered out, too. I got a feelin' he's gonna be makin' that trip often."

From under lowered lids he watched Roxanne's face flush angrily. He hid his satisfaction and mumbled, as though to himself, "All this courtin' goin' on, it's time I go visit Ruth."

Roxanne would have flounced off to her room, but at that moment Lettie announced supper was ready. There was nothing she could do but go and sit at the table.

As she sat picking at her food, she was fully conscious of Gideon's sly glances as Malcolm continued to talk about how smitten Caleb was with Seth's sister.

She wanted to jump to her feet and shout, Shut up, for God's sake! But she knew that Gideon waited for just such an outburst. So she continued to bring the fork to her mouth, hardly knowing what she was eating.

Finally, Malcolm ran out of words to say about the courtship of Caleb and Nell. The rest of the meal was eaten in silence.

Roxanne caught her uncle looking at her several times and knew then that he had talked about Caleb deliberately. Again it was borne to her how much he desired Caleb as her mate.

She sighed and rose from the table. Wishing didn't

make it so. "I'm going to freshen up a bit," she said and left the room.

Her relatives' eyes followed her. "Does she strike you as being happy, Uncle Malcolm?" Gideon asked.

Malcolm shook his head. "No, son, she don't."

Lettie had just dried the last dish and hung the towel to dry when Seth's knock sounded on the door. She let him in and he greeted everyone pleasantly. However, apprehension grew on his face as Roxanne only smiled coolly at him.

Lettie took his hat and coat, and he sat down beside Roxanne, reaching for her hand. She moved her hand up to her head and toyed with her hair. He watched her with a half-quizzical and half-disapproving gaze. He did not like her haughty attitude and decided that that was one of the first things he must teach her, once they were married. If anyone was to have a lofty manner in his home, it would be himself.

And another thing, he decided, her temper was much too fast. She must learn to control it. She must learn to be submissive to him in all things.

An embarrassing silence grew in the room as Malcolm and Gideon watched the pair, an amused gleam in their eyes. Seth squirmed uncomfortably and finally leaned over and whispered, "What's wrong, Roxanne?"

She ignored his question and turned to her uncle. "Uncle Malcolm, would you mind if I took Seth into my room? I have something private to discuss with him."

At first it seemed that Malcolm would laugh at her request. His face took on the squinty look that always preceded his roar of laughter. But Roxanne's expression was so determined, and somehow begging, that he did not laugh. Instead, he quickly straightened his features and said seriously, "Of course, Roxy. I trust you . . . and Seth."

Seth looked at her strangely, but followed her silently into the bedroom. Inside, he moved to the fireplace and stared down into the flames. He meant for his stiff back to intimidate her and thus lessen the flow of questions that he suspected she wanted to fire at him. At least she would be unable to see his face if she should throw a query at him he didn't expect.

Roxanne remained by the door, leaning against it. Some time passed and she still did not speak. Seth felt nervous perspiration gathering in his armpits and wished that she would get on with it. He was afraid that his strategy was being reversed on him.

Finally, into the silence, she blurted out reproachfully, "Why did you have that red slut in your home?"

He sighed in relief. Nell had warned him that Roxanne might question him about White Star. He had been half-afraid that someone had seen him take the squaw into the barn before he came here—and that they knew she was waiting for him now.

He turned around and faced Roxanne. "I knew that was bothering you," he smiled. "But just like Nell explained to you, I hired the girl to clean the cabin for me. Naturally, when you told my sister what White Star had done to you, she ordered her to leave the house. And I might say, Roxanne, I was horrified to learn what you had experienced at the hands of Ez Johnson. I must thank the Indian, Long Step, for protecting you."

Roxanne ignored his words about Johnson. Long Step had been thanked by her uncle and that was sufficient. She was only interested in reading Seth's face. Did he know that the young squaw had returned to his cabin after she had left. Suddenly, she grew warm and confused. For the first time, out of nowhere, it occurred to her to wonder if White Star had ever told Seth about the night she spent with Caleb. She looked away, afraid that he might read her confusion.

Then common sense came to her rescue. If White Star had told, Seth would have braced Caleb about it a long time ago. Not only that, he also would have told Uncle Malcolm. No, the girl definitely hadn't talked. As she brought her gaze back to Seth, she wondered why.

Dismissing White Star from her mind, she asked sharply, ''Will you explain to me why Nell let her return after I had gone?''

Her question caught him off guard and his eyes widened. For a split second he faltered then quickly gained control of himself. Turning to the fireplace, he asked sullenly, ''Do you spy on my place, Roxanne?''

She gave his back an annoyed look. ''You know that I don't, Seth. Now, why did White Star return to your place? And why did Nell greet her in such a friendly manner?''

Seth realized that becoming defensive with Roxanne wasn't the answer. This stubborn and willful girl would not buckle under, nor would she rest until he gave her a satisfactory answer. He took a deep breath and turned around.

''Nell told me that she returned to get her money. And since my sister is afraid of Indians, she didn't want to chance making her angry. She hurried up and paid her, and then I guess the squaw left.''

His story had the ring of truth in it, and yet Roxanne

wasn't fully satisfied. Nell hadn't looked frightened to her. There had been a familiarity between the two women as White Star had been ushered into the cabin. And besides, once and for all, she wanted the truth about Ruth's revelation. More and more she believed the woman's story.

She moved to the chair beside the hearth and sat down. With her eyes fixed steadily on him, she related to him what Ruth had said. She ended by saying, "Is it the truth?"

Her words took Seth with such surprise that he involuntarily turned and stared at her. She read the guilt on his face. Her fingers gripped the arms of the chair and she sat forward. It was true then. He did prefer the arms of an Indian squaw.

Inwardly, she directed a laugh of ridicule at herself and blushed in embarrassment recalling the times she had tried to arouse him. Her body went limp and she leaned back, resting her head on the back of the chair. There must be something wrong with her. First Caleb seeks someone else, and now she learns that Seth prefers an Indian girl.

Her usual glowing eyes became dulled as she asked in a low voice, "Why? Why an Indian girl, when I was here?"

Seth stared at her, misunderstanding her question. He took the step that separated them and knelt beside her. "Oh, Roxanne, you little innocent," he murmured, taking her cold hand in his. "Don't you know that men have a drive that you women know nothing about?"

Roxanne wanted to laugh in his face. What did this arrogant, insensitive man know of a woman's drives! Gazing at him now she realized that she would never be able to let herself go and enjoy an act of love with him. If he should suspect that she enjoyed the act, he was the type that would hold it against her and think her no lady.

The picture of a wild long-hunter taking her into his arms swam in front of her eyes. This man knew that women had the same desires as a man, and he gloried in the fact that his hands and lips had the power to make her body throb and ache for fulfillment.

She realized suddenly that Caleb had never really taken her against her will. He had knowingly waited until she was willing and eager.

Seth was pressing her hand urgently and she brought her attention back to him.

"I couldn't release my lust on you, Roxanne. You realize that, don't you?" he pleaded earnestly. "With a squaw it is different. It don't mean a thing. She is just a means of relieving yourself."

She wanted to slap his hateful face and turned away from him before she did.

He tugged at her arm, adding hastily, "I haven't touched her since we're engaged."

Roxanne sighed. What difference did it make anyway . . . she really didn't care. She now knew there would always be another woman waiting on the side for Seth. One that he could approach with wild abandonment because the woman was no lady. If not an Indian squaw here in the wilderness, it would be a fancy woman in some city.

Mind weary, she smiled weakly at him. "Yes, Seth, I forgive you."

The worried frown disappeared from his face and he leapt to his feet in relief. "That's my good girl!" he exclaimed and pulled her out of the chair. He put his arms around her and she leaned, limp, against him.

Before he released her, he asked with a worried

note in his voice, "Did you mention White Star to Malcolm?"

When she shook her head against his shoulder, she wondered at his sigh of relief. Uncle Malcolm wouldn't hold it against him if he slept with a dozen squaws.

Back in the main room, Seth put on his coat and picked up his hat. Without haste he said good night to Malcolm and Gideon, and, ignoring Lettie, kissed Roxanne lightly on the forehead and left.

Roxanne closed the door behind him and leaned against it for a moment. Malcolm, watching her, noted her pale face and wondered why. She must have caught his look, for suddenly she smiled and moved toward him. She circled her arms around his neck and leaned to kiss his cheek.

"Good night, Uncle Malcolm," she murmured.

Before she could leave, Malcolm caught her arm and held her. "You look upset, lass. Did that mealymouth say or do anything to upset you?" he growled.

She forced a small laugh. "Not at all, uncle. You know Seth. He would never do anything to upset me."

Malcolm wasn't convinced, but he smiled and patted her arm as he said, "Good night, Roxy."

Lettie and Gideon called, "Good night," as she went to her room.

Outside, Seth had swung into the saddle and jabbed the horse hard in its flank. If Roxanne could have seen him, she would have known that behind his suave, polite manner was a hard, ruthless man.

He took the trail in a cold black fury, one that beat against himself. He had been forced to plead with a woman. Never before had he done this. For a moment he hated Roxanne, too, and couldn't wait until they were married. He would soon teach her that she was never to question him!

When he arrived home and rode the horse into the barn, his mood had grown until he was blinded by it. Dismounting, he called loudly, "White Star, where are you?—you red slut!"

Her eyes wide in dread, the girl moved apprehensively out of the shadows. He advanced on her, his hand raised threateningly. She raised an arm to cover her face and cringed. A hideous joy lighted his face and his hand flashed out, catching her sharply across the mouth. She gave a low whimper as he continued to slap at her, his blows falling on her face and head.

His onslaught crushed her finally to the floor of the barn. He stalked her. "Dirty rotten slut," he panted, ripping her clothing apart.

When her firm brown breasts stood free, he began scratching and punching at them while vile, ugly words continued to pour out of his mouth.

White Star's whimpering turned into loud cries of pain as he hit her faster and harder. Finally he stopped and stood limp over her, his breathing rasping and heavy. The girl huddled away from him, knowing that it wasn't over.

When he sank to his knees and tore open his pants, she began to tremble in dread. His lips drawn back in a wolfish grimace, he grabbed her by the hair.

"You know what's coming, don't you, slut?" He sneered and jerked her face down between his legs. "Take it, you Indian whore, and don't let go—until daylight!"

CHAPTER 17

The winter days passed slowly, tedious to the cabin-bound women, but enjoyable to the men who trapped and hunted.

Caleb Coleman awoke each morning eager for the day to begin. He was in his element in the snow-clad hills as he ran his traps or tracked a deer or moose.

Before the sunrise of each new day, he made his way to a flat-topped hill, about a mile from his cabin, and spied on the Hale homestead. If he saw Seth moving about the barn in an unhurried way as he went about his chores, he would shoulder his rifle and break trail on a new hunt.

But if, from his cover of brush, the stall door stood open and he caught a climpse of Nell struggling with a pail of water or an armful of wood, all plans for the day were forgotten. He would return home, saddle the stallion, pick up Hale's tracks, and follow him.

Time and again during the past three months he had tracked the man. Many times he would spend an entire day on the trail, only to have it lead to nothing. Seth's sign would stop either at the post or at one of his neighbors. And though throughout the day he would stop at the Hale place, only an occasional neighbor man, and twice Gideon, to his surprise, came around. Either Seth had become suspicious that someone was onto him or he and the Indians were laying low until spring.

On this midmorning, in late February, Caleb waited on a hill above Malcolm's place for Gideon to join him. For almost two months now, they had gone hunting regularly, every Friday. On this day, they hunted meat for their tables.

Their ripening friendship had come about in a bone-chilling manner. Caleb had been running his traps late one afternoon, moving swiftly from one trap to the next. To the north, dark clouds were gathering—another snowstorm. He had one last trap to inspect, then he would head for home and warmth.

Caleb struggled up a steep knoll. The weight of the dozen or so stiff bodies of beaver, mink, and weasel made a hard pull through snow above his knees. He wondered if he wouldn't be better off turning to farming.

Certainly the man who worked the land lived better, and longer. The rigors of a hunter's life soon took their toll. Sleeping out in all kinds of weather made a man's bones stiffen at an early age. He knew many ex-hunters who, though still young, hobbled like men in their seventies.

Caleb sighed and shook his head. We're a crazy bunch, all right.

He stopped beside a stunted oak to adjust his shifting load on its deerskin skid. Then, in reaching for his rifle, his hand had just closed over the smooth hard stock when a yell came from the top of the next hill.

He straightened up and listened. There was no sound but the moan of the wind that was building. Had he been mistaken, he wondered. Wasn't it maybe the wind he had heard in the first place? It made many weird sounds, racing and bounding through the hills. And, too, he mustn't ignore the fact that it could be Indians trying to draw him into a trap.

As he stood undecided, the call came again. He nodded his head. This time the call for help was clear and was definitely the voice of a white man. He broke into a half run, slipping and sliding as he climbed the ice-spotted hill.

At the top of the rise, standing alone, was a small stand of walnut trees. A movement at the base of a half-grown tree caught his eyes and he froze in mid-step. He had spotted a gray shaggy form leaping and snapping at a pair of dangling buckskin-clad legs. The head and torso of the man were hidden by the bole of the tree; only an arm circling the trunk was visible.

Then the shaky voice of Gideon called a warning. "Watch it, Caleb. He's hungry as hell."

Caleb dropped behind a boulder, but the wolf had seen him. It growled close to the ground, its long fangs bared and dripping saliva. Then it was snarling and walking stiff-legged toward him.

Caleb sucked in his breath and fumbled behind him. Where in the hell had the rifle gone to? The animal was bunching itself and getting ready to spring when his fingers finally closed on the weapon. He brought it quickly to his shoulder and took aim, squeezing the trigger gently. The animal twisted in mid-air as the bullet caught it between the eyes.

The wolf lay motionless in the snow, but Caleb approached cautiously. Maybe the varmint was dead. Maybe it was playing possum. But its tongue lolled out between its teeth and its blood stained the surrounding white.

Gideon had scrambled down from the tree and stood shivering beside Caleb. "God, I'm cold," he sputtered through chattering teeth as he put out a foot and nudged the wolf. "This bastard had me up a tree since early this morning. He surprised me at one of my traps

and like a damn fool I had left my rifle leanin'
against a tree, out of reach."

Caleb hunkered down beside the animal and pulled
the powerful jaws apart. The wolf was young. He
looked up at Gideon and asked grimly, "Ain't no one
ever told you to keep your fire-piece by your side at all
times?"

Gideon blushed an embarrassed pink and looked
away. "Yeah, I know," he said, "but I had to scramble down into this sinkhole—and with my bum ankle,
I needed both hands to steady myself."

With the toe of his boot, he gave the animal a swift
jab. "I had one hell of a time gettin' to this tree and
out of his reach. He caught my heel one time, goin'
up."

"Well, you were mighty lucky, and I think you've
learned a hard lesson. Let's skin this varmint and get
to my shack. It's gonna start snowin' at any minute."

He grinned to himself when Gideon went first, to
get his rifle.

The snow had come, and Gideon had spent the
night with him. They talked of many things, sitting in
front of the snapping fire—of hunting, trapping, and
even whoring; but never once was Roxanne's name
mentioned.

Caleb thought of this now as he waited impatiently
for his young friend. It had taken him a long time to
get the memory of Roxanne out of his mind. He had
worked hard at it and, gradually, the weeks had gone
by. Now, sometimes days would pass without him
thinking about her. Of course, regularly seeing Nell
Hale helped. He grinned, thinking about her fiery
passion.

He glanced at the sun and his grin turned into a

frown. Where in the hell was Gideon? They should have been on their way an hour ago.

''The little bastard is probably foolin' around with Lettie and has forgot the time,'' he muttered.

But at that moment he saw the Sherwood barn door burst wide, and Gideon's horse sprang through the opening. Gideon clung to its back like a monkey, racing wildly up the hill. With chunks of snow flying from under the animal's hooves, he plunged to a stop in front of Caleb.

He grinned. ''I'm sorry I'm late, Caleb, but that damned Roxy kept me back on purpose. Had to change every piece of furniture in the cabin around for her.''

Caleb's face took on a dark scowl. ''She do that because you were goin' with me?''

Gideon looked away from the hurt in the dark eyes. ''Yeah,'' he grumbled. ''She says you are turning me wild . . . just like you are.''

The expected pleasure of the hunt was gone for Caleb. Roxanne still thought poorly of him. But when Gideon said, ''Yeah, she thinks everyone should act like Seth and have his gentlemanly ways,'' a dark anger came over him. If her ideal man was Seth Hale, she could go to hell. Damned if he'd be compared to a turncoat like that one.

He picked up the stallion's reins and said gruffly, ''Come on, let's get started, if we're goin' huntin'.''

CHAPTER 18

In early March the ice went out of the river, and the melting snow that trickled into it swelled to overflowing. Patches of green began to appear on the brown earth, and the willows along the creek became a lacy chartreuse. The frogs had finished their long sleep, and their croaking went on incessantly along the many streams and wet bottom lands.

It was sugar-making time and every homesteader's wife tended a pot of boiling syrup. In lieu of a wife, Lettie made sugar and syrup for the Sherwood family. Roxanne watched, helping whenever she could. It was her job to scum the top of the sweet, boiling liquid and to feed wood to the fire that blazed under a large black kettle.

Since early morning, Malcolm had been boring holes in the young maples, then hanging a pail under the spout he had placed in the holes. As the pails filled with the sweet water, it was Gideon's job to carry them to Lettie and the waiting pot.

Noticing that the fire was burning down, Roxanne shoved a stick of wood under the kettle, then stepped back, drawing an arm across her moist flushed face. She sat down on a stump, wondering who was making sugar at the Hale place. I suppose I should be doing it, she thought inwardly. It would be to my benefit, seeing as how I'll be living there soon.

Her lips curled in contempt. It was certain that the

"Lady Nell" wasn't standing over a steaming pot out in the chip yard.

She had seen the woman only the one time. Although Nell had issued an invitation through Seth, Nell had never made the cold trip to return her visit. Seth had made the excuse that his sister couldn't stand the cold weather. "You two will have plenty of time to visit after we're married," he had added.

Roxanne's face clouded. How would she ever be able to put up with having that woman under her feet all the time? It was bad enough that she didn't like her; but to also have Caleb stuck in her face in the evenings was too much.

At first, she had been noncommittal, merely shrugging her shoulders when Gideon would mention that Caleb rode quite often to call on Nell. But as the winter wore on and Caleb continued to go there more and more often her jealousy grew to where she was sometimes physically ill.

Angry with herself for letting the hunter creep into her thoughts, she stood up, determined to push him from her mind. She took a step—and a cold sweat broke over her, and the earth seemed to float up. She quickly sat back down and choked back the nausea that rode in her throat. Bit by bit, the spinning earth stood still and her stomach grew quiet. She drew a handkerchief from her pocket and patted her upper lip and forehead.

She frowned. This was the third time she had experienced this faintness. The first time had been a month ago when Lettie was frying salt pork for breakfast. She had blamed her queasy stomach on the odor of the meat. It was probably old and rancid, she had told herself. But the dizziness had passed and she thought no more about it. The second time, a week or so later, it had come again, for no apparent reason, and had remained with her for a full morning.

And now, here it was again. For the first time, she stopped and gave it serious thought. Her face drained when she realized that she had missed her monthly for the third time. Was it possible? Could she be with child?

Lettie called out that she needed more wood, then stopped short at Roxanne's white face. She carefully propped the long-handled spoon on the rim of the pot and hurried to her.

Kneeling beside Roxanne, she asked anxiously, "What's wrong, Roxy? Don't you feel well?"

Roxanne plucked nervously at her apron and avoided Lettie's eyes. "I'm alright," she mumbled. "The heat got to me is all."

Lettie studied the pale face and made a pitying sound to herself. She had seen this drawn look on her mother's face too many times not to recognize what it meant. She lay a rough, reddened hand on Roxanne's clenched fingers and urged gently, "Are you sure that's it, Roxanne?"

It took the sympathetic tone to send Roxanne into Lettie's arms, crying wildly, "Oh, Lettie, what am I going to do?"

Lettie rocked the sobbing girl back and forth as though she were a child. "Hush, hush," she murmured softly.

When the tears subsided, Roxanne blew her nose. Lettie smoothed back the hair from the girl's wet face. "I didn't think that Mr. Right and Proper ever did anything but kiss you good night."

"He doesn't," Roxanne hiccuped against her shoulder.

Lettie pushed Roxanne's head back and looked into

her face. "You mean that it's not his?"

Roxanne shook her head mutely, and fresh tears began to flow.

Lettie's face took on a look of dread. "Good Lord, child, who then?" She paused, then barely whispered, "Not one of the help . . . not that rotten Ez?"

"No, no. Not them."

Lettie gave her a little shake. "Who then, for God's sake?"

Roxanne's hands came up to cover her face and she cried through her fingers, "Oh, Lettie, it was that Caleb Coleman. That awful hunter."

Lettie sat back on her heels, sighing in relief, but with bewilderment on her face. "When?"

"The night that Ez attacked me."

Lettie's expression darkened. Damn all men to hell—and back! They were all the same. Caleb was no better than Ez, after all. What Ez had started, he had finished. She jumped to her feet, swearing loudly, "Son-of-a-bitchin' men. They ought to all be hanged!"

She stopped her pacing and turned to Roxanne, yelling furiously, "Mr. Sherwood will take care of that hunter bastard. He'll take a rifle to him—and I can't wait to tell him."

Roxanne jumped up and caught at her arm. "Lettie, please. You mustn't tell him."

"But what about you, child? And what about the baby? It's gotta have a name."

Roxanne gave a ragged sigh. "You forget, Lettie, that I'm getting married next month."

Lettie sat down on the chopping block, her shoulders drooping. "I had hoped that you wouldn't go through with marryin' that cold stick." She brushed at a bee flying around her head, then added disappointedly, "I guess you'll have to now."

Unnoticed by the women, Gideon had appeared at the edge of the forest, a pail of sugar sap in each hand. Noticing their agitated behavior, he set down the buckets and stood watching them. Lettie looked like the end of the world had come, and Roxanne was crying. Then his cousin's face arrested his interest and he stared at her strangely.

Anger shot into his eyes. Roxy had that same look that White Star wore, damn it, and the squaw was five months gone with child.

He spat out the maple twig he had been chewing and swore softly. "Damn Coleman. Leaving Roxy with a wood's colt."

His eyes took on a sly twinkle. He'd let Caleb know about this. And if he knew the man, Caleb wouldn't like the idea of another man raising his child, especially if it should be a son. Then the humor of sticking Seth with another man's child struck him, and he laughed out loud.

Both women stared. "Gideon," Lettie said sharply, "what's the idea, slippin' around, scarin' a person to death? I almost jumped out of my skin."

"Hell, I didn't slip up. You two were so busy talkin', you couldn't have heard the crack of doom." He handed the pails to Lettie and sat at Roxanne's feet. "What are you cryin' about, Roxy?"

While Roxanne nervously fumbled for an answer, Lettie broke in smoothly, "She got to thinkin' about her maw and paw."

Gideon squinted up at Roxanne and felt irritated and a little hurt. Why did she feel that she couldn't confide in him? Well, he thought inwardly, while standing up and stretching, if that's how she wants it. . . .

He lay a hand on his cousin's shoulder and

squeezed it reassuringly. "Don't worry about things, Roxy. Given time, everything works out alright."

Roxanne gave him a surprised look. Was he referring to her parents, or had he overheard her and Lettie, after all?

Gideon took the empty pails and sat them under a tree. "Tell Uncle Malcolm that I'll be back shortly," he said and walked toward the forest.

They watched him disappear among the trees, and Roxanne turned to Lettie. "Do you think he heard us?"

There was indecision on Lettie's face as she answered. "I don't know, Roxy; but even if he did, I don't think he'd tell your uncle."

"Oh, I'm not worried about that. I just don't want him telling Caleb."

Gideon was halfway to Caleb's place, just approaching the hill above the Hale cabin, when his àttention was caught by a movement at the barn. He stepped behind a tree and watched. Maybe the hurrying figure was Nell. He grinned and rubbed his loins. He hadn't seen her for a couple of days now. Seth was always hanging around. Maybe she was going for a ride and he could delay her for some fun under a tree.

On peering closer, he grunted and spat. It was Seth. He was saddling his horse, his movements hurried. "He's in a hurry to go somewhere," Gideon thought vaguely.

He grinned. It would be more fun taking Nell in bed than on the hard ground.

Seth's horse tore out of the barnyard, kicking up mud and gravel as it headed toward the river road. Gideon hitched up his buckskins and started for the cabin. Then a drumming of hoofbeats to his left caused him to stop and swear angrily. Someone else had been waiting for Seth to leave.

He recognized big Zebe Stevens on the powerful horse that raced across the clearing. Kicking out at a rock, Gideon muttered darkly, "That damned old bastard will stay there all day."

He sighed. He wanted to see Caleb anyway.

As he neared the old shack, Gideon could see, through the still-leafless trees, Caleb sitting on a stump in a spot of sunlight. Traps were spread around his feet and, when Gideon first spotted him, he had just put down a trap and picked up another. He was rubbing bear grease into the mechanism of each, preparing them for next winter. Without this protection, the humid summer would soon rust and ruin them.

Gideon halted at the fringe of the small clearing and called a greeting. It didn't pay to sneak up on Caleb Coleman.

Caleb lifted his head and smiled. "Howdy, Gideon. I was just gonna have a cup of coffee. Come join me."

The coffee was still hot from breakfast and they carried their cups outside, to sit in the warmth of the morning. They sat and leaned back against a stump. After a few swallows, Caleb looked at Gideon. "What brings you over this morning? I thought you folks were makin' sugar and syrup."

Gideon looked quickly at the hunter, then down to the coffee cup in his hand. He blinked, uncertain, almost sorry that he had come. Now that he sat here with his friend, he wasn't so sure that he wanted to revenge Roxanne against him. If given the chance, Caleb would marry his cousin, he was sure.

But damnit, a voice inside nudged him, he raped

Roxy and he shouldn't have. After all, she's not some whore to be used so lightly.

He cleared his throat a couple of times, then in a voice feigning sorrow said slowly, "I just found out something over at our house and I had to get away for a while."

He stopped and brought the cup to his mouth, watching Caleb from the corner of his eye. Caleb was gazing at him quizzically, a frown on his face. Finally, he snapped, "Well, do you want to tell me about it, or are you gonna swig at that coffee all day?"

Still playing his role, Gideon set down the cup and rested his chin on his bent knees. "I just learned that Roxy is expectin'."

He glanced up in time to see Caleb's face go white and a terrible look enter his eyes. He slammed his cup down and jumped to his feet. "I'll kill the bastard!"

Gideon hid his pleasure. Roxy was revenged. The hunter ached with an agony that was tearing him apart. Gideon stood beside the trembling man and picked up his rifle. He'd better get home before Uncle Malcolm came looking for him.

But before he left, he gave Caleb one last jab. "Don't get all riled up, Caleb. It don't make no great difference, when you think about it. They're gonna get married next month, anyway."

Caleb's big shoulders drooped, and he gave a ragged sigh as he nodded his head. Gideon turned to leave, then stopped after a dozen or so steps. "On my way over here, I saw ol' Seth. He was tear-assin' away from his place, in a hell of a hurry to get some place."

Caleb started and drew in a long breath. Then with a short, "I'll be seein' you," he wheeled and hurried to the shack.

Gideon stared after him a moment, then shrugged his shoulders and continued on. "Caleb sure acts strange sometimes."

The spiral of smoke was some distance away when Caleb stopped to study it and the surrounding area. He would have to put landmarks in his mind. Once he descended a few hills, he would lose sight of the thin spiral.

He mentally marked a stand of young maples, showing their first new leaves. Then a few miles on he marked a group of towering pine. And directly in front of the smoke, a mile or so away, a lone beech tree standing in the middle of a clearing. Beyond that would be the gleam of the river, and he felt satisfied that he would find his man camped there.

He had been trailing Seth since yesterday morning, minutes after Gideon mentioned seeing him ride out. Hale had tried his best to hide his tracks once he left the main trail and had, for a city man, actually done a good job of it. But Caleb's knowledge of the wilderness was unequaled even by the Indians, and he had had no trouble tracking the man.

However, this sureness of himself had almost lost him his quarry. This morning the sun had topped the forest for at least an hour before he rolled out of the blankets. He had hurried to the glen where Seth had made camp that night and found him gone. He followed the hoofprints to a wide creek, swollen with the melting snow. Having no idea how long Seth would keep to the water and having no desire to force the stallion to wade its icy depth, he rode the animal to the highest hill and waited patiently for signs of Seth's noon meal. Unlike himself, the city man would want his three regular meals.

With the trail marked firmly in his mind, Caleb swung into the saddle and, keeping the maples in view, tried to ride in a direct line to them.

As the horse's long legs stretched out, eating up the distance, Caleb pulled some parched corn out of his pocket and munched contentedly. A warm meal wasn't necessary to him, he thought contemptuously.

Within the hour he came to the stand of maples and cautiously circled them. He saw evidence of sugar-making paraphernalia lying about. From the construction of the rocks forming the fire pit, Indians had been here, maybe as recently as yesterday. And the amount of trees still untapped suggested they might return today.

Not knowing if they were friendly or renegade, he gave the trees a wide berth as he took a bearing on the tall pines a few hills away. He hadn't gone far when, from through the forest, he spotted a small party of Indians. Three braves rode shaggy ponies while four squaws plodded along on foot. All the necessary gear for sugar-making was strapped to their backs. One young squaw was almost bent double under the cumbersome bundle attached to her shoulders.

Holding the stallion quietly behind a boulder, Caleb shook his head. Poor dumb women, he thought. Treated worse than animals.

As the last squaw disappeared around a knoll, he rode the stallion into the open. The sun was quite warm now and, before continuing on, he unbuttoned his coat and loosened the collar of his shirt.

He was in rough country now; so rough, no one had bothered to homestead the land. Time and again he had to abandon his direct route because of an obstacle. Usually it was large gullies, but sometimes it was boulders, larger than a cabin, that would stand in his way. But by keeping the pines in sight he always came back to his planned course.

It was way past noon when he finally reached the pines. He halted the horse and sighed in relief. The lone beech was just a short distance away. And as he had figured, the river showed plainly. Its waters rushed and swirled out of view around a bend.

From the water that had drained in the past week, it was swollen to double its normal size. "Neither man nor beast could swim it now," Caleb mused.

At this distance, looking down, he discovered that the smoke rose from beside the river. For a city man, Seth had chosen wisely. Besides supplying his camp with plenty of water the stream teemed with fish.

Caleb lifted the reins and moved on. This time he moved more slowly and more carefully, making his way from one screening shelter to the next, each time scrutinizing the area before moving on.

He heard voices before he came in sight of the camp. A male and female talked in a low murmur. He swung from the horse and dropped to the ground. On his elbows, he wriggled through the underbrush and dried grass until he came to the edge of the river bank. A wafting of smoke moved slowly overhead, and the aroma of cooking meat drifted up the five-foot bank and teased his nose.

He lay quietly and listened. There was not a sound. He frowned. Had Seth heard his approach and given him the slip again? Slowly he raised his head and shoulders and peered over the river bank. The bank dropped straight down to meet a sandy stretch that measured eight feet wide to the river's edge. Its length was not too great before it came to the encroaching forest on each end. In the middle of this small clearing, the fire burned. Suspended over the low flames was a pot, probably some kind of a stew.

Caleb dropped back to the ground. This was no fast camp made by Seth. It was a well-made established camp. From the amount of ashes around the fire, someone had been here a long time. His breathing became faster. Was he finally going to learn something? Was Seth meeting the enemy?

Then the hair on the back of his neck prickled. Where were they? Were they watching him at this moment, with rifles trained on his heart?

The dull thud of stamping hooves sharply broke the silence. Caleb raised up again to let his eyes fly around the camp. At first he saw nothing. Then the stamping came again and his eyes darted to the sound. In a small glade of cedars he spotted an Indian pony staked out in a grassy patch. And close by, tied to a branch, was Seth's mount. The animal switched its tail at the tiny spring gnats that swarmed around him and tossed his head restlessly.

A cold chill broke over Caleb. He had been lured into a trap. At any moment a bullet would come zapping into him. But as he cursed himself for a fool, his eyes were caught by a movement alongside a boulder half-concealed between two trees. He held his breath and leaned closer, then smothered a curse.

Seth Hale was leaning against the boulder, facing Caleb, his pants down around his ankles. He stood spraddled-legged, hands on hips, and head bent to watch White Star kneeling in front of him.

Caleb's eyes quickened. I knew he was layin' with that red bitch, he almost said out loud. He's the one that made her belly big.

For over an hour Caleb watched Seth keep the girl on her knees, twice deriving his satisfaction. But all this time, not once did he so much as give White Star an affectionate pat.

When at last he was sated—unaware of Caleb's angry stare—he placed the flat of his hand against her face and pushed viciously. As she fell over on her back, he reached down to pull up his pants. He fastened them, walked around the girl, and moved to the bedroll. Sitting cross-legged upon it, he ordered brusquely, "Bring me a bowl of that slop."

The young squaw hurried to the fire, and, because she was frightened, her trembling fingers splashed the meat and vegetables she was ladling.

By God, she's scared to death of him, Caleb thought in surprise.

Seth was glowering out of narrowed eyes at the girl as she moved toward him, carefully holding the steaming bowl.

Caleb watched closely. That mean-eyed bastard isn't finished with her yet, he thought.

White Star timidly placed the bowl of stew before Seth and watched anxiously as he lifted some meat to his mouth and began to chew. When he made no remark about it, she dropped to the ground beside him. She had just settled herself comfortably when, without warning, Seth's arm came up and swung sharply against her breasts. She gasped and tumbled backward.

Her stomach, big now, lay helpless to his gaze, and his contemptuous glance said plainly that the mound was offensive to him. Suddenly, he hawked and spat upon it.

White Star raised upon an elbow, staring at him wide-eyed. "Why you spit upon your child?" she whispered. "Maybe a son."

Anger, in a red flush, spread over Seth's face and he flung away the bowl. "Red slut, you'll bear me no half-breeds," he ground out between clenched teeth. And before Caleb's unbelieving stare, the enraged man pounced on her legs and began striking her in the stomach with his closed fists. The blows were hard and deliberately planted to do the most damage.

White Star screamed in pain and fright, the thin wail ringing through the forest as she tried to get away from Seth. But the sound only incensed the maddened man, and he began to rain blows on her face, smashing her rapidly in the mouth.

Sick to the pit of his stomach, Caleb raised to his knees. "That bastard means to kill her," he muttered angrily as he brought his rifle to his shoulder.

But just as his finger touched the trigger, a loud hallo came from the river. He dropped to the ground and lay still, eyes searching the stream.

His body stiffened. Hugging the river bank glided a canoe with two men kneeling in its bottom. A red man and a white one. Caleb's eyes slitted. The white man was a British officer. The red of his uniform glared in the bright spring sun.

What a sitting target he makes, Caleb thought, and fingered the trigger.

At the first hail of the camp, Seth had left off beating White Star and stood up. He shaded his eyes against the sun, then hastened to the canoe and stepped in, beside the officer. And as Caleb stared popeyed, the canoe shot out of sight behind the trees and brush that edged the river.

Mumbling curses, he scrambled to his feet and raced along the screening growth, trying to locate them through it. But the vessel had disappeared as though it had been swallowed by the river.

"Damn it to hell," he panted and leaned against a tree to catch his breath. "I don't see how that damned Indian could paddle so fast."

He was pushing himself away from the tree when his attention was caught and held by a winking light out in the middle of the river. Peering intently, he spotted the canoe, halfway across the river, making for the other shore. The sun was striking the officer's brass buttons, reflecting the light.

Furious curses ripped from his tight lips. Two days of trailing for nothing. He hadn't learned anything except that Seth was involved with the enemy, and that was no surprise.

He watched the canoe land on the other shore and saw the figures of several men move out of the forest to greet them. But the distance was too great to determine whether they were white or Indian. But he could see plainly that the red British uniform was not among them.

Caleb hunkered down and brought out his pipe and tobacco. "How had that one lone officer made his way to the hills," he wondered out loud. Someone had to have brought him. Was that someone Seth Hale?

Puzzled, he shook his head. Only yesterday, Malcolm had heard at the post the British had cleared out. That General Washington had brought in heavy cannon to Boston and had forced Howe to leave. Rumor had it that Howe had taken 7,000 British troops with him, along with 1,000 Loyalist civilians who had opted to go with him.

It was believed that Washington was moving his general headquarters from Boston to New York, where he expected the British to attack later in the spring. If this were all true, why then was this redcoat slinking around the Kentucky hills?

. Something was in the wind and Seth Hale was deeply involved. He thought of Nell Hale and her soft warm body and hoped that she was ignorant of her brother's associates.

He remembered White Star and knocked out his pipe. ''I hope the bastard didn't kill her,'' he muttered, and he made his way back to the camp.

But when he arrived at the spot, only blackened, charred wood met his eyes. Somehow the young squaw had managed to break camp and disappear. He debated a moment if he should follow her . . . try to find out what she knew.

He smiled grimly and kicked at the burnt wood. It would be a useless trip. To get information from Indians was almost impossible when they didn't want to talk.

As he climbed the bank to the horse, a large dark cloud blacked out the reach of the sun. Glancing to the north, he saw more and large clouds gathering. The long spell of cold spring rains was about to resume. He spoke to the horse, urging him on, even though he knew he would find no other shelter than the forest.

CHAPTER 19

The rain held off until dark, except for an occasional drizzle that pattered gently on the newly opened leaves and on Caleb's dampened clothing.

When evening came, the rain began in earnest, so he searched for and found a wide-spreading cedar with dense branches. Bending forward, he rode the stallion beneath it. He dismounted and found the small area dry and warm.

As he unsaddled the horse, he talked to it. "You're gonna have to go without supper tonight, fella." He gave the ears a playful tug and added, "It won't be the first time, will it?"

Close to the trunk he made his bed and sat down. Pulling some beef jerky from his pocket, his strong white teeth bit into it. When hunger was satisfied, he filled his pipe and leaned against the tree, puffing contentedly. The pelting rain was the only sound in the forest, and its steady beat soon had him yawning. He put out the pipe, rolled up in the blankets, and within minutes was asleep.

But his sleep was fitful, filled with crazy dreams, where he was chased by Seth and hundreds of redcoats. Toward dawn Roxanne entered his dream world, and when she snuggled in his arms, he relaxed and slept deeply.

It was hard to tell when he awakened the next morning. The rain still fell steadily and the sky was gray and overcast. He lay a moment in the now-damp blankets and stared up through the branches of the tree. A dozen or so mourning doves roosted in the topmost branches, sending out their soft cooing.

He sighed, dreading the wet ride ahead of him, and crawled out of bed. His muscles were stiff and he became chilled almost immediately in his still-wet clothing. He tied up the bedroll, then searched his pockets for his breakfast. Deep in one corner, he found some kernels of parched corn. Popping them into his mouth, he saddled the horse and again rode out into the wet world.

As he moved through the steady rain, his eyes and ears strained for any sound. These days the forest was full of renegades, eager to put a knife between the white man's shoulder blades.

Twice from the top of a hill he caught glimpses of the river. It had swollen and had a sullen roar now. He wondered what side of it Seth Hale was on. "I wish the bastard was on the bottom of it," he grumbled as the rain increased.

The wind sprang up, strong and cold, lashing him in the face and adding to the misery of his hunger. He tried to push it from his mind as the horse plodded on mile after mile. Then, just before dark, he began to make out landmarks that were familiar to him. He smiled in relief. Two hills away was Malcolm's place. He would stop there first. The thought of a warm meal and a pot of hot coffee brought him sitting straight in the saddle with a more relaxed look on his face.

Descending the last hill, through the semidarkness a dim wavering light became visible. Caleb's spirits jumped. It was candlelight coming from Malcolm's cabin.

To the right of the cabin, and several yards beyond,

his eyes caught the swinging light of a lantern as someone moved about the barn. He heard Gideon rip out a string of curses, and he grinned. The milch cow must have kicked over the bucket, he thought.

He halted the stallion at the hitching post and dismounted. Tying the reins loosely, he leaned over and unhooked the gate of the picket fence that Roxanne had insisted on being erected. She would not have the chickens roosting on the porch, she had declared.

On the porch Caleb lifted the latch without knocking, as was custom in the hills. He closed the door softly and gazed toward the fireplace.

Roxanne knelt there, unaware of his presence. She was adding something to the contents of a pot, and the aroma that floated out of it made his mouth water. He watched the fire play on the bent golden head and his heart raced.

I had forgotten how lovely she is, he sighed inwardly.

Lettie came out of the bedroom and he lifted a silencing hand to his lips. The hired girl gave him a dirty look but said nothing as she moved to the table.

Her look surprised Caleb. Why this sudden change in Lettie? She had always been so friendly before.

His drenched clothing had dripped water on the floor and, when he stepped away, his moccasins made a squishing noise. Roxanne looked over her shoulder and came whirling to her feet.

"You!" she gasped. "What do you want?"

Caleb's eye's twinkled and he barely managed to keep from saying, I want you.

But she had read his mind, anyway, and slammed the lid on the pot. Turning away from him, she snapped, "Uncle Malcolm and Gideon are in the barn. You'll have to go there if you want to talk to them."

"I can wait," he murmured, walking toward her.

She began backing away, crying out in a small voice, "You stay away from me, you . . . you wild long-hunter. I'll call Uncle Malcolm."

He threw her a cool smile. "Calm your feathers, Roxanne. I never bother other men's women. I just want to get warm." He knelt by the fire and reached for the coffeepot. "Do you think you could spare a wild hunter a cup of coffee?"

Roxanne blushed for her inhospitality. Even the Indians were offered food and drink when they happened along. She went to fetch him a cup from the table, which was set for supper. When Caleb took it from her, their fingers touched, and to Lettie, who watched them, it was hard to tell which was more affected by the touch.

As he drank the hot bitter brew in long draughts, Caleb studied Roxanne over the rim of the cup. "You've put on some weight, haven't you?" he drawled.

For a moment Roxanne's eyes blazed. Then telling herself she would not let him upset her, she turned her back on him without response.

The reason she was gaining weight came to him and, in wounded cold fury, he had the driving urge to hurt her. To let his tongue chop her into tiny pieces.

Deliberately, he let his eyes move to her breasts and hold. "Actually, now that I look closer," he mused out loud, "you only look bigger there. I don't remember them beauties fillin' out your dress so. I'd have more than a handful now, wouldn't I?"

She whirled on him, her hand lifted to slap his face. But he caught and held it in mid-air. He gave a low laugh. "When's the weddin' takin' place?"

She pulled her wrist free and snapped, "Soon."

She walked to the fireplace and stared into the flames, trying to hide her trembling. Caleb studied her stiff back a moment, then said quietly, "He'll never make you happy, Roxanne. He's cold and mean to his women."

Roxanne's fingers clenched tightly. How dare he talk about another man not making her happy, after the anguish he had put her through so many times.

She spun around, giving him a withering look as she retorted, "What do you know about making a woman happy?"

His lips quirked into a lazy grin. "Do you have to ask, Roxy? Can't you remember those nights together? Especially the last one. You were a happy woman then . . . remember?"

Roxanne caught her breath as his words came jabbing at her heart. She wanted to fly at his arrogant face and scratch it to pieces with her nails. How dare he throw that night into her face. That night of all nights —when he had so carelessly sowed his seed.

But with a cold determination that she didn't know she possessed, she fought back her anger and answered coolly, "Do you think, long-hunter, that that part of the man is the only part that can make a woman happy? I'm sure you know Seth has the same happy-making equipment."

She saw his face go pale, and, as she studied him through narrowed eyes, she wanted to hurt him more. And she was suddenly hurling words that were deliberately meant to chop away at him. She ended by saying, "For your information, I might add, Seth handles the loving department even better than you do."

Her words had barely left her lips when his open hand caught her across the mouth. She staggered against a chair and, before she could right herself, his fingers, like bands of steel, were gripping her arms. Her head snapped back and forth as he shook her furiously. "Damn you," he panted. "Tell me that you lie. You couldn't enjoy that man."

She stared at him through the tumbled hair that had shaken loose, and her cut and smarting lips spread in a smile. He is jealous! her joyful heart sang.

He gave her another shake. "I'm waitin' for your answer," he panted through clenched teeth.

She looked at him, debating. Should she tell him the truth? Tell him that Seth had never done more than give her a good-night kiss. But that would never do, she remembered. If she told him that, he would know later that it was he who had fathered her child. She could not do that to Seth. She would not let Caleb walk around with that smug knowledge.

She was spared an answer by the sounds of footsteps on the porch. Caleb pushed her away and sat down, his face like a storm cloud.

Roxanne started for her room, a worried and upset Lettie at her heels.

She stopped the woman. "I'm alright, Lettie. Go ahead and put supper on the table so Uncle Malcolm doesn't become suspicious."

Inside her room, she poured water from the pitcher into a wash basin. With a cloth, she bathed her swollen lip until it was almost back to normal. Then, brushing her hair in quick movements, she grinned at her image.

"You still don't know, Mr. Caleb Coleman," she whispered. "And you can just sit out there and wonder."

The door had barely closed on her back when Malcolm came stamping into the cabin with Gideon on his heels. Their faces lit up when they saw Caleb, and they called out friendly greetings.

"Where you been off to?" Malcolm questioned. "I was over to your place yesterday and today."

For a moment Caleb looked at Malcolm from under glowering brows. Then, his voice flat and expressionless, he muttered, "Been trailin' a polecat the past four days."

"I thought you'd been gone for a while, from the whiskers on your face," Gideon spoke, hunkering down to the fire and holding his fingers to the flame.

Caleb ran his hand over his rough chin. "I expect I look pretty much like a bear," he growled. Suddenly, he was angry at himself for allowing Roxanne to see him looking so woodsy. Seth Hale would never let himself be seen with four days' growth of whiskers.

Because of the irritation at himself, his voice was brusque when he snapped at Gideon. "When you get old enough to have some whiskers, bucko, then you can talk about mine."

Gideon shot him a look of surprise. Caleb was certainly in a black mood, he thought, and looked at Roxanne's closed door. They've been at it again, he observed inwardly.

He looked back at Caleb and gave him a small smile. "I didn't mean nothin'." He studied his friend another moment, then remarked, "I think you're gettin' cranky from being alone too much. Maybe I'll move in with you."

"That's a debatable cure," Caleb muttered. "Wrong company can be worse than loneliness."

Gideon's hot temper flared up. Caleb was going too far with his surliness. "If that's the way you feel about it, I'll keep in my own territory from now on," he retorted.

Caleb chuckled dryly. Gideon is a proud young rooster, he thought, and I've pushed him too far. He lay a hand on the youth's shoulder. "Don't mind me, Gideon. I'm tired, wet, and hungry, and to top it all off, I lost my polecat."

Gideon immediately gave him a forgiving grin. "That's alright, Caleb. I shouldn't have ragged you about your whiskers."

Malcolm looked at Caleb quizzically. "Anything you care to talk about?"

The hunter gave a small warning shake of his head. "Not right now, Malcolm. I'm too hungry to talk."

Malcolm scooted around in his chair. "Supper about ready, Lettie?"

"I'm gonna put it on the table right now, Mr. Sherwood." She looked at Gideon. "Would you call Roxy to help me?"

As Roxanne bustled around helping Lettie to get the meal together, she shot many glances Caleb's way. One time she stopped with a bowl of potatoes in mid-air, just over the table. She had noticed for the first time a sadness in his countenance when he was relaxed and resting. It was hard to believe that this hard and uncaring man would ever have a moment of sadness.

But tonight he was different from any way she had ever seen him. He seemed drawn into himself somehow, as though only half of him was here as he talked in low tones to her uncle and cousin. She wondered silently if her words about Seth had brought about this strangeness. She knew that he was still angry with her. Once when she had knelt by the fire to rake the potatoes out of the coals, she shot a sharp look at him. But her challenging glance had only met a cool stare in return. She had bubbled pleasantly inside. He still boiled with his jealousy, she had thought at first.

But then the nagging doubt came that maybe he was merely angry. Angry because he thought she had found someone better than he in bed.

She sighed raggedly now, wishing that he would leave the hills.

Lettie called them to the table and the meal was a silent one, out of respect for Caleb's hunger. The stew and potatoes vanished as if by magic, and the pile of hot biscuits dwindled at a rapid pace. Finally, after three cups of coffee, he leaned back and patted his stomach.

He smiled at the hired woman. "That was the best stew I've ever eaten, Lettie."

"You should compliment Roxy on that," Lettie said. "She made it."

Caleb said, "Oh?" and looked at Roxanne curiously.

She kept her eyes lowered, refusing to meet his probing glance. But he drawled mockingly, "You have many talents, don't you, Miss Sherwood?"

Her voice trembled with anger as she snapped back, "More than you'll ever know, Mr. Coleman."

Malcolm, watching the pair surreptitiously, saw Caleb's face go pale and red spots of rage appear on his cheekbones. Then slowly his color came back and, as he calmly filled his pipe and tamped it, he said softly, "Don't count on it, Roxy."

Too angry to answer, Roxanne jumped up and plopped into the rocker beside the fire.

Caleb grinned and winked at Gideon. "I think I'll get on home now," he said. "I gotta get cleaned up before I go see my girl."

Gideon fell in with the badgering. "That Miss Hale is sure some looker, Caleb. All them pretty clothes she wears. But I've been wonderin'—is she as pretty with them off? Sometimes them long skirts are hidin' thick ugly legs.''

Caleb reared back in his chair and puffed smoke toward the ceiling. "Gideon, my boy, you wouldn't believe them legs of hers . . . if you know what I mean.''

"I get your meanin', Caleb." Gideon laughed and sneaked a look at Lettie. Lettie blushed and looked uneasily at Malcolm. But Malcolm was smiling into the fire, enjoying the remarks meant to make Roxanne angry.

"Yeah," Caleb was continuing, "I can't wait to get over there."

He waited to see if Roxanne would make some concession that his remarks had irritated her. But the rhythmic rocking of the chair didn't miss a beat, and a small frown appeared on his forehead.

Malcolm, not missing it, grinned to himself. If he was trying to best Roxy, he might as well give up. That mulehead would never let it be known that his words were tearing her apart.

But Lettie wasn't smiling. And if she could help it, Caleb wasn't going to get the best of Roxanne. Women had to stick together in this man's world. Besides, she was very fond of the young girl and, since she was carrying the hunter's child, he had no business traipsing off and sleeping with that no-account Nell Hale.

She waited until a small silence built in the room, then spoke quietly to Roxanne.

"Roxanne, shouldn't you be changin' your clothes? Didn't Seth mention that he'd be over tonight to finish the wedding plans?"

Roxanne had to force herself not to fly to Lettie and

hug her. She understood what the woman had at-
tempted and, from the dark scowl on Caleb's face, she
had succeeded.

She rose from the chair and stretched lazily and
seductively, purposely turned so that Caleb could see
the proud tilt of her breasts. A fast glance revealed that
he was watching her.

She smiled serenely and murmured, ''Thanks for
reminding me, Lettie,'' and moved toward her room,
her slim hips swaying gently.

But once the door was closed behind her, she threw
herself onto the bed and let loose the tears that had
trembled on her lids all night.

After awhile she heard the chairs scraping as the
men rose from the table and heard Caleb say he had
better be getting home. After he asked Malcolm to
walk a piece with him, she heard the outside door
close. Then only the low murmur of Gideon and Lettie
was heard in the room.

CHAPTER 20

The rain had finally stopped when Caleb and Malcolm stepped off the porch and moved toward his horse. The sky was clear and the moon was a bright yellow, lighting up the surrounding area.

"Damn, my rump is sore," Caleb complained, limping a bit. "I must have rode a hundred miles the past few days."

The stallion whinnied, and Malcolm murmured a "tsk, tsk" as he walked closer to the mount. The handsome animal was thoroughly drenched, and its head drooped wearily as it stood on three legs.

"We didn't see your mount out here, Caleb, or we'd have stabled him for you. Let's get him in the barn and you can ride one of mine home."

"Naw, Malcolm, thanks just the same. This black fella can stand worse things than gettin' a little wet. But I would like to take him in the barn and dry him down."

"Yeah, come ahead. We'll give him a bite to eat, too."

While Caleb briskly rubbed the rippling satiny skin with a piece of old blanket, Malcolm went to bring a pail of shelled corn for the animal. Then, sitting on a milking stool, he asked casually, "Care to put a name to that polecat you was chasin'?"

Caleb made a last swipe with the blanket, gave the

saddle a tug, then looked grimly at Malcolm. "Seth Hale," he said bluntly.

"I kinda figured that would be its name."

When Caleb finished telling him all that had happened, not forgetting Seth's brutal treatment of White Star, Malcolm stood up and paced the barn floor. Running his fingers through his rough, shaggy hair, he stopped and asked in a voice that was rough with anxiety, "Caleb, what am I gonna do about Roxanne? She's plannin' on marryin' that bastard in a couple of weeks."

Startled, Caleb stammered, "So soon?"

"Yeah. Seth's been pushin' her to push up the date. I think I know why, now. I think he wants to get married and carry her off to England as soon as possible."

A curse ripped from between Caleb's lips as he struck out at a supporting beam. Two weeks didn't give him much time to pin the bastard down.

"What am I gonna do?" Malcolm asked again. "If I tell her what we suspect, she might not believe us—and then go and tell him. I'm sure she thinks he's too much of a gentleman to do anything against his country."

"Damned little fool," Caleb snorted. "She's sure got some mixed up ideas about human behavior."

"I know, Caleb. It's her parents' fault. They didn't know any better, either, always livin' in the city."

Malcolm looked so downcast and depressed that Caleb lay his hand on his arm and squeezed it reassuringly. "For the time being, Malcolm, let's just let things ride. A lot can happen in a couple of weeks. I gotta feelin' that Seth is gonna make his move any day now."

Malcolm nodded his head reluctantly, still unconvinced. "I hope you're right, Caleb. I know that

Roxy's a hellcat and rubs you the wrong way lots of times, but I love her dearly.''

Caleb climbed into the saddle and looked down at his friend. Very quietly he said, ''Your love for her, Malcolm, could not touch mine.''

He rode the horse out of the barn and guided it up the hill, leaving Malcolm staring after him.

The stallion took the hill easily and moved into an easy lope once it gained the top. Caleb held the reins loosely, letting the animal choose its own speed. His mind was occupied with other things.

Foremost in his thoughts was how to catch Seth Hale red-handed with the enemy, then turn him over to the authorities. Outside of killing the man, that was the only way of making sure Seth would never walk these hills again. He would gladly shoot him outright if it weren't for Nell. That he didn't love Nell made no difference. He had used her often and freely and felt that he owed her.

Horse and rider topped another hill and, faint and far off, he heard a hound baying. Caleb smiled at the sound. He would be glad when his friends returned with his hound. He missed the old scamp.

Then he reined in sharply. Another dog had taken up the chase, joining its voice with the other. Cocking his head to one side, Caleb listened intently. His smile grew wider. That ringing yowl belonged to his own hound, Coon. The hunters were returning.

He spoke to the horse, urging him on. His heavy mood was lightened. His friends were back and things would become lively around here. Together, they would rid these hills of redcoats and enemy spies.

On the last hill, before he descended to his old cabin, he stopped the horse again to peer off in the direction of the Hale place. A dim light glowed in a win-

dow and he thought of Nell and her winning ways.
He'd go visit her ,after all, he decided.

He hadn't intended to, when he teased Roxanne
back at the supper table, but the rocking motion of the
horse had rested him, and now he had a growing premonition that he would learn something tonight.

He lifted the reins and turned the horse in the direction of the Hale cabin. But halfway across the clearing
he brought the animal to a sudden halt. His eyes had
caught the soft glimmer of lanterns bobbing back and
forth in the barn area. So many lanterns—something
was going on. Then the noise of hungry, barking dogs
floated up to him and he relaxed. Of course. Seth's
hunters were back, also. Most likely just gettin in.

"There's no use tryin' to see Nell tonight," he
spoke to the horse. "Them hunters will be goin' in
and out half the night, reportin' their catch."

Not overly disappointed, he turned the horse and
once more headed toward home. As the stallion loped
along, Caleb hummed a tune under his breath. He
hadn't felt so good in a long time.

Soon he was dismounting at the rear of the cabin
and leading the horse into the canting shed. He unsaddled the animal and pitched down some hay.

The cabin smelled musty and old when he pushed
the door open. Its air was heavy with dampness, and
he gave a slight shiver. In the dark, he fumbled at the
table for the candle and flint. When the length of wax
spluttered and flamed, he carried it to the fireplace.
Rummaging in the wood box, he brought out twigs
and small pieces of wood. Laying them loosely in the
fire grate, with a long splinter lit from the candle, he
soon had a roaring fire going.

The flames lit up the room and Caleb glanced
around. Everything seemed in order, but still he had

the distinct feeling that someone had been poking around the place. The box of sugar, for instance, seemed to be just a bit off from where he always kept it. And the candle, when he had searched for it in the dark, seemed to be more in the center of the table than where it usually sat. He walked over to the shelf where he kept his clean clothes stacked neatly, and they appeared slightly rumpled.

After a moment, he shrugged his shoulders. There was nothing missing. "Probably some homesteader's young'un been nosin' around," he mumbled.

The dampness gradually dispelled and the room became warm. Filling a basin at the dry sink from the pail, he took off his shirt and scrubbed himself with a bar of homemade soap. Whistling tunelessly, he scraped off the growth of whiskers on his face.

Then filling his pipe, he sat down in the lone chair and stretched his feet to the fire. He would relax awhile, smoke a bit, then retire.

But he was restless, the pipe wouldn't draw right, and his thoughts were constantly pulled to the Hale place. An inner voice kept urging him to go there.

"Hell," he finally exclaimed into the silence, "I might as well go. I won't get no sleep tonight if I don't."

As he donned a fresh set of buckskins, he thought of all the work that had gone into them. He had watched the Indian women make them when he was a prisoner in the renegade camp.

The first step in tanning the hides had fallen to the old squaws. They worked long hours rubbing deer brains into the green hides. Once the hides were cured, they were turned over to the younger women, possessing strong teeth. These women would spend days chewing the hides to make them soft and supple before they were sewn into garments. The old squaw who had gifted him with these had teeth worn down to stubs from the years of chewing deer hide.

Lacing up the trousers, he stepped to the piece of mirror propped in the window and brushed his dark shoulder-length hair. His strong white teeth smiled back at him. He looked good and he knew it.

He saddled the stallion and climbed upon its back. Before he was barely settled, the horse was off, wet gravel flying through the air. But after lunging up the hill his pace slowed, and when they neared the Hale cabin, he was moving at an easy trot.

Midway across the clearing, Caleb's ears caught the sound of trampling hooves. He halted the stallion beside a lone pine. The sound had come from the barn area, and he peered closely in that direction. Then clearly, he made out the shapes of four horses hitched to the side of the log structure. The animals moved about restlessly, anxious to get back to warm stalls.

Were they the hunters' mounts? he wondered. If so, why hadn't they been turned indoors and tended?

A fast glance around revealed no human shape. But as he hesitated, from the cabin came a burst of talk, then loud laughter. He slid from the saddle and tied the reins loosely to a branch. Cautiously, he slipped across the open space and around to the rear of the building. The animals started a low snorting of fear, and he dropped to the ground.

Something or somebody had frightened them. Could it be him they were afraid of, or was it someone slipping up behind him? He lay motionless for several minutes; gradually the horses settled down. He gave a relieved breath. It was he, after all.

Another burst of laughter came from the cabin. Something unusual went on there. It was not Seth

Hale's nature to entertain a bunch of drunken hill men. Flattening himself to the ground, Caleb began to inch his way to the rear of the cabin. As he wriggled along on his elbows, from miles away he could hear the hounds, their baying floating clearly on the night air. That's good, he thought. They would run all night, and he wouldn't have to worry about them coming around and attacking him. A pack of mean hounds was worse than a pack of hungry wolves.

At last he was beneath Nell's bedroom window, and he rose to one knee. He was hopeful that her door would be open and that he would be able to see into the room. A faint light shone out into the night, and his heart leapt. The door was open.

Putting his ear to an open chink between the logs, he caught the low murmur of voices and the rustle of clothing. When the bed creaked, he grinned. Nell was going to bed. He wished that the window wasn't so small. He would like to join her.

Slowly he eased up beside the window and carefully peeked around its edge. Damn, he thought, the door was closed after all. A burning candle on a bedside table had caused the light in the window.

He gave a low exclamation, staring openmouthed. In a dim corner, on the bed, lay two naked bodies. A man lay sprawled on his back, his head in the shadows. Nell Hale knelt between his bent legs, her face buried in the vee of his crotch. As she moved her head up and down, her long hair swayed in a rhythmic motion.

Stunned, Caleb dropped back on his heels. He directed a soundless derisive laugh at himself. All this time he had thought that he had the inside track there. But her days had been busy, also, he knew now.

Hell, that's why Gideon has been comin' over here,

he speculated. I wonder how many others have made this trip?

And who was this man? He had been unable to make out his features. When the unmistakable sound of thumping bedboards reached him, he stood up and peered into the room again. This time it was Nell who lay on her back, her long legs clasped around the man's waist, reaching eagerly to meet his every thrust.

Caleb still could not see the man's face and swore out loud. There was no need of being quiet. The noise going on in there would deaden the approach of an army.

His eyes made a slow survey of the room, then stopped and held. On a chair, draped over its back, was a bright-red coat. On the floor in front of it was a pair of bright shiny black boots.

He crouched down. Nell was laying with a British officer . . . and loving every minute of it. Most likely the same one I saw with Seth, he thought.

The moon was quite high by the time the play on the bed had ceased. Squatting beneath the window, Caleb cursed himself for being all manner of a fool. Nell was as deeply involved with the British as her brother was . . . perhaps even more so. With her ability in the bed, she had more ways of finding out things than Seth did.

Caleb searched his mind for anything he might have said that would help the enemy. Hell, I don't know what I said to her, he raged, mad at himself for being used by her.

Roxanne's lovely face sprang before his eyes. Had she, too, been used? He thought not. It was plain that the cold fish, Seth, was madly in love with her and meant to marry her. Malcolm was probably right about the man wanting to whisk her off to England as soon as possible.

From inside came the rustling of clothes again, as the pair dressed. Their voices came through the cracks quite clearly now, and again he pressed his ear against the logs.

"When do you think we can leave this wilderness?" Nell was asking.

There was a clinking of glass and the sound of liquid being poured, then, "We could leave tomorrow if it were up to me. I've finished my job."

A moment of silence followed, and Caleb could picture the officer lifting the glass to his lips. There was a dull thud as the glass was put down, and the voice continued. "But Seth is so hot to marry that Sherwood wench he won't listen to me."

Nell gave a short laugh. "Yes, I know. I told him to just take her and get married when we reached England. But he became so riled at me for even suggesting it that I dropped the subject."

Liquid splashed again before the officer answered. "I just hope that hanging around here any longer doesn't lead us into trouble."

"I agree," Nell murmured.

"And besides, I don't know how much longer I can stand them smelly Indians. I hate to think of staying with them another two weeks."

"Why don't you stay here?" Nell exclaimed, her voice excited. "You could always climb in the attic if anyone came around."

There was the crisp rustling of taffeta. The Englishman gave a low smothered laugh before he said, "Would you like that?"

During a long silence, Caleb wondered what Nell was doing to show the officer how much she would like it.

But whatever she had done the officer wasn't convinced. "I don't know, Nell. That would be awfully chancy. My bag is full of maps and information—and they must get to England at all costs. If I should get caught here, almost a full year's work would be for nothing . . . not to mention losing my head."

"Oh, but I'm sure you wouldn't be found," Nell urged. "Who would find you?"

"Don't forget that long-hunter, Coleman. He's the leader of these hill men and Seth thinks that maybe he's getting suspicious. He's pretty sure the man has followed him a couple of times."

Nell mumbled some word, but Caleb couldn't make out her words.

Then the officer said, "That devil must lead a charmed life. We've tried to kill him a couple of times, but the bastard always manages to scrape through. Too many of the Indians like him, the renegades included."

The liquid spilled again into the glass before the officer continued. "Our job would have been a hell of a lot easier with him out of the way."

Caleb's face was grim. The mystery was cleared up. They had wanted him out of the way so they could roam the hills freely. He thought of how nearly he had come to going away with the hunters. If he hadn't met Roxanne . . .? Anyhow, he was thankful that his staying had helped the colonies a bit.

Pulling the rifle across his knees, he checked the priming. He would face them now. There would never be a better time to bring this to an end. Also, he wouldn't hesitate putting a bullet in Seth now.

Caleb's hand grasped the knife sheathed at his waist to loosen it. Once he fired the rifle, he would have to rely on the long blade.

On hands and knees, he crawled under the window

and moved to the corner of the house. He stood up and made his way silently along the wall, then turned the next corner. There he dropped to his knees again and crawled beneath the front window. He listened a moment, then stepped noiselessly onto the porch. From within its deep shadow, he could stand unobserved and gaze into the room.

His lips spread in a mirthless smile. Seth and his two companions were roaring drunk. He would have no trouble with them. Seth stood at the fireplace, his elbows on the mantel, staring bleary-eyed at his drinking buddies, whose backs were turned to the window. They were dressed like long-hunters and Caleb peered closer. He knew every hunter within fifty miles and his mind raced, wondering which of the wild bunch had turned against his country.

His attention came back to Seth, who with thick tongue and slurred words was trying to tell some long-winded joke. After many wrong starts and repeated loss of memory, he finally brought it to an end. The tale made no sense, but he gave a braying laugh at its finish and the hunters, afraid of his temper, joined in with insincere guffaws.

Caleb got a good view of their faces then, and his body went rigid. They were Malcolm's men . . . friends of Ez. His forehead wrinkled into a frown. This British spy ring had been thought out a long time ago. These men had been with Malcolm three or four years.

When Seth bent to lay a log on the fire, Caleb made his move. With rifle held ready, he raised a foot and kicked open the door. The three men froze as he jumped into the room.

Seth made a growling noise in his throat and muttered hoarsely, "Coleman."

In a voice dangerously quiet, Caleb snarled, "Flicker an eyelash and you're dead men." .

Seth was sobering up fast and cast a furtive glance toward Nell's bedroom. Then a smooth smile spread across his face, and he took a step toward Caleb, his hand held out. "Good evening, neighbor. Set down and have a drink," he invited.

Caleb ignored the hand and surveyed Seth with contempt. "Don't take another step," he warned.

Seth's face clouded indignantly, and he drew back his hand. But his body went still and his eyes took on a scared look when he saw the cold glitter in Caleb's eyes. He sensed the violence that could erupt at any minute and let his hands hang loosely at his sides.

Caleb laughed lowly. "You didn't expect to see me tonight, did you, turncoat?"

A dread fascination came into Seth's eyes, and he stammered, "I don't know what you're talking about, Coleman. Why shouldn't you drop in? You've been doing it all winter."

"But not when you've had other company. Come to think about it, this is the first time I've ever seen anybody here at nighttime. You haven't been what you might say, real neighborly, with the homesteaders."

Then, still watching the three warily, he called out, "Nell, you and your redcoat can come out now."

No sound came from the bedroom, and Seth was suddenly brave. "When did you start talking to empty rooms, Coleman?" he sneered.

Caleb's eyes flicked toward him coldly as once again he called out, "If you two aren't out here immediately, Seth gets my knife in his heart."

His face white with terror, Seth yelled, "He means it, Nell. For God's sake, get out here!"

There was the sound of a scraping chair, then the

pair appeared in the doorway. Nell's face was sullen and she avoided Caleb's eyes. He gave her a mocking look and drawled, "Shame on you, Nell. Playin' around when my back is turned."

He saw the startled officer stare at the guilt on Nell's face. Caleb grinned wickedly. The Englishman hadn't been aware of Miss Hale's little side adventures, and here was his chance to get back some of his crushed ego.

"Didn't you notice, Englishman," he drawled lazily, "that our little Nell has become more adept with that devilish tongue of hers? I've been givin' her lessons all winter. She's turned out to be the best student I've ever had."

The officer's face had grown beet red, and only the pointing rifle kept his fingers from grasping Nell's slender throat. She opened her mouth to hotly denounce the words as lies, but he interrupted her with a stinging laugh.

"I think she betrayed us both, redcoat," said Caleb. "It's been hinted to me that a young friend of mine, only seventeen, mind you, comes over here regular to see our Nell, too."

Nell's fury and confusion had turned her livid. With an animallike cry of rage, she leapt at Caleb. But he had expected it and the back of his hand caught her across the mouth.

As she fell to her knees, he gazed down at her. She closed her eyes against the contempt in his eyes as he said, "Get to your feet, woman, and tie these gentlemen's hands."

He tossed a ball of narrow-sliced rawhide at her feet. "Start with your lover," he snapped, "and do a good job of it, because I'll examine the knots when you're finished."

When the officer was tied to Caleb's satisfaction, he motioned her next to one of the hunters. When that one was tied, he nodded to the other, and then only Seth was left unbound.

"Now," he said when Nell straightened up, "gather up all the rifles and stack them in the corner behind me . . . and don't forget the one in your room."

When the four rifles were placed against the wall, he spoke quietly. "Now go sit down out of my way."

Carefully Caleb lay his own rifle on the floor, and Seth's jaw dropped. When Caleb started to remove his coat, his eyes widened in apprehension. He had heard many stories of this man's rock-hard fists and of how he could use them.

Caleb's narrowed eyes bored into Seth's, and he nodded his head. "That's right, Hale. Me and you have got some settlin' up to do before I turn you over to the authorities. First, I'm gonna beat hell out of you for movin' in on Roxanne. Then I'm gonna shoot you in both legs. I'm takin' no chances on you ever bein' able to treat her like a squaw."

Seth tried to stare down the hate-filled eyes, but quickly shifted them to a spot above Caleb's head. Finally, he muttered, "I don't know what you're talking about. I don't know any squaws."

"You know what I'm talkin' about, you bastard. I'm talkin' about White Star. Did you tell Roxanne about her?"

"Yes, I did. She knows all about that red slut, and she understands."

"Oh? Did she understand that you fathered White Star's child and that you beat her unmercifully, tryin' to make her lose it . . . and in all likelihood were successful."

There was an ugly sound from the hunters. Long-hunters were known for their rough treatment of women, especially of Indian squaws, but an expected baby of any color was a special event to the rough backwoodsmen.

Caleb saw the grim looks shot at Seth, and grinned. The sneakin' spy would most likely be killed by one of his own men.

Seth had caught the looks, also, and his eyes fairly blazed as he tried to make excuses for himself. "I . . . I was a fool. I never dreamed she'd get with child. I thought Indian women knew what to do."

Caleb took a threatening step toward him. "You lie in your teeth, you bastard. You know that squaws are as ignorant as sin about such things. Only whores like your sister know how to keep that from happenin'."

Nell gasped and sprang at Caleb. Again, with his open hand, he knocked her to the floor. But his action had given Seth an opportunity. With an unexpected movement, he dived for Caleb's rifle.

The dammed-up wrath that had smoldered in Caleb all winter burst loose. With pantherlike swiftness he charged toward Seth, knocking the rifle from his hands. They smashed together, each struggling to clench the other's body. Then Caleb managed to free an arm. He pulled back his arm and drove his fist into Seth's face with the force of a kicking mule. Seth howled in pain as he hit the floor, hard.

Seth rose to his knees, shook his head, then staggered to his feet. Caleb waited for him, fist clenched. When Seth stood straight, like lightning he let fly to the pit of the man's stomach. Seth gasped and doubled over, and quickly Caleb brought up a knee, smashing Seth under the chin. He went limp and fell unconscious to the floor.

Caleb stood over him, breathing fast. Then Nell's voice rang out. "Caleb!"

Startled, he looked up—into the barrel of a pistol. She had tricked him. She had concealed the officer's firearm in her clothing.

As in a dream he watched her finger curl around the trigger and tighten. Then he was staggering and clutching at his chest as the loud report filled the room. Gunsmoke burned his nose and eyes. Then he was sinking slowly to his knees, and, the last he knew, the floor was coming up to meet him.

What must have been hours later, for the sky was pink in the east, Caleb became aware of a swinging motion. Dimly he could make out the ground, moving only inches from his face, and slowly realized that he was on a horse, riding head down. The burning throb in his chest turned into acute pain, and he was once again sliding into oblivion.

Later he was again drawn back into a half-world as he was dragged roughly from the horse and tumbled to the ground. He groaned and opened pain-blurred eyes. A leg, clad in buckskin, was coming toward him and the moccasined foot kicked out sharply.

Caleb felt himself rolling and tumbling down a steep incline. After what seemed forever, he hit bottom and lay in stuporlike silence, limp and still.

CHAPTER 21

The tears flowed unchecked from Roxanne's eyes and soaked the pillow beneath her cheek. They were a mixture of grief and anger. Grief that the hunter was going to visit Nell Hale and anger that she could do nothing to ease her overwhelming desire to punish him. She brought her fist down into the pillow with a soft thud. Caleb Coleman was the most hateful man she had ever known, and she wished that he was dead.

"That's not true, Roxanne Sherwood," she sniffed aloud and wiped her eyes on the corner of the pillow-case. "I just wish that I could hate him."

Then ashamed at herself for even thinking about him, much less caring, she willed herself to stop crying. Once and for all she must put the cold and uncaring hunter from her mind. From now on she would think only of Seth. She owed him that much. After all, wasn't she playing a heinous trick on him as it was. Palming Caleb Coleman's child off on him.

I should be glad that such a man as Seth wants to marry me, she scolded herself. He is everything that mama and papa would approve of in a man. He is a gentleman in every way, considerate of my well-being, and treats me with utmost respect.

Still, when Gideon and Lettie entered the room a short time later and sat on either side of the bed, bitter tears were falling again.

Comforting a crying woman came awkwardly to

Gideon. For several moments he sat scowling down at the floor in indecision. But as his cousin's slender shoulders continued to shake gently, he reached over and patted her shoulder. Letting his hand move up and down her arm in a soothing manner, he spoke to her softly.

"Don't take on so, Roxy," he coaxed, "Caleb don't care nothin' for that Nell Hale. He knows what she is."

Roxanne's tears stopped, and she turned over on her back. Lettie leaned forward, and both women stared at him.

"What do you mean, Gideon?" Roxanne asked sharply, a hint of hope in her query.

Lettie moved impatiently, echoing Roxanne's words. For some time now, Gideon had been leaving the cabin almost every afternoon around two o'clock. He would be gone the rest of the day, returning only at suppertime. His lean young face would always wear a relaxed and pleased air when he sat down at the table. She had suspected that he had found himself a new Indian girl.

But Lettie's mind had argued that if this were the case, would he continue to seek her out every evening? She had argued back that the time she spent in his bed lately had shortened a lot. These nights, after one fast tumble, Gideon was fast asleep. It seemed strange to go back to her own bed still fresh and not dog tired.

Since the age of twelve, when she had been forced into sexual acts with an older uncle, Lettie had grown used to being used nightly. The acts demanded from her were demeaning and long lasting.

The nightmare had started with her first experience ten years ago. She still shuddered when she thought about it. Her parents' home was a one-room shack, small and crowded, with the seven children who ran underfoot.

As far back as Lettie could remember, every spring, like clockwork, a new puling baby was delivered in the poverty-stricken cabin. Beside the seven living, three were buried upon the hill.

When the last baby was a month old, the old midwife who tended all the women in the hollow had warned her mother that another baby would be her death. Darting an angry glance at Lettie's father, she had said, "Your body has been abused too long and too much, Meg."

But the father, in his usual state of drunkenness, hee-hawed the midwife and, before her disapproving stare, had pushed his wife onto the bed and entered her roughly. When at last he rolled off the crying woman, he sneered, "I planted you good, you snivelin' bitch. We'll see now if you die."

His words were meant for the old woman, but she had left the cabin almost immediately upon his onslaught. The cowering children watched him with frightened eyes, but he staggered to a chair and sat down.

They settled down quietly on the floor as he turned to the man at his side. "I showed that bossy old bitch, didn't I, brother? Ain't nobody gonna tell me when I can take my old lady to bed."

As her father had slammed in and out of her mother, Lettie became aware of her uncle's eyes upon her. She read the message in the fat, cruel face, and looked away when he opened his homespuns and pulled himself free. She knew without looking that he was fondling and stroking himself. It was a favorite practice of his, and he did it often.

She glanced at him now and became nervous when she saw that he was paying no attention to his brother's bragging, but still had his pig-eyes upon her. She put the new baby into the much-used cradle and started across the floor to aid her mother, still lying in bed. But as she passed her uncle, his arm darted out and encircled her waist. As he jerked her to him, she pulled back, reluctantly leaning against him.

When his coarse hand slid up her thin and worn dress, she blushed and strained away from him, but his arm tightened. She threw a pleading look in her father's direction. But he had only frowned at her warningly.

"It's alright to be friendly with your uncle, girl," he growled, then tilted the jug of corn whiskey to his lips.

Ashamed and trembling with fright, she remained at her hated uncle's side, suffering his rough hands to slide over her thin thighs and flat stomach. Then his thick grimy hands moved up to her immature breasts and gave a tender nipple a sharp tweak. She cried out and cowered away from him. But the two men only laughed loudly as they passed the jug between them.

Then the uncle sat the jug on the floor and staggered to his feet. Leaning his great weight against her small frame, he muttered under his sour breath, "Come on, girl, you're old enough to be diddled."

She gasped and struggled to pull away. But he grabbed her thin arm and dragged her, crying and pleading, across the room and pushed her down onto the cot where she slept.

She had tried to fight him off, but her puny muscles were nothing against his burly strength. He had pinioned her wrists over her head and roughly pushed her legs apart with his knees. Firmly established between her legs, he released her hands and reached down and guided himself to her small opening. Then he thrust deep within her. The excruciating pain that ripped through her body sent her scream ringing through the room.

And as he used her, time after time, none had come to her rescue. The ailing mother had not dared.

When at last he rolled off her and fell into a drunken sleep, she managed to get off the low cot and crawl painfully out of the cabin and into the forest. Resting every few minutes, Lettie at last came to the cave where she and her younger sister played with their cornstalk dolls. Like a sick animal, she crept into a corner and curled up. At dusk of the same day, the sister, one year her junior, came to her. For the next three days she brought food to Lettie while her ravaged body healed.

But immediately upon returning to the cabin, she was ordered to the cot by the dreaded uncle. Bit by bit the act became less painful and as time went by, she learned to endure his savage attacks.

Toward the end of summer the uncle tired of her and began to eye the young sister. The time came when he passed up Lettie's cot and lay down beside her frightened sister. Moments later pain-filled screams rent the air. And Lettie, helpless to aid her sister, clenched her fists in the agony of her mind.

The next day, as if on signal, her male cousins began to arrive, five in all. One after the other, each in turn had crawled onto her weary body and stolidly pushed in and out, making noises like the hogs at the slop troughs.

One day, a month later, a change came into Lettie's life. A long-hunter, bewhiskered and mean of eye, showed up at the cabin. He and her father talked for some time out in the chip yard, with the hunter throwing glances her way. As she watched from her seat on a stump, she saw the stranger open the pouch at his side and hand over some bills to her father, who pocketed the money and turned and motioned to her.

When she stood at his elbow, he snapped curtly, "Go get your duds together. You'll be leaving with this gent."

His words brought a singing gladness to Lettie. Just the thought of getting away from her male relatives made her heart race. Going away with the devil would be better than the hell she had endured the past months.

But she had been mistaken. It turned out that the man had appetites that were strange to her and that he derived pleasure from treating her cruelly.

When she had returned to the chip yard with her pitiful amount of clothing tied up in a cloth, the hunter picked up his rifle and gave her a hard shove. "Get on, whore, we've got a long way to go."

They traveled all night without stopping. The sky was turning a light gray and Lettie didn't think she could take another step when they came to a sloppily made camp. Rolled in blankets around a low-burning fire were two men and two women. The hunter walked over to one of the figures and kicked him in the side. The man sat up and rubbed his eyes, then spread his lips in a toothless smile when he saw Lettie.

"Well, Ez," he snickered, "I see you got what you went for." He came close and peered into Lettie's face. He licked his thin lips and murmured, "She's young." Then reaching out he grabbed one of her small breasts. "She any good, Ez?"

"I don't know. I ain't tried her yet."

"Well, damnit, hurry up and try her. I want my turn."

"Got no time now. I just got our orders and we gotta move on."

The two women, haggard and gaunt, pulled themselves wearily out of the smelly blankets. And Lettie, thinking that surely now she could rest, dropped to the ground. But Ez, a hard gleam in his eye, swung his foot back and slammed it hard into her thigh. "Get over there and help them other sluts make breakfast," he ordered.

After a hurried meal, camp was broken and they started off through the forest, the women carrying the gear.

By late afternoon, when Lettie was staggering in weariness, they arrived at a well-kept homestead. The buildings and farm animals milling around a large barn indicated success.

Ez raised his hand, motioning them to stop. "This is the place," he said to the men. "You all stay here while I go talk to the owner."

At Ez's "hallo" the door opened and a man stepped onto the porch. He was middle-aged, big and rangy, with a pipe clenched in his teeth. Ez joined him on the porch and they talked quietly for some time. Then they shook hands and Ez returned. His face wore a pleased smile, and the hint of smug satisfaction reminded Lettie of a cat.

"We're hired," he spoke to the men. "We can live in that cabin over there."

Lettie followed his pointing finger and was thankful

that the place looked sturdy. And from its large size, she judged it to have two rooms.

"His name is Malcolm Sherwood," Ez announced, swinging open the door. As Lettie passed through, he had halted her. "You're to work for him in the house. If he wants to use you, you treat him good, do you hear?"

As his fingers tightened around her arm, she grimaced in pain and nodded her head.

She and the two women made a desultory inspection of the cabin, and Lettie found that she had been right. There were two rooms. In the smaller, window-less room, one bunk bed was attached to two opposite walls. Other than three shelves, built one above the other, there was nothing more. In the other room, somewhat larger, a good-sized fireplace, well-built, took up most of one wall. The room boasted one window, looking out toward the Sherwood home. A crude bed was in one corner, with a low table beside it. In another corner stood a long table, with benches of equal length on either side. Two pole chairs completed the furnishings.

"It all looks so nice," Lettie thought yearningly. "If only I could live in it by myself."

She and the women unpacked the gear and settled into their new home, and lived for the next four years a life of hell.

Then Ez's sudden death had released her, and for the first time in her life Lettie began to live normally. It was during her relationship with Gideon, where cruelty didn't exist, she found that she hadn't hated the actual act of sex after all. She had hated and dreaded the brutality that had always gone with it. Gideon's slackening demands had surprised and alerted her to the fact that that part of the man was very essential to her well-being. She had already started to cast her eyes about for his replacement.

The low murmur of that young man's voice brought Lettie back to the present. Her attention was caught by the tail end of a statement he was making.

"That Nell Hale is nothin' more than a fancy whore, in my opinion," he was declaring. "The only difference bein' she smells good while she's doing you."

Roxanne gasped, too astounded to even chide him on his vulgarity. "Nell Hale does that?"

His tone boastful, Gideon retorted, "I'll say she does." His eyes twinkled teasingly at Lettie. "She's almost as good as somebody else I know."

Lettie made a small distressed sound and slapped him on the shoulder. "Gideon, hush up."

"How did you know she would do this?" Roxanne urged him.

"Do you remember that peddler that came through here several weeks ago?"

Both women nodded, eager for him to get on with the story.

"Well, just before he left, he mentioned to me that he had spent a very nice two hours with Miss Hale. When he rode off, he called back, 'You ought to look into that, lad.' So I got to thinkin' on his words and decided to ride over and test her out."

Roxanne and Lettie leaned forward, their eyes intent on his face. "And?" they breathed.

Gideon grinned broadly. "The peddler was right. And I'll tell you somethin' else. That one takes a heap of pleasurin'. I was real tickled that first day to hear a horse come gallopin'."

"Was it Seth?" Roxanne asked.

"Naw, it was our neighbor, Zebe Stevens, from over on Baldy Creek."

Interested, Lettie asked, "What did he want?"

Gideon snorted. "What in the hell do you think he wanted? He wanted the same thing I did. When I passed him on the path, he was already loosening his pants."

Gideon paused a minute. A tickled grin came over his face. "I said hello to him, and he just frowned and growled at me, 'I hope you didn't wear her out, boy.' "

"Shame on him," Roxanne exclaimed. "He's in his fifties and has a cabinful of children."

Gideon and Lettie howled their laughter.

Finally Lettie managed to say, "Roxy, haven't you heard that old saying, 'the older the buck, the stiffer the horn'?"

"No, I haven't heard that one," Roxanne grinned. "But I have heard, 'It's all in their heads, all they have to do is blow their noses.' "

Gideon and Lettie stared at her, surprised that she could come back at them with such a fitting remark. They laughed.

Gideon said, "It's a good saying, Roxy, but I don't think it applies to Zebe Stevens. That randy old bastard has worn out three wives and is lookin' for the fourth."

"Men!" Roxanne spoke angrily and gave her pillow a hard whack.

But Lettie was silent. In these harsh hills, the wives usually died before the husbands, and it was not unusual for the man to start casting his eyes about for a replacement before his wife was barely cold in the grave. And this was especially true if there were young children left behind. A homesteader had to work from dawn to dark and had no time to look after small children. There were a few who, unable to find a white woman, had taken to himself an Indian squaw. But his neighbors frowned on this practice, and it was slowly being discontinued.

More than once Lettie had given thought to making up to Zebe Stevens. With youth in her favor she believed that she could keep up with the lusty man with no trouble at all. Hadn't she managed to muddle through with Ez and his friends? And certainly Gideon was always ready to go to bed.

I'd put up with anything, she thought to herself, just to have the security of a husband and a home.

She made silent plans to seemingly, accidentally, run into Zebe some day.

Gideon rose and stretched, then remarked that he was going to bed. He glanced at Lettie, his look asking if she was going with him. But she avoided his eyes. She was going to another man tonight. After everyone was asleep, she would slip away.

But she was not going to Caleb Coleman to crawl into his bed. She was going to visit the hunter to tell him a few facts she felt he should know about. If someone didn't interfere in the lives of these two people, they would never get together.

But later, lying on her narrow bed, fully clothed, waiting for the cabin to sleep, Lettie had fallen asleep. The morning sun, streaming through the window and shining in her eyes, awakened her.

It wasn't until around ten o'clock that she managed to get away, telling Roxanne that she was going to pick a mess of greens for supper.

With a basket and a knife swinging on her arm, she climbed the hills to Caleb's place. She could tell before she knocked on the door that no one was in the

place. It wore that total quietness that spoke of emptiness. Disappointment on her face, she stepped off the
rickety porch. She started to walk around the building,
but at the corner of the cabin, she stopped short.
Caleb's stallion, fully bridled and saddled, stood
cropping the tender new grass that grew around the
shed.

Thinking that Caleb must be nearby, her face relaxed and she called his name. When no answer came,
she called again, louder. But only the twittering of
birds high in the treetops answered her.

"That's strange," she muttered, walking over to
the horse. "Why would he go away and leave his
horse saddled and walking around?"

Talking softly to the animal, she picked up the reins
and rubbed the sleek neck. Then her eyes saw the
large dark stain that covered the saddle and part of the
horse's belly. She ran her fingers over the saddle, and
they came away red and sticky. "Blood!" she gasped
and stepped back.

Renegade Indians! raced through her mind. She
could feel the hair on the back of her neck rising and
gooseflesh breaking out on her arms. She was sure
that every bush and boulder concealed a red body
ready to spring out and scalp her.

But calmness returned to her as she reminded herself that if renegades were around she would have
been killed immediately upon nearing the cabin.

Caleb was either seriously injured or dead. There
was only one thing to do. She must backtrack the stallion and try to find Caleb.

Lettie had been walking for at least an hour, having
no difficulty following the large prints, when the
tracks led up a steep incline. Near the top, and coming
from an eastwardly direction, many tracks mingled

with the stallion's. Her face took on a puzzled expression. There was only a sinkhole at the top of this rise. She had discovered it one day last summer while picking blackberries.

She stopped short, bringing her hands to her cheeks. "Dear Lord," she whispered, "they've dropped him in the hole."

The spring sun had become quite warm, and she opened the top two buttons of her blouse as she hurried up the hill. Her legs ached from the steady climb when she finally reached the top. The ground leveled off to a width of five feet around the depression.

Dreading what she might find, Lettie moved to the rim of the sinkhole. But when she peered down into the deep and sunny pit, she could see nothing but large boulders scattered about and, in the very center, a small pool of water.

She was about to leave when her eyes caught on an object that was foreign to the surrounding terrain. Shielding her eyes from the sun's glare, she stared intently. Then she grew rigid. From behind a boulder protruded a hand and part of an arm.

"Oh, my God," she exclaimed and started a plunging descent. Slipping and sliding, she reached bottom in a swirl of dust and gravel. Picking herself up, she ran behind the sheltering boulder and stared down at Caleb.

Low groans came from his throat. His breathing was harsh and heavy. She knelt beside him and lifted his head. His eyes were closed and she laid him back down and carefully undid his blood-soaked shirt. A small moan escaped her lips when she saw the gaping hole. Dried blood surrounded the slowly seeping red, indicating that he had bled for some time.

Shaking her head, Lettie hurried to the pool a short

distance away, tearing a wide strip from her petticoat as she ran. After dipping the cloth into the clear water, she raced back, water dripping on the ground.

She wiped away the matted blood, then shook her head. The wound meant death in a short time if Caleb didn't get help almost immediately. She tore off another strip of cloth and went to the spring again. Back once more, she let the cool water trickle over his mouth. The cracked, blood-smeared lips opened and his tongue came out to catch at the life-giving liquid.

As she continued to give him water in this manner, his eyes would open momentarily and, from the light in them, she knew that he was aware of who she was. Heartened, Lettie made one last trip to the pool and soaked the cloth. Returning to the wounded man, she folded the cloth into a square and placed it on the gunshot wound. Pressing his shoulder, she said calmly and clearly, "Lie perfectly still, Caleb. I'm going for help now."

Caleb made a struggling motion and feebly raised his hand, trying to catch her arm. His lips moved soundlessly and his fevered eyes fairly blazed at her. Thinking that he was afraid to be left alone, she patted his arm and said softly, "Don't fret, Caleb, I'll be right back."

His eyes still pleading with her, she stood up and turned to go. Then she gasped and stood still. A tall, wide-shouldered Indian stood in her path.

The thin lips on the stony face moved. "You stay here."

CHAPTER 22

Roxanne stood on a hilltop, inhaling the bracing breath of the mountains. She felt the fresh wet dew of the early morning on her face and hands and felt invigorated. She stood there a long time, her dress gathered up above the damp grass, her blonde hair tossing in the wind.

Twice Malcolm had called to her from the cabin below. But she had only looked down and shook her head. This was her special time of the day and she would allow no one to interfere with it.

Looking out over the valleys that lay at her feet, she wondered when her feelings toward the hills had begun to change. It must have been a gradual thing, for she could not pinpoint the time to any special month or event. It must have been merely the day-by-day living in the hills.

It had grown on her in a silent, subtle manner, slowly awakening her to the glorious beauty of the hills and valleys. A derisive smile, directed at herself, curved her lips. How could she have ever thought that masses of houses on crowded dirty streets surpassed this panorama of new green leaves and white-flowering dogwood.

And more surprisingly, she became accustomed to and liked the rough yet gentle men of the hills. Many times lately she had caught herself curling her nose in contempt for the simpering dandies back in Boston.

What a poor showing they would make against the stalwart, rugged men whom she now knew. How could she have ever thought that the Boston men were gentlemen? She had finally learned that perfect manners did not make the gentleman.

A frown gathered on her forehead as she realized that she had begun to learn this when she and Seth had discussed White Star. He had been so callous about the girl . . . as if the color of her skin kept her from having feelings.

A long soft sigh came through her lips. Seth had disappointed her so many times lately that she hardly dared to think about him. If she mused too hard on him, she would find it impossible to go through with her marriage, and then what would become of her baby?

Caleb flashed into her mind, but she angrily pushed him away. He had left the hills, gone back to the wild bunch, Uncle Malcolm had announced sadly. And although her uncle and cousin never talked about it, she knew that they were both hurt that Caleb had not bothered to say good-bye.

She would not even think about the disappointment, then anger, that had gripped her. Lettie had dropped the news one night at the supper table.

"I stopped at Caleb's today to get a drink of water," she began, "and he's gone."

Malcolm had looked at her from under his shaggy brows and inquired, "What do you mean, he's gone?"

"I mean he's gone . . . cleared out. The cabin is bare as a bone. All his gear and grub is gone."

The subject had been dropped and never mentioned again. But the next day she and Gideon had ridden to the old cabin, and it was as Lettie had said. It was bare, just as though Caleb had never lived there.

Returning home she had fought back the bitter tears and had finally reconciled herself to the idea that Caleb Coleman had gone out of her life for all time. From now on she must think only of Seth and their approaching marriage.

"Rox . . . y," came Malcolm's loud ringing call again. And this time it carried a commanding tenor that Roxanne heeded.

Down the grassy hillside, her toes crimping against its slippery surface, she moved toward the cabin. Halfway, she spotted Seth's horse tied to the hitch. Shifting her glance to the porch she saw Seth and her uncle talking, and the corner of her lips quirked. Uncle Malcolm became fidgety if he was stuck with Seth too long.

Her mind now made up to always be pleasant to the man she was about to marry, Roxanne smiled sweetly and murmured, "Good morning, Seth," as she climbed the three steps to the porch. "Isn't it a glorious day?" she continued.

But Seth only nodded briefly, as, with a frown puckering his forehead, he looked at her bare feet.

Roxanne felt herself blush and quickly let go of the skirt bunched in her hands. But as the skirt fell to the floor, covering her wet and grass-stained feet, she became angry for feeling guilty over her lack of shoes. She tilted her head proudly and gave her grinning uncle a cold stare as she moved past them and on into the cabin.

When she joined them later, her hair neatly brushed and black slippers tied neatly around slim ankles, Seth smiled, pleased. He would have no trouble keeping her in line, after all.

He rose and took her arm. "Let's take advantage of

this beautiful morning and walk as we finish our wedding plans.''

They chose the wide wagon trail that led to the river. For some time they walked in silence. For though Roxanne had made her face calm and relaxed, inside her rage still burned. She would start no conversation. If Mr. Right and Proper wanted to discuss anything, then he could start it.

She was startled when he did speak. ''You're awfully quiet this morning,'' he said, bending his head to look into her face. ''Is there something on your mind . . . someone been telling you stories again?''

She gave him a weak smile. ''No, I haven't heard any stories recently. I just don't have anything to say.''

Seth patted her hand. He disliked chattering women, and that Roxanne talked little pleased him. ''I'll do the talking then,'' he smiled at her.

They strolled on and, after a moment or so, Seth said, ''I ran into the new minister yesterday and had a nice chat with him. He has agreed to a candlelight service.''

Roxanne hadn't met the new minister, and she now thought of the old one, Preacher James. Poor old fellow. Toward the end of winter he had been found by a hunter, crumpled over beside his dead campfire, scalped by the Indians. She had felt dreadful on hearing about it and had recalled how kind he had been to her that awful day of the Indian attack. She had wondered guiltily if his helping her had led to his death.

Seth was talking again and she brought her attention back to him.

''What do you think?'' he asked.

''Oh, I'm terribly sorry, Seth,'' she apologized. ''I'm afraid I was thinking about old Reverend James.

Please tell me what it was that you said?''

Seth's face clouded, but he made no mention of her inattentiveness. ''I was saying that I told him we would like the ceremony to be held at your house. Do you agree?''

Actually, Roxanne had given no thoughts to her wedding day . . . other than it would happen. She hadn't experienced that all-over excitement of planning where it should be and at what time. Sadness crept over her, and she would have liked to cry. A young woman's wedding day was supposed to be the biggest event in her life, outside of the birth of her first child.

She suppressed a sigh and looked away from Seth so that he could not read the guilt in her eyes.

But a stubborn defiance was taking hold of her. It was still the bride's privilege to make her own wedding plans. And, even if she weren't all that interested, she was going to claim that right. In her opinion Seth had been too high-handed. He had no right making the arrangements without first consulting her.

Her voice was a bit sharp when she answered. ''I'm sorry, Seth, but that is not how I planned my big day.''

The dark cloud flickered again on Seth's face, but he kept his displeasure inside. He, too, knew that it was up to the bride and her family to plan every detail of the wedding.

He forced a smile to his lips and murmured, ''Of course, dear. It was thoughtless of me to go ahead and take such matters into my own hands. It's only that one so seldom finds the preacher about, I thought that perhaps I should make the plans while I had him.''

When she made no response, he asked, ''How did you want your day to go?''

Caught off guard with no plans of her own, Roxanne fussed nervously with her hair while her mind raced crazily. Luckily Seth thought that she was just being shy, as any young bride might be, and he waited patiently for her to speak.

Haltingly she spoke her thoughts as they came. "I would like to be married right after church services so that my friends and neighbors could witness my happy day. I would have the sun shine brightly on that day, and the church should be decorated with wild-flowers."

Seth fell silent as they walked along. He made no response until they were almost to the river. Roxanne's plans did not fall in with his, and he fumed inwardly.

There was an important purpose in him wanting an evening service. He needed the cover of darkness to carry out his well-laid plan. At this very moment, a boat lay concealed along the river only yards from Malcolm's cabin. It waited to take him and his new bride to Boston. From that city they would set sail for England, where they would make their home.

His frown deepened. Too many things could go wrong before nightfall. It was imperative that nothing stood in the way of the British officer and his sister leaving these hills as soon as possible. At any time now, Caleb Coleman's body might be found and an investigation started. The hunter had many friends, both red and white, and they would not let his murder go lightly.

His mind raced with new plans and, when the river flowed across their path, he was ready with a new one. Taking a handkerchief from his pocket, he spread it on a log, then took Roxanne by the elbow. "Sit here, dear."

Sitting down beside her, he picked up one of her hands and continued, "I was going to wait until after the wedding to give you your surprise, but I've decided to give it to you now. You will need time to get things together."

Roxanne looked at him quizzically. "What is it, Seth?"

He squeezed her fingers, and she noticed how clammy his hands were. Why is the nervous? she wondered.

Then suddenly, his words rushed out at her. "How would you like to go to England on your honeymoon?"

Roxanne stared at him, her mouth open. Then her eyes lit up and her lips spread in a wide smile. Seth relaxed with a long sigh.

"Oh, Seth, I think that's wonderful," she exclaimed, returning the pressure of his hands. "Imagine, a honeymoon in England."

His voice eager now, Seth began to tell her of the things they would see and the places they would go. And once, he barely caught himself in time from describing their new home.

He ended by asking, "It's all set then?"

"Yes, yes."

He continued, "Be all packed and ready to go, for we'll be leaving immediately after the service."

"Oh, I will. I can hardly wait. Uncle Malcolm will be so happy for me."

A wary light appeared in Seth's eyes. He stammered a bit, then cautioned, "Let's keep it a secret for a while, dear. I don't want word to get out that I'll be away from my place so long. You know . . . Indians and all."

Roxanne wasn't sure that she understood, but,

being carried away with the excitement of seeing England, she readily agreed.

Seth helped her to her feet, mentioning that he had a lot of things to attend to and some business to take care of.

"My sister will be traveling with us," he said casually, then laughed lightly. "I'll have to keep an eye on her packing or she'll take too much. She won't want to leave anything behind."

Roxanne glanced at him from hopeful eyes. "Will she be staying in England?"

Seth averted his eyes and said shortly. "Yes."

A great weight lifted from Roxanne. Nell's absence would go a long way in making her marriage a more successful and happy one.

They were halfway home when they rounded a bend and ran into Lettie. A small cry of confusion escaped the hired woman's lips, and Roxanne and Seth looked at her curiously.

"My goodness, Lettie," said Roxanne, laughing. "You still look like a little tyke that's just been caught stealing pie. Did we frighten you?"

"Only for a moment." Lettie laughed. "I was woolgathering and didn't know there was anyone around for a hundred miles."

"See you back at the cabin, then," Roxanne smiled as she and Seth continued on.

Lettie's gaze followed them, a hard glint in her eyes. She spat on the ground contemptuously and muttered, "You rotten dog," her eyes boring into Seth's back.

Hiking up her skirt and holding it away from the brush and brambles, she left the trail and moved off through the forest. Deep in a pocket of her apron she felt the meat and bread there. When she had run full tilt into the pair, she was sure that they would see the bulge it made. They could have asked questions that she would have been hard put to answer. Especially that cold stick, Hale.

Lettie was on her way to see Caleb. She had gone this way for a week. Usually she couldn't get away from the cabin until after the noon meal. But today Mr. Sherwood and Gideon had gone downriver to help a neighbor clear a field and would be taking lunch with that family.

As she hurried along, she thought of Caleb and hoped that he would continue to mend. He had looked much better yesterday. There was a tinge of color to his cheeks and he had been able to sit, propped up, for the better part of an hour. Thanks to Long Step and his knowledge of Indian medicines, Caleb would soon recover completely.

She recalled with a shudder the day she had found Caleb so near to death. If the brave hadn't come along when he did, she doubted if the hunter would be alive today. But Long Step had come, like some huge red angel, grunting short sharp orders to her. She had brought him the buds from a tall balm of Gilead, crushed the leaves of the mayapple, and finally, handfuls of cool soft mud from the pool. The mayapple had been mixed with the mud, then spread on the seeping wound. Again she had donated a piece of her petticoat to bind the wide chest.

Then Long Step had knelt and scooped the hunter into his arms and, as though Caleb's weight was nothing, started climbing out of the hole with Lettie scrambling after him.

They had walked but a short distance when the brave stopped in front of a dense clump of sumac. Its new green leaves stood out against the large boulder directly behind it. When Lettie looked at the Indian questioningly, he pointed his toe to the center of the bush and grunted, ''Part the branches here.''

She gave him a doubtful look, but did as she was bidden. The branches parted easily and she stared at the wide, dark opening in the stone.

''A cave,'' she whispered.

Behind her, Long Step growled impatiently and she quickly swung aside, holding the bush apart. The brave bent his head and stooped until his wide frame and burden could fit the opening. With Lettie at his heels, he moved down the sloping floor for about five feet and was then able to stand erect. After another few feet, Long Step bent into the semidarkness and lay Caleb on the stone floor. Lettie could make out the Indian's fingers groping along on a ledge, then heard the scratch of a flint on steel and presently a candle burned brightly in his hand. He moved to the wall and carefully sat it in a niche. He dusted off his hands and returned to Caleb.

As he carried his white friend to a bed of bearskins placed near the candle, Lettie glanced around the roomlike structure. It was of good size, equaling a normal cabin room. It was warm and dry, and a small stream ran through its middle. The cave was a fine place for a man to mend in, she thought.

Still, she wondered why the Indian had carried Caleb here instead of taking him home. But she had learned a long time ago that the Indian's ways were strange to the white man, and she dismissed the thought. She was sure that Long Step had a good reason.

As the brave worked over Caleb, straightening his arms and legs into a more comfortable position, Lettie whipped off her apron and rolled it into a makeshift pillow. When Caleb's head was lifted to receive it, he groaned and opened his eyes. Long Step hung over him anxiously. "Who do this to you, Coleman?"

His voice barely above a whisper, Caleb had slowly and painfully related what had happened to him at the Hale place. When Long Step gave a derisive grunt and rose to his feet, Caleb put out a hand and stopped him.

"Not yet, friend. Let me mend a bit. The man is mine."

Long Step looked undecided a moment, then dropped down beside Caleb. He started to speak, but the hunter was unconscious again. The brave scanned his face, felt his brow, and then rose. He moved to the narrow stream and squatted beside a piled stack of dry leaves and twigs. Using his flint, he soon had a flame eating at the leaves. Piling on larger pieces of wood that lay waiting, he coaxed the fire into glowing coals. Then going to a dark corner, he dug out a battered pan and silently left the cave. He was back in a short time, the pan full of roots that Lettie did not recognize. Scrubbing them clean at the stream, he put them in the pan and filled it with water. Sitting it on the fire, he added the buds of the balm of Gilead to the other contents. After it began to boil, a strange and pungent odor filled the cave. Lettie's nose and eyes began to run, and she gave a small cough.

The Indian turned from the bubbling mixture and studied her. His gaze was so intense that she began to squirm uncomfortably and became a little afraid. She was almost ready to turn and run when he finally spoke.

"You go home now. Say nothing to no one. Come back later with broth made from deer meat."

Wordlessly, she nodded her head and, after a fast glance at Caleb, left the cave. Hurrying along, she worried where she would get some venison. None was at the cabin, and the men folk had gone to the post and wouldn't be home until late. And even if they were, it wouldn't be her place to tell them to go shoot a deer.

She wondered if she dared kill one of Malcolm's chickens. Could she have it boiled and hidden away before he returned? It wouldn't matter if Roxy were about. These days she wasn't aware of anything that went on around her.

Lettie now recalled how she had stepped up her pace, thinking that she must hurry if she was to catch one of those wild chickens. She smiled and her face had a tender look. It was then she had met Zebe Stevens.

She had been almost running when she rounded a bend and bumped hard into a large, sturdy figure. Strong hands came out to steady her and piercing eyes had gazed down into her startled face. She stared back as though hypnotized by the probing, penetrating gleam of them. She had never seen him close and felt overpowered by his large size.

"Zebe Stevens," she finally gasped.

His firm lips spread in a smile that showed surprisingly sound white teeth. "You know me, do you, big eyes?" he asked. "I hate to admit that I don't know such a handsome woman."

His hands were still on her arms, but in a more caressing way now. His warm fingers were striking nerves throughout her flesh and she felt herself begin to tremble. And when his eyes told her that he was aware of what was happening to her, she became confused and dropped her eyes. She murmured lowly, "They call me Lettie. Lettie White. I work for Mr. Sherwood."

A mocking light appeared in his eyes. "Just what

do you do for Mr. Malcolm Sherwood?''

An angry flush spread through her and she tried to draw away. But the large hands held her firmly and she spit out, ''I don't do what you're thinkin'. I work. I work hard.''

Still smiling in a lazy manner, he moved a hand up to caress her throat, stopping at the throbbing pulse, resting his fingers lightly. ''Lettie, girl,'' he teased, ''didn't anyone ever tell you that it's not good to work all the time?'' He tilted her chin. ''You've got to play a little in between.''

His gaze moved to the two opened buttons, his hands quickly following. Then fingers moved slowly, undoing the remaining ones. The material parted and her heavy breasts hung free: For a long moment he gazed at their ripe fullness, then began to fondle them. Lettie felt herself becoming weak and could only lean against him.

Wordlessly, he swept her into his arms and buried his face between the white mounds. Her hand came up to stroke the black hair that was turning gray.

He dropped to his knees and laid her on the ground, thick with pine needles. His eyes questioned her hungrily, and she nodded eagerly. His face came down and his lips covered hers as his hands slid beneath her skirt, pushing it up. In his hot haste, his fingers fumbled at his buckskins and she reached down to help him. The lacings opened and he sprang free. Lettie's lips formed an O, and she leaned on her elbows and stared at the size of him.

He saw her startled look and gave a low, uneasy laugh. ''I'm hung like a bull, Lettie, but I'll try not to hurt you.''

But Lettie's instant feeling for this large hill man was such that she would have taken more had he had it. When she did not cry out as he carefully eased into her, but rather pressed closer, a glad smile lit his rugged face.

He gathered her writhing buttocks in both hands and began a rhythmic drive that frightened the birds in the trees. But Lettie relaxed and loved every plunge, rising to meet each one.

And when he reached his release, she held him close, not even attempting to obtain her own. This first time would be his alone—a complete fulfillment.

She felt his weight slump onto her, his breath coming fast. Then, still keeping himself locked inside her, he lifted himself to an elbow, letting her body rest. Smoothing the tousled hair from her forehead, he studied her comely face and a look of tenderness came into his eyes.

"Lettie, in all my years of layin' with women, you're the first to hold me close and ride out my storm."

In all of Lettie's experiences with men, Zebe was the first to look at her with the eyes of a lover. Always before only lust or impatient anger had gazed out at her. Even Gideon had taken her roughly, with no real thought to her as a person.

She gazed up at him and the wonder on his face reminded her of an adolescent boy who had just received his first rifle. She lifted her hand and let a finger trace lightly around his face. "Those women were such fools, Zebe," she murmured.

His eyes kindled and she pulled his face down. Covering his lips with her own, she gently grabbed his tongue between her teeth and sucked it slowly. When she felt him growing inside her, she brought her legs back up around his waist and held him tightly.

This time Lettie rode the crest with him, mingling

her low moans with his soft grunts.

He had refused to let her leave until she promised to meet him again that night. She had hoped that he would want to see her again and had only hesitated, to tease him a bit.

It wasn't until she was about to leave that she saw the dead bodies of several squirrels lying next to his rifle. Her breath quickened. They would make such rich broth for Caleb. Zebe saw her eyes fastened on the small animals and leaned over and took two from the pile.

"Take these home and stew them," he said. Then grinning, added, "Make sure you eat a lot of it. You're gonna need your strength tonight."

Taking them from him, she grinned back. "Don't worry about me. I'll keep up with you, big man."

He had laughed deeply and reached for her. But she evaded his hands and ran down the trail, her happy laughter trailing behind her.

A soft happiness came over Lettie's face as she remembered the glorious nights spent together this past week. She grew warm just thinking how much she loved the big man who was older than her father. And better yet, he loved her, too. They were to be married a week after Roxanne was.

The screening bush to the cave came in view, and she stopped to give the bird whistle that Long Step had taught her. But this time it was Caleb who stuck his head through the sumac and motioned her in.

Back in the cave, she inquired anxiously, "Should you be moving about so much, Caleb? You must be careful that your wound don't start bleedin' again."

"I feel fine, Lettie," he assured her.

But she noted that he quickly sat down and leaned

his back against the wall. Fine beads of sweat were gathered on his upper lip, a sure sign of weakness.

She hurried to spread out the generous chunks of meat and bread. His appetite was good, and he soon had it polished off and was looking for another cup of coffee.

When he had filled his pipe and puffed on it until it was working smoothly, Lettie nervously cleared her throat a couple of times, then went to sit beside him.

He looked at her questioningly through the swirl of smoke and asked, "You got somethin' on your mind, Lettie?"

She hesitated, took a deep breath, and began slowly. "Yes, Caleb, I have. The day I found you wounded, I had gone to your place looking for you. I wanted to tell you something I felt that you should know."

Again she hesitated and stared down at her folded hands lying in her lap. Caleb looked at her and wondered at the apprehension on her face.

He lay a hand on her shoulder. "Lettie, you want to tell me something that you're afraid I won't like, right?"

When she nodded dumbly, he continued, "Well?" When she still didn't speak, he became impatient and spoke sharply. "Get on with it, woman. Spit it out."

Lettie looked up at him, her eyes wide. "Roxanne is gonna have a baby," she said in a rush.

For several seconds Caleb was strangely quiet. His eyes took on a look that made Lettie draw away from him. Then he slumped back against the wall, a look of total defeat on his face.

Finally, he muttered, "I know. Gideon told me."

Lettie glanced at him, not too surprised. She had suspected that Gideon had overheard some of her and

Roxanne's conversation that day. She firmed her lips. Just like a man—he had hurried to tell Caleb about it.

In the silence that grew, anger began to build in Lettie. In her opinion, Caleb was taking a churlish attitude about Roxanne's pregnancy. His stony face seemed to say that it was all her fault. That she had deliberately gotten with child.

Lettie shot Caleb a look of dislike. Who in the hell did he think he was? Did he think he was king of these hills, and, as such, had the right to strew his seed all over the countryside and not have to hear of its consequences? Well, by God, this time it was different. Roxanne Sherwood was no Indian squaw—and Caleb Coleman was going to realize that fact.

But just as she opened her mouth to speak, Caleb got to his feet and began to pace back and forth. Then, his voice rising truculently, he said, "I'll kill the bastard! I should have a long time ago."

At first Lettie stared at him, half thinking that he had gone mad. Then the truth of his anger became clear, and her laughter rang through the cave.

When Caleb stopped his pacing and glared at her, she gasped out, "You fool. Do you think she's carryin' Seth Hale's baby?"

Her question made him reach out for the wall's support. Hope and doubt fought in his eyes. Then haltingly, he asked, almost begged, "Lettie, are you . . . are you tellin' me that the baby is mine?"

She gave him a saucy grin. "That's what I'm sayin', Caleb. Seth has never laid a hand on her."

He settled to the ground, joy transforming his face. "Me, goin' to be a father," he whispered. He ran trembling fingers through his hair. "Can you imagine it, Lettie?"

"Why not?" Lettie laughed. "You've got all the

equipment for baby-makin', ain't you?"

Almost dizzy in his happiness, he laughed back. "Yeah, but always before I was so careful that that equipment didn't do its job, I didn't know if it worked properly or not."

Lettie studied his beaming face, then asked gravely, "That being the case, why did you experiment on Roxy?"

A pensive look came over his face. "I knew from the beginning that she was the only woman in the world for me, and I knew that I would try every possible way to get her. I'll tell you the truth, Lettie, until now I had just about given up hope."

"I'm afraid you're still out of luck, Caleb," Lettie said quietly. "She and Seth finished their wedding plans this mornin'. It's going to take place next Sunday morning."

"Even though she knows the baby is mine?"

"Yes, even though."

"Does Hale know?"

"No. We decided it best not to tell him . . . him bein' so proper and all. Roxy is afraid he wouldn't accept and love the child if he knew."

A deep sadness came over Caleb's face. "Does she hate me so much, Lettie?"

Lettie gazed at the hunter and felt sorrow for his grief. She sat down beside him and patted his arm. "She doesn't hate you at all, Caleb."

"Alright then, does she love Seth so much?"

"Huh! She doesn't even like him."

Bewildered, Caleb stared at her, trying to read her face. "I'm all at sea, Lettie," he finally said. "If she doesn't love the man, why is she marryin' him?"

"She's marryin' him because the man she loves hasn't asked her."

"The man she loves . . . ?" Then hope flared in his eyes and he pressed, "Do you mean, Lettie, that. . .?"

But before he could finish, Lettie interrupted.

"All I'm gonna say is that she don't hate you. It's up to you to find out the rest."

"Then, by God, she'll never see the day she mar-. ries Seth Hale."

Lettie squeezed his arm. "Oh, Caleb, I pray you're right. That man would crush her wonderful spirit."

A cold calmness settled over Caleb, and he reached over and threw a cedar knot on the fire. He had a new lease on life. The freshly created flames showed the intentness on his dark face as his mind raced with. plans and schemes. Lettie remained quiet, knowing that he wasn't even aware she sat beside him.

But after several minutes he remembered her presence and gave her a quick smile. "You won't have to be makin' more trips back here, Lettie. I'll be comin' a lot from now on. I'll be lookin' up my old huntin' friends and layin' my plans for next Sunday. In the meantime, you carry on just like you've been doin'."

Lettie was not completely convinced, but she nodded her head and left the cave for the last time.

CHAPTER 23

Roxanne walked out on the porch just as the sun, falling behind the tall pines on the distant hill, threw a red glow over the cabin and the hills. Down in the valley, the dark-green gloom of pine buried itself in evening shadow.

She stood at the edge of the porch until the gloaming crept up, deepening the shadow on the cabin door. She sighed raggedly. This was the last time she would see this magnificent sight.

Seth lived in a valley and the sunsets came quickly and left early there. Beginning tomorrow, she would be his wife, and after her honeymoon in England would spend the rest of her life there.

She sighed again, then turned when Gideon spoke at her elbow. "The sunset is somethin', ain't it?"

"It is, indeed."

"I guess you'll miss it?"

"Oh, so much, Gideon."

There was a long silence as the cousins continued to gaze out over the wilderness, each hating to break the mood. They both knew that there would be few, if ever, times of such closeness again.

Gideon dropped an arm across Roxanne's shoulder, drawing her near. "Roxy, do you think you're doing the right thing . . . marryin' Seth, I mean. Are you sure that you love him?"

Roxanne slipped an arm around his waist. "I'm

doing the right thing, Gideon. Maybe I don't love Seth wildly and completely, but I have a deep respect for him and will do my very best to make him a good wife."

"But do you think respect will be enough over the long years?"

"I hope so. I'm counting on it."

There was silence again, then Gideon spoke abruptly. "Caleb's back. I saw him at the post yesterday."

He felt the tremor that shot through her body and sensed that she was peering at him in the near darkness.

At last, she asked, "Has he gone back to the wild bunch?"

"I believe so. He was with several of them."

Gideon was silent a moment, then continued in a puzzled voice, "I don't think he wanted me to see him. At first he acted like he didn't see me. But when I went up to him and spoke, he was as friendly as ever."

Roxanne gave a short "Huh" and moved toward the door. But before she went in she asked over her shoulder, "I don't suppose he mentioned me?"

Gideon fidgeted nervously with a piece of loose bark on a cabin log, avoiding her eyes. When she remained waiting for his answer, he muttered, "Not really. He asked me if I was goin' to the wedding."

He looked away as she stiffened and her lips quivered. When she wheeled and half ran to her room, he sighed and returned to his seat beside the fire.

Malcolm halted his rocking and looked over at him. "Roxy ain't very happy tonight, is she?"

"That she is not." Gideon crossed an ankle over a knee and stared gloomily into the flames. Then as though talking to himself, said angrily, "I know she's makin' a mistake tomorrow. She's gonna be standin' in front of that preacher with the wrong man."

"I feel the same way, lad. But I can't hog-tie Caleb and make him stand at her side."

Gideon felt like telling his uncle that he could, in fact, make Caleb stand at her side if he was a mind to. But knowing that Roxanne was too proud for such an action, he kept his silence.

Malcolm resumed his rocking. "I gotta say, though, I sure thought them two would get together. Caleb as much as told me so."

Gideon stretched his feet to the fire. "I guess he changed his mind."

The room grew quiet, with only the slow creak of the rocker breaking the silence. After several moments Malcolm spoke, doubt edging his voice. "I guess Roxy could do worse. Regardless of what Seth may be, I'm sure Seth loves her and will be good to her."

Gideon looked at his uncle. "What do you mean by 'regardless of what Seth may be'? What is he, exactly?"

Malcolm shifted uncomfortably. "I mean he's not like the hill people . . . too proper."

"Yeah, he's different, alright."

Malcolm tapped out his pipe against the fire wall, then rose and stretched. "I'm goin' to bed," he announced. "We've got a big day ahead of us tomorrow. Make sure you bank the fire before you turn in."

He turned at his bedroom door and added, "Make sure the latch is up for Lettie. She and Zebe will be comin' in before long."

Roxanne awoke with the first shaft of sunlight pouring through the open window. The spring mornings were still chilly, and she snuggled deeper into the blankets.

Then swiftly, she leaned up on an elbow. Today was her wedding day. By noon she would be Mrs. Seth Hale. She let her gaze roam around the cozy little room and wondered how she could ever leave it. So much of herself was tied up within these four walls. Tears and happiness, long talks with Uncle Malcolm and Gideon, and the many card games with Gideon and Lettie.

She heard Gideon's bed squeak, as he turned over, and she wished that she could creep into bed with him and cry on his shoulder.

But she was a big girl now, about to be married and soon to be a mother. She must stand up to her fears and disappointments like an adult woman.

When the family assembled for breakfast, they were not an especially happy group. Malcolm tried to be jovial, attempting to crack jokes, hoping to get a smile from Roxanne ... . or even from Gideon.

But Lettie went about in her usual manner, a smile on her lips and humming a tune in her throat. Malcolm frowned at her. She was acting as though this was the biggest day in Roxanne's life. Couldn't she see how pale and drawn the girl looked?

Finally, Roxanne glowered at the woman and snapped, "Don't be so damned jolly, Lettie."

Lettie smiled and pressed Roxanne's shoulder as she placed a plate of ham and eggs on the table. "Don't wear such a long face, little one," she coaxed. "Before this day is over, you're gonna be the happiest woman in these hills."

Roxanne tossed her an impatient glance and jabbed at the yellow eye of the egg staring up at her. Lettie was only thinking of her own wedding that was taking place next week.

The meal was silent after that, with very little eaten by anyone. Gideon washed the dishes and cleaned the kitchen area while Lettie went with Roxanne to help her dress.

The white dress lay across the bed. It was made of ivory-colored satin, in a very plain style. It was, in fact, the same dress she had worn the night of her graduation from the fancy girl's school she had attended for four years. She had almost left it behind in Boston. Mama had said, ''Take only your simplest clothes, dear.'' But something had urged her to pack this particular dress. Perhaps it was because she had been so happy the night she wore it.

She thought now of all her bright fancy gowns hanging in a closet so far away, and a tear trickled down her cheek. Then her spirits brightened with an idea. She would have Seth stop at her old home and she would choose some to take with her to England. She had to go there anyhow, sooner or later. There was the furniture to dispose of and the house to sell. She sighed, dreading the heart-rending chore.

''There, you look beautiful,'' Lettie was saying, giving the skirt a final smoothing pat. ''You'll take your husband's breath away.''

Roxanne murmured, ''Thank you, Lettie,'' and looked at the clock on the small table beside her bed. It was time—and she could put it off no longer. Her uncle and cousin waited in the yard.

Malcolm helped the ladies into the light wagon, then climbed in beside them. He snapped the reins and they were off, with Gideon riding alongside them.

When they arrived at the church, its small yard was full of milling people. Roxanne spotted some neighbors among the mass, but most were strangers to her. When she whispered this to Malcolm, he chuckled and nodded his head.

"News of a wedding travels fast, Roxy, and hill people will travel as far as thirty miles to attend it. If you look over there to your right, just at the edge of the woods, you'll even see some Indians."

She glanced in his nodded direction and saw a dozen or more Indian braves. They stood silently, with arms folded across their chests, their eyes inscrutable.

"There's Long Step," she exclaimed and started to wave to him.

But Malcolm caught her hand. "You'll embarrass him."

Malcolm halted the team just outside the yard and tied the animals to a tree. Gideon helped Roxanne to the ground and turned to assist Lettie. But big Zebe Stevens was already there, swinging her down as though she were a feather.

They started toward the church and the people parted, making way for them. Their friends and neighbors smiled and called out greetings to the bride-to-be. Roxanne pulled an answering smile to her lips and started slowly to the church door.

As she walked through the narrow passage of men and women, she glanced often through lowered lids, hoping to catch a glimpse of Caleb. Would he come to see her married? At the door she gave one last look, but the tall frame of the hunter was nowhere about. Her fingers tightened on the small bouquet of spring violets and she passed through the open door.

Behind her, neighbors and strangers trooped in. For a while there was the sound of shifting feet and scraping benches as they seated themselves. Roxanne's glance strayed across Malcolm, sitting beside her, to the benches across the aisle.

Nell Hale sat there, fancily dressed, looking like a bluejay amid a flock of drab sparrows. She sat scowling down at her hands as she stripped gloves from them, then slapped the leather pieces into her purse.

My, she's in a dark mood, Roxanne thought.

A tall handsome man sat next to her, and Roxanne wondered idly who he was. It was plain from his appearance that he was not from the hills.

Then the church door was opening and she felt a draft of air as Seth and the preacher arrived. Seth glanced at her as he passed and smiled. She smiled back and felt nervous perspiration break out in her palms as he took his place before the altar and waited for her.

Then Gideon was nudging her and whispering excitedly, "Caleb just came in!"

Against her will, Roxanne turned and looked toward the back of the church. Her heart began to race. Along with several of his hunter friends, Caleb was sliding onto the back bench. He caught her eye and winked broadly. Her face went red and she snapped her head around and stared at the back of Seth's head.

She became aware of a stirring in the assembly as Malcolm nudged her. She looked up to see the preacher motioning her to join Seth. She stood up—and thought that her legs would not support her. Then Malcolm was taking her arm and escorting her to the altar.

The minister whispered to them to join hands and opened his Bible. "Dearly beloved," he began, "we are met here . . . "

He stopped in the middle of his sentence to peer

over his spectacles to learn the reason for the sudden whisperings and exclamations from the congregation. Startled, Roxanne looked up at Seth's annoyed face.

After a moment of utter quiet a voice rang out. "Before you go on, preacher, there's a couple of things I want to mention."

Seth's face went black with surprise and rage. "Caleb Coleman!" he ripped out as he spun around.

Roxanne turned with him and stared at the icily smiling face of Caleb as he stalked toward them. And moving threateningly at his heels were six of his friends, long rifles cradled in their arms.

From the corner of her eye Roxanne saw Nell and her companion stiffen and start to rise. But a hunter had stopped beside them to lay a rough hand on the stranger's shoulder, pushing him back down.

The minister, his eyes wide in disbelief, spoke sharply. "Young man, do I understand that you're objecting to this wedding?"

Without taking his eyes off Seth, Caleb answered, "That's right, Reverend."

A buzzing started in Roxanne's head and the room began to tilt. I am going to faint, she thought with surprise.

But Malcolm had hurried to her side at Caleb's first words. And now, with a wide smile on his lips, led her back to sit between him and Gideon.

Caleb stood before the two men and, in the deathly quiet of the room, fixed his eyes on Seth. Then calmly he began to talk.

"I have two reasons to stop this wedding. First, this man is an enemy to this country. I have proof that he, and his sister, are British spies. The man sitting next to Miss Hale is a British officer. You'll find papers on him that will prove my words are true."

A low, menacing rumble was beginning to fill the church. The minister stared at Caleb, his mouth working wordlessly. He was uncertain what to do.

Seeing the hesitation on the minister's face, the congregation became quiet and eagerly watched the melodrama taking place. This was something they could talk about for years. There would be as many different versions as there were people who told the story.

Into the stillness, Caleb reached into his pocket and brought out a folded piece of paper. He handed it to the minister and said, "Preacher, I have a better reason that this man shouldn't marry this woman."

The minister unfolded the legal-looking paper, read it, then gaped at Caleb.

Caleb nodded his head. "That's right, preacher. As you see there, the lady is my wife."

A startled sound broke from every throat, rising to the ceiling in a whoosh. In the Sherwood pew, Gideon let out a hurrahing yell.

At Caleb's shocking words, weakness filled Roxanne and she slumped against the wildly smiling Malcolm. Only half believing, she listened to Caleb's explanation.

"Old Preacher James married us," he began. "It was early one morning when me and her, along with the Indian, Long Step, were pinned down by some renegades."

Roxanne sat erect, remembering that morning— how she hit her head and later had bad dreams for a while. But she realized now that it hadn't all been a dream. She remembered distinctly saying, "I do" over and over.

After staring down at the floor a minute, obviously nervous, Caleb began again.

"I thought that we were all gonna be killed and, lovin' Roxy like I do, I wanted her to be my wife. So when old James came along, I had him marry us. I admit that Roxy was stunned a little from hittin' her head on a rock and didn't quite know what she was doin,' but she answered, 'I do' in all the right places, and that makes us man and wife."

A ripple of laughter ran through the room. The minister had finished reading the document and now looked up at Caleb. "It's all in order, young man. If the young woman is in agreement, you can take your bride home."

Caleb motioned to the men to take care of the captured three and couldn't help the stir of pity that ran through him when he looked at Seth. The man looked crushed, and he knew well that feeling.

As his men marched the prisoners outside, Caleb moved toward Roxanne, his heart racing wildly.

Malcolm rose and pushed him down into the place he just vacated beside Roxanne. But Roxanne stared at the floor, refusing to look at him.

Caleb lifted a hand and gently tilted her chin up, forcing her to look into his eyes. "Don't you want to be married to me, Roxy?"

While the congregation held their breaths, Roxanne gazed at him, searching for and finding the love and devotion that gazed back at her.

"Oh, Caleb," she whispered, "I want that more than anything else in the world."

There was the sighing of breaths released, then a great shout went up. Roxanne hid her blushing face on Caleb's shoulder, and he beamed proudly.

Roxanne flung open the window and stood staring up at the sky, atwinkle with stars. "Mama, papa," she whispered, ''you may not approve of my choice, but he's all the world to me.''

Behind her, the mattress rustled and a voice coaxed huskily, ''Come love me, Roxy.''

A smile formed at the corners of her lips as she answered him. ''I'll love you, long-hunter. I'll love you like you've never been loved before!''